Changing the Station
How One Stray Dog Found Its Purpose

David Homick

"Your purpose in life is to find your purpose and give your whole heart and soul to it."

Buddha

Chapter One

The little pup sniffed every corner of the cardboard box he called home, but his siblings' scents had faded. Memories of climbing over and under the other five pups, relentlessly vying for Mama's attention, were fading as well. Their carefree days had been filled with eating, sleeping, playing, and eating some more. But giant humans with reaching hands had put an end to all that. They showed their teeth and spoke in unusually high voices as they carried the little fur balls away one by one.

Mama looked down at her last pup with sad eyes. He met her gaze and wondered if she missed the others or just felt sorry for him. Why had no one picked him? Although he'd been left behind, he tried to look on the positive side. He held his nose up and sniffed the familiar Mama scent. He couldn't imagine a world without the warmth of her body and the calming rhythm of her breathing that gently rocked him to sleep at night. She was all he had left of his pack. They would be together forever.

But the humans kept coming. They talked in lower voices and showed less teeth. He changed his mind and hunkered down to make himself look smaller, hoping to discourage them from plucking him from the security of his home. Mama smelled different after they left. A dog's nose is never wrong, and his smelled fear. Mama's eyes told him they couldn't stay there, or they might be separated. Neither wanted that to happen.

Mama hadn't had enough time with her other pups to teach them everything they needed to know to survive in a world full of humans. Now they were gone and had to fend for themselves. She said she wouldn't let that happen again.

Pup had much to learn about the world. Mama began by telling him that all pups were born innocent and full of unconditional love, which stays with them for life. Humans were born that way too, but it rarely lasted beyond their childhood. Dogs often learned this lesson the hard way.

Pup looked at Mama, his little face scrunched up into something that resembled a frown. *Does that mean I should avoid humans?*

Avoiding humans is nearly impossible, but be wary of them until they prove themselves worthy.

Her answer puzzled him. Apparently, unconditional love had certain conditions.

He'd had little exposure to humans yet, except for brief encounters with the woman who showed up from time to time to feed them or let them out to play in the yard. She seemed nice enough. Perhaps he should be more wary of her for now.

Mama's lessons became longer and more intense over the next few days. Pup's little brain spun with all the new information.

Can we slow down? I'm getting dizzy. He did a little pirouette and then tumbled to the ground. He looked up at Mama and wagged.

She did not reciprocate. *You must keep up. We don't have much time.*

We don't have much time? What did that mean? He knew what it sounded like. It sounded like their time together was growing short. He smelled fear again, Mama's and his own.

You have much to learn, was her only reply when he questioned her.

Pup picked up a scent and held up his nose. He recognized this one. It belonged to the woman who kept them locked up in the room that she'd added onto the back of the house for her pets. Mama said she'd shared the room with other dogs and even a goat before her pups arrived. They'd had the place to themselves since then.

The door latch clicked, and Pup's tail swung from side to side. He had no control over its movements. The first time it happened, it frightened him, but Mama assured him it was perfectly natural. It meant happiness or excitement, or both. Sometimes, when Pup questioned his feelings, he stole a glance at his tail for validation.

The door swung open, and the woman who fed them stood in the opening on her hind legs. Other than the talking heads that had peered into his cardboard box and snatched his siblings, the woman and her male friend were his only exposure to the creatures Mama called humans. Curiously, both balanced on two legs as they moved from place to place. It seemed like an inefficient method of travel.

"Come on, Lola, time for some exercise."

Pup followed Mama outside into the fresh spring air. He swept his nose in a wide arc, and it exploded with so many intoxicating scents he staggered and nearly fell. He couldn't wait to investigate every one.

A fence surrounded the large yard, allowing him to roam without supervision. Mama could go off on her own adventures, knowing that her pup was safe.

First order of business: rolling in the grass. After sitting in a box all morning, the fresh, earthy smell was heavenly. He didn't actually know anything about heaven, except that Mama had told him it was a wonderful place. He imagined they had plenty of grass there.

Next, he needed to mark his territory. He found a suitable tree, standing tall in the middle of the yard. He squatted and let out a stream. *There.* If any other animals came around, they would know that this yard belonged to him, and, of course, Mama. He'd watched her perform a similar ritual.

Pup followed his nose in every direction, sniffing out little treasures and making sure no other dogs encroached on his territory. From time to time, he smelled other animals and chased after them. They were small and fast, and he never caught any. The one with the bushy tail scampered up trees so quickly it made Pup's head spin.

Then, there were the birds. Most of them were cool, except for the big black ones that danced around the yard and made faces at him. They talked to each other in loud, arrogant voices. Pup didn't know what they said, but the way they said it made him feel like he was the subject of their derision.

After a good sniff around, he looked for Mama, but didn't see her in the yard. *Hmm...* He ran back to their room and found it empty. Is this why she'd been acting strangely? The relentless lessons and the fear he smelled. Had she left him behind? She wouldn't do that. Would she?

No. She's got to be here somewhere. Just because a pup, through no fault of his own, was smaller than the rest didn't mean he was any less smart. He devised a search plan—start at one end of the fence and follow it to the other end. He would look inside and out. Even if she had left, she couldn't have gotten far.

He held his nose high and scoured the air, filtering out any scents that were not Mama's. The woods outside the fence made it difficult to see. Maybe he wasn't so smart after all. He tried to be optimistic, but a whimper slipped out as he forged ahead. At the corner of the property, he spotted her behind a clump of bushes that hid her from the rest of the yard. His heart, which had sunk into his stomach, snapped back into place.

Maybe this was a game where she hides and waits for him to find her. That sounded like fun, but a little heads-up would have been nice.

Mama scratched at the ground near the bottom of the fence.

He barked, which sounded more like a little yip than a bark, to let her know he was playing along.

Mama didn't stop.

My turn to hide.

She clawed harder, tossing clumps of dirt into the air behind her.

Perhaps this was a different game. He barked again, this time a little louder.

Shhh!

Pup inched closer, careful to stay away from the flying dirt.

What are you doing?

She stopped for a moment. *I started this hole yesterday. If I dig a little every day during our yard time, soon we'll have a hole big enough to crawl through and be free.*

But I like my yard. Wait. What's free?

Please let me work. We don't have much time.

That was the second time she'd mentioned running out of time. Mama reeked of fear, so he let her continue. He didn't know what free meant, but he had a feeling it wasn't something that the woman would approve of. He crawled under the bush to keep an eye on the rest of the yard.

Mama panted hard as she threw more dirt into the air.

The woman stepped out of the house and scanned the yard. Pup stifled the urge to run out and play with her after remembering Mama's warning.

"Lola," the woman called.

Pup tilted his head. *What's a lola?* He'd heard that word before.

She put two fingers to her mouth, and a shrill sound filled the yard. "Lola. Come on, girl. No time for games."

No games? Pup dug his paws into the dirt and pushed himself backward. *Ouch!* He'd gotten himself stuck. The more he tried to wriggle out of it, the more it hurt. He stopped and looked into the yard.

She's coming.

Get out of there. Now! Mama yelled.

He took a deep breath and shook as hard as he could, like Mama had taught him to do when he got wet. A branch snapped. Pain shot up his back, but he was free. He scampered out from under the bush.

The smell of fear and fresh dirt filled the air as Mama clawed at the edges of the hole. It didn't look big enough for both of them to fit through.

Mama said, *I need to know where the woman is.*

I can't see her.

Listen carefully. I want you to run out from behind the bush. Let her see you walking toward her. She will stop. That will buy us some time. Don't get too close to her. When I bark, you run back here as fast as you can and jump into the hole.

That sounded like fun.

Pup did what Mama said, and the woman stopped. They stared at each other as he ambled toward her. Mama barked. He turned and ran. When he neared the fence, he leapt through the air and slipped through the hole like a Steph Curry three-pointer. He hit the ground with a thud and rolled out the other side.

Mama followed. She made it halfway through before she stopped.

Hurry, Mama. Don't stop now.

She wriggled her hind-quarters frantically. *I'm stuck.*

The woman appeared from around the bush. Her eyes doubled in size when she saw Mama wriggling under the fence. "Oh, no you don't, Lola. Not again."

Mama!

The woman lunged forward and grabbed Mama's tail with both hands.

Chapter Two

Pup's heart raced. He didn't have the size or the strength to pull her through. *What can I do?*

Mama's eyes were wild with fear. *Run!*

What? And leave you here? No way.

Mama winced in pain as the woman pulled her back against the chain-link fence.

Pup climbed up behind one of Mama's front legs, dug his little paws into the dirt, and pushed with all his might.

Mama kicked her back legs one at a time as if running. Dirt sprayed backward into the woman's face. Her hands slipped a little on Mama's tail. Mama kicked harder and moved forward again, shaking her tail to free it.

Her tail slipped from the woman's hands, and the two escaped convicts rolled down the small embankment, then quickly gained their feet.

Pup looked at the woman on the other side of the fence, then at Mama. *NOW we can run.*

The woman shook her fist. "Come back here!"

They were free, whatever that was. They ran and never looked back.

Mama, can we please stop? I can't run anymore.

They'd put enough distance between themselves and the woman to stop for a rest. Crystal-clear water slipped and danced over a rocky creek bed nearby and they drank their fill.

We can rest for a few minutes, Mama said while they reclined next to a mighty oak.

Pup had never run so much in his life. He rested his head on his paws.

How did I do, Mama?

She gave him an affectionate lick. *I'm proud of you, Son.*

Pups were all about making their mamas proud. His little heart swelled in his chest as he snuggled up against her. He wanted to close his eyes and sleep, but he had more questions.

Mama? What's a lola?

Mama smiled. *It's a name. My name.*

Why?

Humans like to name things, including animals.

What's my name?

Mama hesitated. *You don't have one yet.*

Why not?

The woman didn't name any of the pups. That's up to the humans who took them. They'll give them names, and hopefully, good homes.

Why do we need names?

We don't. Humans use names because they have a poor sense of smell. We can tell each other apart by our individual scent. We can also communicate telepathically.

Tele-what?

Telepathically.

Pup tilted his head.

It means we can communicate without speaking.

He paused for a moment. *Is that what we're doing now?*

Mama smiled and licked her pup. *You are VERY smart... and very lovable.*

Pup sighed before he continued with his questions. *Why did the woman say "not again" when you crawled under the fence?*

I escaped once before. That's how I met your father.

Pup tilted his head. *What was HIS name?*

I don't know. Like I said, we don't need names.

What happened?

I didn't get far enough away, and the woman found me. That's why we need to keep moving. I don't want to go back there again.

That makes two of us. Pup scrunched up his little face. *We don't need humans.*

I didn't say that. We all need each other. Mama paused for a moment. *It's like we're pieces of a very large puzzle. Some are humans and others are animals, but we all fit together to make the puzzle whole.*

Pup tilted his head. He couldn't understand why they ran away if they needed humans.

You have much to learn.

After a long silence, Pup spoke again. *Where will we go now?*

I don't know, but wherever it is, we'll be together.

He liked the sound of that.

Soon, hunger gnawed at their bellies. The woods ended, and a row of houses became visible in the clearing. They walked from yard to yard looking for scraps of food as rain fell. The water coated everything and made it difficult to pick up scents. Mama's nose worked better than Pup's, but even she had trouble.

Unfortunately, freedom meant no one to feed them and take care of them.

The rain fell harder, accompanied by a clap of thunder. He'd heard the dreadful sound before in his box and burrowed his way under Mama for protection. Pup let out a whimper and scampered between Mama's legs, nearly tripping her.

Mama stopped and looked down at her frightened pup. *We need to find a place to wait out this storm.*

I'm scared, and I'm hungry.

We're making things worse wandering around aimlessly in this storm. We'll rest now and conserve our energy for better weather.

They ducked inside a shed behind one of the houses and shook themselves off. The thunder wasn't as loud, and their sense of smell worked better inside where it was dry.

Mama held up her nose. *I think I found something.* She knocked over a big plastic can, spilling its contents onto the floor.

Pup smelled it, too. His mouth watered while he watched her paw through the bags. Lucky for them, humans were notoriously bad at finishing their meals. She backed up and dropped a mouthful of flat brown strips on the ground.

What's that?

Mama's tongue made a big circle around her mouth. *Bacon.*

Pup sniffed it. *Oh, boy.* He hesitated, afraid it couldn't possibly taste as good as it smelled. He tried a piece. *Ho-lee cow!* Even better. It created a flavor explosion in his mouth like nothing he'd ever eaten. He gobbled up two more strips, then looked for more.

They dined on enough scraps to satisfy them for the time being. Unfortunately, there'd been no more bacon. Mama said it wasn't stealing if they took something that someone else had thrown away. The storm had moved on, so they decided to make a quick exit in case the humans didn't see it the same way.

By nightfall, they were hungry again and in need of shelter. They found an old barn to sleep in, but no more food.

Mama, I'm hungry.

I know, dear. Tomorrow we'll find food.

How do you know that?

Mothers know things.

He considered her answer. *That's why I'm never leaving you.*

She smiled. *That's a nice thought.*

It's not a thought. It's the truth.

Someday you'll know things too. You'll grow big and strong and, like all dogs, you'll find your purpose. You won't need me anymore.

I want YOU to be my purpose.

That's not how it works. You, my pup, will do great things someday and bring joy to others in your life.

I don't want to do great things. I want to stay with you forever and ever.

Mama smiled and stroked his back with her tongue. *Shhh. We need to get some rest.*

A bed of straw made for adequate accommodations, but their empty stomachs kept them up most of the night. The morning would bring a serious search for a more stable food supply.

· · · · ● · ● · · · ·

Pup grew quickly throughout the summer, despite his poor diet. Mama made sure he had enough to eat, even if it meant she went without. They lived on the streets most of the time. Finding food and rudimentary shelter was easier in the city than the country.

But the city brought a new set of problems. Humans everywhere. And giant metal boxes on wheels that whizzed past.

Mama, what are those?

Humans call them cars. They're dangerous. They will kill you if you get in their way.

Pup tilted his head. *Do they chase dogs?*

Only if they get in the way. The cars generally stay in the black areas with the white and yellow lines. We'll be safe over here.

The constant undercurrent of energy and unfriendly sounds frightened him, and he stayed close to Mama. Everyone and everything moved quickly. The humans appeared distant and unfriendly. Most didn't even notice him sitting on the sidewalk. Occasionally, he would lock eyes with a kind-hearted soul, their features softening with empathy if only for a fleeting moment.

Pup didn't like the city. There was no grass to roll in or trees to chase squirrels into. Cars and buildings meant no room to run and play. The smells were oily, not earthy. And where were the other dogs? Occasionally, one would walk by tethered to one of the humans. They never looked very happy.

Days became shorter and cold temperatures made sleeping in open alleys and bus shelters almost unbearable. After three days of waking up to a layer of frozen white flakes that had fallen from the sky, Mama said they needed a roof over their heads if they had any hope of making it through the winter alive.

Most people stayed off the streets during the cold months. They hunkered down in their warm homes with their packs. The ones that did venture out were in too much of a hurry to notice a couple of hungry, stray dogs in the street. Except for children, of course. If children ruled the world, there would be no stray dogs.

The wind-chill had dipped to twenty degrees the night before, causing Mama and her pup to double their efforts to find relief from the unforgiving winds.

We need to find a way into one of these buildings.

Pup agreed. Even a damp basement would be a tremendous improvement.

They sniffed up one alley and down the next. A half bag of stale potato chips and a blueberry muffin they found near a dumpster had breakfast written all over it. They had barely finished when a large human dressed in blue and carrying a big stick yelled at them, his voice gravelly and mean.

Mama's eyes filled with fear. *Run!*

They ran until they couldn't run anymore.

Who was that? Pup asked when they caught their breath.

A dangerous man. There are many of them on the street. They're called cops. If a man in blue ever catches you, he will take you to a terrible place where you'll never see me again.

They continued on, eyes ever vigilant. Pup saw it first. A broken window. Mama had trained him well in the six months they'd been on the streets. They peered into the darkness, then looked at each other and nodded. At least inside, they had a chance.

Mama jumped into the abyss with no idea how far she might fall or where she might land. Pup barked, which no longer sounded like a yip.

Mama's face appeared in the window. *Shhh!*

She stood on the cardboard box that had broken her fall. It sat atop other boxes piled in front of the window. *It's safe to come in.*

They both survived the leap to the floor. Pup looked up at the window and wondered how they might get back out of this underground room.

Pup had never been in a place like this before. Mama said it was safe, but the strange sounds and shadows on the walls made him second-guess her initial assessment.

They turned a corner to find a fire-breathing octopus sitting in the center of the large, mostly dark room. It belched and hissed as they approached. Neither had ever seen such a monster. On the positive side, the heat from its massive metal body felt wonderful.

Pup barked.

Mama gave him a stern look. *Shhh!*

A few moments later, a door creaked, and a shaft of yellow light filled one corner of the room.

Mama thrust her nose in the air. *Humans!*

Chapter Three

Mama looked at her pup. *Hide!*

Pup swung his head from side to side and back again. There were so many places to hide in the big room. His legs slipped out from under him as he scrambled to find cover.

A boy stood at the bottom of the stairs, surrounded by the yellow light.

Pup's paws scratched at the slick concrete floor. A whimper slipped out.

"Who's there?"

Mama watched the boy approach her defenseless pup.

"How did you get in here?" He looked around, his gaze stopping at the broken window.

Pup's heart pounded in his chest as the boy squatted next to him. Mama had warned him about humans. He didn't know this one. It had short hair and smelled different than the woman. The boy's hand reached out toward him, and Pup pressed himself to the floor.

Mama stepped out, brave and ready to defend her pup. She barked, and the startled boy fell back onto the floor. Mama barked again.

The boy held up his hands. "Relax. I'm not going to hurt you."

Mama stepped between the two and stood firm. *If you want him, you'll have to go through me.*

The boy couldn't hear her, but he appeared to get the message. He looked as frightened as the pup. He put his hands up again and shuffled backwards. "No one is going to hurt anyone. Got that?"

Mama's muscles relaxed, and Pup gained his feet. He stood behind her and watched the boy from a safe distance.

"You guys look hungry." He hesitated. "Wait here. I'll go see what I can find."

Bacon would be nice.

Mama shook her head. *He can't understand you.*

Pup watched the young human walk away, moving gracefully on only two legs.

Look on the bright side, Mama said. *We're finally going to get some proper food.*

Unless he comes back with the cops.

Mama glanced at the window and the stack of boxes, too tall to climb. *We're trapped. We'll have to trust him.*

Wait, I thought you said all humans were bad.

Mama shook her head. *Not all humans are bad. They need to earn our trust.*

Did this one earn our trust?

This is a complicated situation. First, we don't have much of a choice. But I believe this one is sincere. I smelled fear when I barked, then compassion. I think his heart is big, and he truly wants to help us. Besides, he is still young. The younger they are, the more they can be trusted. The littlest ones are the closest things to dogs in the human world.

Pup realized he still had a lot to learn.

The boy returned and set a big bowl of water on the floor. Pup lapped up the cool, clear liquid while he kept one eye on the human, who showed his teeth as he watched from a safe distance.

The boy opened a small container with his front paws. They were long and slender with an extra digit on the side. He gracefully manipulated objects using those elegantly shaped appendages.

Mama, why are his paws different from ours?

They're called hands because they come in handy when humans need to pick things up.

Pup's nose drew his attention to a fresh scent. Some kind of meat—proper food, not dumpster scraps. His mouth watered.

The boy removed a flat disk that flopped and wiggled in his hand. He rolled it up and held it in front of them. "Bologna. I think you'll like it."

Mama went first, probably to make sure the food was safe. Apparently, trust only went so far. She sniffed it, then quickly gobbled it up. He rolled another, and she nodded her approval.

Pup snatched the next one from his hand and devoured it. The closest thing to bacon he'd ever eaten. They each wolfed down four of the floppy pieces of almost-bacon.

The boy reached out and gently stroked Mama's back. Pup waited for her reaction. She closed her eyes and went limp, like she might melt all over the floor. No fear.

Pup took a few steps toward the boy from his protected position behind Mama. The boy showed Pup his teeth and stroked Pup's head and scratched under his chin, which made his tail wag so hard he had trouble staying on his feet. It felt SO good. It was the closest thing to the love he felt when he cuddled up next to Mama. Were humans capable of love, too? This world kept getting crazier.

The boy said his name was Brian. He was thirteen years old and lived upstairs with his pack. He said the other members of his pack wouldn't approve of any new members, so Mama and Pup needed to stay in the basement. Pup wanted to be scratched like that for hours, but Brian said he had to go to a place called school. He promised to return later with more food and water.

They waited. And waited. And waited.

How could school, whatever that was, take so long? Pup need-ed a distraction, so he got up and sniffed around the room. Nothing but a lot of dust and boxes and oily things. He gave the octopus a wide berth in his travels. A fire glowed inside its mouth, and he feared the monster might turn him into charcoal with one mighty breath.

The heat felt wonderful, though, so he circled around to its backside. He looked for a hole to sniff, hoping to gather some information. The beast had no butt, which confused him. Oh, well. He lay down in the warmest spot he found and fell asleep.

He awoke to the sound of footsteps and held up his nose. Brian had come back. Just like he promised. Mama had been right about him, after all.

He ran to the boy, who showed him his teeth again, which must be some kind of greeting. Pup opened his mouth and reciprocated.

Brian set down the box he carried and scratched behind Pup's ears.

Oh, boy! I could get used to this. Wait. I smell meat. He stood on his hind legs and scratched at the top of the box.

"Be patient, my little friend." Brian moved the box.

Pup scolded him with a loud bark.

Brian's eyes widened. "Shhh! You'll get me in trouble."

You're already in trouble.

Mama nudged Pup aside with a mind-your-manners look. Pup lowered his head. Message received.

Brian opened the box, then closed it again. "I'll let you stay here, but you must be quiet. If someone hears you, you'll both be back out on the street. Got it?"

Pup didn't understand everything he said, but he knew by the tone of his voice he meant business. He backed up a couple of steps, despite the meat box. Suddenly, a powerful urge to pee made it difficult to keep his legs still.

"What's the matter?"

I need to pee.

"You look like you could use some food."

I said, I need to pee! At times, certain bodily functions took precedence, even over food.

Brian gave him a blank stare, so Pup showed him.

"Hey, where are you going?"

Pup realized he hadn't yet marked his territory and sniffed out a spot in the corner. Brian said they could stay, so he didn't want any other dogs to steal his room or his almost-bacon. When he found an appropriate spot, he squatted.

"Stop!"

That wasn't going to happen in mid-stream. He'd have to deal with whatever Brian wanted when he finished.

Brian blocked his return to the meat box. "Bad dog." His brow wrinkled above a scrunched-up face.

Pup hadn't seen this expression before and didn't care for it. He liked the teeth much better, but he wagged his tail, anyway.

"You can't do that in here."

Pup sensed Brian's anger and lowered his head. He hoped he hadn't just blown his chance to see inside the meat box. He raised his eyes without lifting his head. Brian stared, hiding his teeth.

Brian's shoulders slumped. "I'm sorry. I should have known that you'd eventually need to go to the bathroom. We'll need to work something out."

He opened the box, and they ate pieces of tube-shaped meat. Then he pulled out two silver bowls and filled them with water from a sink on the other side of the room. Pup assumed things were back to normal.

While they drank, Brian came up with a plan. He moved some boxes around to make steppingstones up to the window, which he opened to give them more room to get in and out when they had to do their business. Apparently, that meant no more peeing, or anything else, inside.

He also laid down a thick blanket to sleep on in a hidden spot that only the three of them knew about. If any other humans came down the stairs, Mama and Pup were to hide in their secret spot and not make a sound.

One day, Brian taught Pup a game called *tug-on-the-towel*. He dangled a soft cloth just above Pup's head. When he grabbed it in his teeth, Brian would try to pull it away. Pup didn't understand, so, at first, he let him have it. Pup didn't think it was a good game at all. After he got the hang of it, he decided it was the most fun he'd ever had.

They stayed in Brian's basement through the winter months. Brian appeared every day before and after school to feed them, and the octopus kept them warm at night. Only once did someone else venture into the basement, and Mama and Pup stayed out of site. Mama said it didn't feel like a proper home, but it beat living on the streets.

She also said all good things must end, and this one did abruptly. After a walk on a beautiful spring day, Mama and Pup returned to find Brian in the basement when he should have been in school.

"I have some bad news." His eyes leaked. "My family has to move. I'm sorry, but you won't be able to stay here anymore."

Brian's eyes sprung another leak two days later as they said their goodbyes and climbed out the basement window for the last time.

Street dogs once again, they realized they didn't know how good they'd had it until it was gone. Pup didn't just miss the roof over his head and the big warm octopus and his tugging towel, he missed his friend Brian. Brian had loved them and taken good care of them. Pup fell asleep every night for a week praying he'd find another Brian.

Two weeks passed, drinking from puddles and dumpster diving for their meals. Occasionally, a kind soul noticed the downtrodden mother and her pup and fed them some proper food.

But there were more bad humans than good, it seemed, and everything in the city moved so fast and loud. Mama told Pup they needed to find a quieter place.

One dreary day, something that looked like a giant metal snake roared behind the buildings on the opposite side of the street.

Pup stopped and looked at Mama. *What's that?*

I don't know.

They went to investigate. Pup ran across the street, and Mama followed. He reached the other side and turned just in time to see a car slam into Mama and toss her aside.

Mama!

She didn't move. He ran to her side, dodging other cars along the way. He nudged her. She must be asleep. *Mama, please wake up.*

A crowd of humans gathered and muttered in hushed tones.

Mama, we need to go now! She didn't move. Pup noticed her legs were bent in different directions. A strange, not-Mama smell replaced her familiar scent. Something was VERY wrong.

Why didn't he wait for her? She had taken such good care of him, but who took care of her? Perhaps he'd been selfish. Perhaps he should have taken better care of Mama. But he was just a pup. How could he take care of anyone?

The crowd parted, and a large man in blue with a big stick walked toward them.

Cop! Pup looked down at Mama. Still no movement. *What do I do? What do I do?* Mama couldn't help him this time.

The cop towered over them, his big stick dangling from his waist. Mama had warned him about such men.

Argh! Reluctantly, he turned and ran.

Chapter Four

George Baxter swept the sidewalk in front of the apartment building he owned in a quiet little northern California town. His once-strong frame now carried the burden of age, causing him to move a little slower, but his deep, soulful eyes, like portals into an untold story, still held a glimmer of determination and strength.

He'd once taken a great deal of pride in the converted train station hotel he bought with his own money in 1974. Back then, people of color were treated as second-class citizens, and his return from fighting an unpopular war had been another strike against him. After the third bank turned him down for a loan, he used some of the money he'd saved while deployed, plus the proceeds from his father's life insurance policy, to buy the tired old building.

Over the years, he'd fixed the place up, but kept the rents low. He used the name of the original hotel, *The Station*, hoping, as the name implied, it would be a temporary stopover on his tenants' journeys to bigger and better things.

When his wife died seven years ago, his entrepreneurial spirit, and just about every other manner of spirit, died with her. The demons that had followed him home from Vietnam years ago once more darkened his doorstep, and he sought refuge in alcohol.

A beagle meandered down the street under George's suspicious glare. Probably looking for a place to drop a deuce. Not in my yard! He'd picked up more than his share of poop over the years, and he wondered why anyone would willingly own an animal.

"Keep moving," he warned as he shook his broom.

The dog cut a wide berth around the crazy man with the make-shift weapon.

"Damn dogs," George muttered under his breath.

He finished his chore and turned a tired eye toward the old building. It would need a new roof in a couple of years. He shook his head. He wasn't getting rich from the place, that's for sure. It had been his wife's idea to keep the rents low. The income from the commercial space he leased to the coffee shop on the ground floor kept him afloat.

George walked back inside to the owner's apartment. He'd lived there for the past forty-nine years, most of them with his beloved Dorothy, who preferred Dottie or Dot. After nearly seven years, the plaster walls still echoed her sweet voice and playful laughter. He relived the remnants of moments shared with her as he gazed at old photographs or listened to their vinyl records. The melodies transported him back to a time when life was simpler, and his heart felt lighter.

Dottie had been his muse and the inspiration for the three novels he'd written in his late fifties. He'd stopped work on a fourth when she became ill. For five years, he abandoned his literary pursuits to care for her. He'd made a modest amount of money from book sales, which helped with Dottie's medical bills. The rest he mostly invested in his building, beer, and scratch-off tickets.

He poured himself a cup of coffee, part of his morning routine. The first cup he took black, with two eggs, two strips of bacon, and a slice of rye toast. He preferred the second with a shot of Baileys and the morning newspaper. George read the words through a large magnifying glass as he followed each line across the page. His eyes weren't what they used to be.

He never read much past the headlines on the first page. Too depressing. He moved on to the obituary section to see if anyone he knew had died. He figured the more people his age that died, the better his chances were to go next.

"Nobody we know," he said aloud as he folded the paper and set it on the table. "What do you want to do today, dear?"

George often talked to Dottie as if she were in the room. Some habits took time to break.

He rinsed his coffee cup and did what he did every other day of the week. After he donned his cap and pocketed his keys, he commenced his daily walk to the market. It had taken a while to get used to walking alone, and truth be told, most days, he still missed the company.

George didn't need to buy vegetables. He grew his own. In fact, he didn't even like most vegetables. The garden had always been Dottie's thing, but he'd loved spending time with her, working in the summer sun. Watering and pulling weeds had been another daily ritual.

George deposited a six-pack and two bags of cheese popcorn on the counter, then picked out two cigars from a display case.

The clerk smiled. "Hey, George."

George nodded. "And I'll take one of those scratchers." He pointed at the rolls of colorful lottery tickets hanging on a metal bar behind the counter.

"What kind do you want?"

That used to be Dottie's job. "You choose."

The clerk shrugged and tore off a ticket. "Do you ever win anything?"

"I buy them for my daughter."

George strolled home along the quiet, tree-lined streets, paper bag in one hand and cane in the other. He only used the cane on days when the arthritis in his seventy-two-year-old knee acted up.

Two young girls stepped off the elevator as he unlocked his door.

"Hello, Mr. Baxter," the little one said. The older one didn't look up from the cell phone in her hand.

George nodded. "Hello, girls."

He hung his cane on the hook he'd installed next to the door and put his groceries away. The lottery ticket went with the others in a big jar on the counter.

The grandfather clock in the living room chimed twelve bells, so George prepared a sandwich before heading back out to make his rounds in the building. Every day, he checked the common areas to make sure they were clean, and that doors and windows were in good condition and locked. He checked the mechanicals in the basement and inspected the exterior. Rarely did he find a problem, but it kept him busy and his mind from slipping back into darker places.

After rounds, he grabbed a rake and headed out back. He looked out over the lush green garden, alive with new growth. In every bloom, he saw a reflection of her spirit and a connection to the woman he loved so deeply. He had no doubt she was watching from above.

"Looks like another bumper crop this year," he said, half expecting Dottie to comment. He made his way up one row and down the other, turning up the weeds that grew like, well, weeds.

Chapter Five

Pup didn't stop until he reached the alley across the street. He ducked inside and peeked around the corner at the scene of the crime. Mama lay still in the street as Pup's heart raced. The cop bent down and picked her up. Her legs hung limp as he carried her to the sidewalk and gently set her down.

More than anything, Pup wanted to believe she was asleep. He imagined calling to her from the alley. She would escape and they'd run off together on their next adventure, far away from the city.

His heart sank into his stomach when he realized that wouldn't happen. He had eyes and a good nose, and both told him Mama was gone. The reality of being alone hit him with a crushing blow. Fear pinned him to the wall of the alley.

He watched until he couldn't watch anymore, then pried his weary body from the wall and turned down the alley. He put one paw in front of the other and walked away from everything he'd ever known. It felt like walking in a dream. A very bad dream.

He emerged from the alley and encountered a patch of tall grass that ended at a mound of gravel beneath two steel rails. They were warm from the sun and stretched out in either direction as far as he could see. What were they? Where did they end? Were they real or part of this strange dreamland?

Too exhausted by fear and grief to investigate, he returned to the tall grass and lay down his head. One dreamland turned into another. His young life played in his mind like a movie—the Mama show, with himself as her co-star. Brian played a part, as well, feeding them meat tubes. But in this movie, he had an endless supply. He didn't move away, and they all lived happily ever after.

Pup awoke to a deafening sound. He crawled to the edge of the grass to take a look. The sun had disappeared, and the ground shook as a giant metal snake, like the one they'd seen earlier, slithered along the rails. He watched until the flashing lights on the tail of the beast disappeared in the distance.

The sky ahead looked mostly gray, while the city lights burned behind him. His stomach growled and clawed at him from the inside. He must have fallen asleep, but for how long?

When he returned to his resting spot, his stomach pleaded with him for food, but he willed himself back to sleep to see Mama again. They were back in the basement having a conversation about heaven.

It's a wonderful place where all dogs go when they die, Mama said.

Do they have bacon there?

She nodded. *Of course they do, more than you could ever eat.*

He doubted that. *When can we go to heaven?*

Someday, we will both be there, although you may have to wait a little longer than me.

They don't have cats there, do they?

I don't know. She paused. *Probably not.*

They laughed so hard his head shook and his eyes opened. He squinted against the rays of the morning sun. Thankfully, he'd made it through the night. If his stomach had knees, it would be down on them praying for food.

He walked cautiously back down the alley toward the loud and smelly city. A faint, but unmistakably meat-like scent drew him from the alley. He tried not to look at the place where Mama had been hit, but he needed to sneak a peek and face his fears.

There were no cops, no crowd of humans shaking their heads and muttering, and no Mama. Cars whizzed by like nothing had happened—like Mama's life hadn't mattered. In his experience, humans didn't care much about dogs.

The meat smell brought him back to the present. He followed the scent for a couple of blocks, filtering out all others. There, in the middle of the street, sat a lump of meat. He sniffed harder. A side of cheese accompanied the main course. His mouth watered, and his stomach did a cartwheel.

He had a dilemma. Cars whizzed past, bringing terrible memories with them. His legs trembled as he considered leaving the relative safety of the sidewalk and making a mad dash into the heart of the cars' black space. Hunger battled fear. He stepped off the curb, then jumped back. His heart pounded in his ears.

He kept an eye on the traffic, trying to time his run. Another dog watched from across the street. *Oh, no, you don't. That meat is mine.* A low, gravelly sound he hadn't heard before oozed from between his clenched teeth as he prepared to fight for it.

His gaze alternated between the traffic and the meat. A space opened up, and he leaped off the curb, legs churning and heart racing in unison. He opened his mouth and scooped up the gooey mass. A car screeched to a stop and looked down at him, eyes flashing on its angry face. He ran back the way he'd come.

When he returned to the safety of the sidewalk, he wolfed down his meat and cheese combo before anyone else could get their paws on it. Across the street, the other dog stared and licked his chops before hanging his head and walking away. On these streets, it was every dog for himself. He didn't like it, but he didn't make the rules. He hoped Mama couldn't see what he'd become.

What was he doing? This was no way to live. He preferred to play with other dogs rather than fight with them over scraps of food. He considered running back into traffic, hoping to join Mama, but he wasn't sure how that worked.

Pup's belly, though not quite full, no longer complained out loud. He found a few more scraps and a puddle in the alley. When he returned to the tracks, he looked both ways for the giant snake, then walked in the same direction the snake had gone. The scary sounds of the city diminished the farther he traveled, and eventually disappeared altogether. While he found much to explore in the endless woods and fields on either side of the tracks, he found little in the way of food or adequate shelter.

Fortunately, small groups of humans with their homes and farms appeared from time to time on either side of the tracks. The people in these settlements moved slower and had fewer cars. He'd stop for the night, or perhaps for a few days if food was readily available, but something told him he needed to keep moving.

Some humans were nice, but most kicked at him and shooed him away, which was ridiculous. He was not there to hurt anyone. He only wanted to play and eat and feel loved. Was that too much to ask? Other than his friend Brian, he'd never seen a human play, or show love for that matter. It wasn't the type of world in which he wanted to grow up.

With his pack gone, he felt a desire to belong to someone or something. Otherwise, what's the purpose of being alive?

Mama had told him that all dogs have a purpose, which revealed itself at different times in their lives. Some found it early in life, others needed more time. Pup believed he was destined to be more than a vagabond, so he moved on, hoping the next settlement might be where his special someone waited.

Walking the rails gave him plenty of time to think and relive old memories. He pushed away the ones that were too sad. Mama had taught him many things before tragedy took her, and he went over them again so he wouldn't forget. He imagined there were plenty more lessons yet to learn.

Alone and left to fend for himself, he found it difficult to share Mama's optimism about life. She'd said it's a dog's nature to be positive and full of unconditional love. Perhaps he'd been born that way, but after literally being kicked around and going to sleep hungry many nights, his once positive attitude had met its match. His puzzle had too many missing pieces.

Another week passed, and he thought about the place called heaven. All dogs go there when they die, so it seemed logical that Mama must be there. It changed the trajectory of his journey, if not his life.

Pup no longer wandered around aimlessly. He had a destination in mind. Unfortunately, he had no idea how to get there, and he couldn't just stop and ask for directions. So, how does one find heaven?

He slept during the day and traveled at night through the brutal summer months. He stopped and searched in every settlement along the way, foraging for food and hoping to find a clue.

This was not how he pictured his life moving forward. He wanted a name and a safe place to call home. He wanted a special someone to love and take care of, much like Mama had loved and taken care of him. Given his present circumstances, it seemed like an impossible dream, and he wondered how much longer he could go on like this.

A dog needs to give love and attention as much as he craves it, to take care of someone as much as he needs to be taken care of. Without an outlet for all that love, he was afraid his poor heart might hold on to it until it grew too big and exploded. Or worse, it might shrivel up and harden from lack of use. Neither scenario appealed to him.

Just when he thought he might never find Mama, he stopped at a small settlement where he spotted a sign that read, *Heaven 20 miles*. His tail wagged, which it hadn't done for some time. Despite his weary bones, he picked up his pace. He was on the right track. Literally.

Chapter Six

Most folks in the little town of Heaven, California, knew George Baxter. He'd been a fixture there for as long as most folks could remember. Before Dottie passed, he could talk anyone's ear off. Their morning walks to the market, which should have taken an hour, stretched into two or three.

George had loved to tend their garden and work on his apartment building almost as much as he loved to talk. That all ended when Dottie passed. He still made his daily trips to the market, but the people he met along the way rarely received more than a courtesy wave or a quick hello. Some avoided him altogether. He kept up with the garden for Dottie's sake and did his best to keep his tenants safe.

After a reasonable amount of time had passed, some suggested he find a new lady friend. Their advice was aways met with the same response.

"Dottie will always be the only girl for me."

So, poor George continued to muddle through life with a profound loneliness etched across his face, a sorrowful testament to the void left in his heart. He stood on the sidewalk in front of his building, cigarette in hand. Normally a cigar man, on this day every year, he abstained.

Dottie had never cared for the smell of cigars, so he smoked a cigarette or two instead on the anniversary of the day she passed. His long-time tenants knew enough to give him some space around that time of year. He stared off into the distance as he exhaled a cloud of hazy gray smoke and questioned the God that had mercilessly taken her from him.

Sam Nguyen stepped out of the building. "Hello, Mr. Baxter."

George continued to stare, busy giving God a piece of his mind about how He conducted business.

Sam, a sixty-something Vietnamese immigrant who worked in a nearby restaurant, had moved into 3C six months ago. He lived alone and kept to himself, which left him unaware of the building's early September protocol. "Nice day, huh?"

George took a long drag, turned to Sam, and blew a cloud of smoke in his direction.

Message received. Sam moved on.

George had nothing against Sam personally. The man had shown up on his doorstep, looking for a place to live. He seemed nice enough, but he reminded George of the VC with their slanted eyes and pointy helmets. They popped out of the jungle and shot at him and blew up his friends. He still heard their screams some nights.

Sam had good references, so George had no reason to turn him away. There were laws against that kind of thing, and George had always been a law-abiding citizen. He took one more puff, licked his thumb and forefinger, and extinguished the glowing ash.

George pocketed the butt and set off for the market. He dropped his usual order on the counter.

The clerk offered a knowing smile. "And a scratch-off ticket?"

George nodded.

He retrieved the ticket while George picked up two boxes of Jujubes and placed them on the counter.

"Those things are bad for your teeth."

George raised an eyebrow. "You're quite the salesman, aren't you?"

The clerk frowned and rang up his order.

On the way home, George told himself that once he made it past Dottie's anniversary, things would get back to his new normal. As he approached his building, he spotted a dog sniffing around his front yard. "That little son of a biscuit is looking for a place to squat." He picked up his pace.

Sure enough, the dog bent his hind legs and assumed the position.

George shook his cane and shouted. "Hey. Stop that. Get the hell out of my yard."

The dog paused for a moment to stare at the crazy man who hobbled down the sidewalk waving a big stick. He turned and ran.

"Caught you just in time, didn't I?" George muttered while he inspected the grass where the dog had been. Perhaps he needed to put up a fence.

Jasmine, from 2B, watched from inside the front door. If you asked her what she did for a living, she'd tell you she lived for what she did, not the other way around. A spiritual guide by trade, she defied the stereotypical image of a senior citizen with her vibrant and eccentric personality. Unconstrained by societal norms, she embraced her individuality, which often made George a little uneasy, though he never admitted it.

She held the door open as George approached. "It's just a natural bodily function. You do it, too, I'm sure."

"Not in other people's yards."

She smiled at George as he passed. "Have a blessed day," she called over her shoulder as she stepped outside.

The woman in 2B had been unusually kind to him since she moved in, always trying to engage him in conversation and occasionally showing up at his door with a home-cooked meal. While he appreciated the food, he hoped she wasn't hitting on him.

George unlocked his door, hung his cane on the hook, and made himself a ham and cheese sandwich, which he chased down with a cold beer. After a brief nap, he spent the rest of the afternoon in the garden. His failing eyesight made it increasingly difficult to tell the weeds from the plants.

George wondered what to do with this year's bountiful harvest. Years ago, Dottie had come up with the idea to set up a free vegetable stand in the first-floor lobby. The tenants loved it, but George didn't have the same motivation after she'd passed.

After the weeds had been removed, he washed up and popped his dinner into the microwave. George had spent some time as a cook in the army before they shipped him to Nam. He knew his way around a kitchen, but with no one to cook for but himself, it hardly seemed worth the effort. A freezer full of microwave dinners provided adequate sustenance.

Marie Callendar's chicken pot pie was a close second to homemade without all the fuss. When he finished, he dropped the empty plastic tray in the trash and rinsed off the silverware. No muss, no fuss. That left plenty of time to putz around with his model trains before *Jeopardy!* and *Wheel of Fortune*.

He hadn't needed a hobby while Dottie was alive. You could say *she* was his hobby. A few years after she'd passed, George pulled an old Lionel train set out of storage. He'd found it under the Christmas tree when he was seven. His father worked for the railroad and passed his love for trains on to his only son.

The antique set had an engine that belched smoke as it made its way down the tracks. Similar models fetched a pretty penny on eBay, but George had no intention of selling. He invested in more tracks and built a little village and countryside for it to meander through. The train station was a replica of the station that had once been attached to his building. He did less intricate work as his eyesight deteriorated and sometimes joked that he was blind in one eye and couldn't see out of the other, but it was no joke.

George spent his evenings in his favorite chair, pushed up close to his sixty-inch television. The *Honeymooners, Gunsmoke, I Love*

Lucy, and *Bonanza* were some of his favorites as a child. Dottie had been a fan of the *Burns and Allen Show*. Naturally, he was George, and he'd playfully call her Gracie. "Say goodnight, Gracie." George Burns said it at the end of every show. Gracie Allen replied with a smile and a simple "goodnight." The same could have been heard many nights when George and Dottie's heads hit the pillow.

Wallowing in the past was worth the price of cable.

Chapter Seven

After months of walking the lonely tracks and sleeping in the weeds, the smell of dirty dog made it difficult to sniff out food and detect dangerous situations. Technically, he wasn't a pup anymore. He'd grown bigger and stronger and, well, stinkier. What this dog needed more than anything was a bath.

The rails bent around the end of a small lake up ahead. Dog jumped the tracks and ran for the cool, clear water that reflected the sunrise like a mirror. He jumped in and splashed around. The water invigorated his dry skin and tired muscles as it washed away the months of grit and grime that clung to his fur. Once he'd been thoroughly cleaned, he splashed some more, just for the fun of it. He felt like a pup again, a feeling that had been missing since Mama had left him on his own.

He stepped out of the water and gave his body a good long shake before searching for food. The trash cans that dotted the shoreline proved too tall for him to breach. Luckily, humans had little regard for etiquette and dropped their half-eaten lunches and empty water bottles wherever it was most convenient. You wouldn't catch a dog acting like that.

His search turned up enough scraps to satisfy for now. He found the perfect tree to mark with his scent, then picked out a shady spot to get some much-needed sleep before he continued his journey.

After another night of walking, the early morning sun illuminated the weathered sign that signified the end of his journey. *Welcome to Heaven.* It hung on a brick building behind a crumbling concrete platform. The place looked deserted, and he momentarily doubted the validity of that old sign until he smelled the bacon. His tail wagged as he searched for a way inside.

Dog followed the scent to a door on the side of the building. Two trash cans guarded the entrance. He knocked one over and rifled through the contents. No bacon, but an array of slightly used pastries. *Bon appétit.*

Before he'd finished, the door opened. A large man wearing a dirty white apron stepped outside and shouted some words he didn't understand. However, the man's tone gave Dog a general idea of his intention. The low, gravelly noise Dog made, and a good look at his teeth, made apron man retreat. He shouted something from behind the screen door, and Dog ran.

He stopped out front and surveyed the building. It appeared to be an impenetrable fortress of brick and stone. A sign next to the door read *Apartments for Rent.* Mama never mentioned having to pay to get in.

He studied the letters painted on the glass of another, smaller door. *Heavenly Café, Serving Fine Pastries and Breakfast Fare.* The smell was heavenly—apron man, not so much. He crept up to the door and peeked inside. Plenty of humans, but no Mama. Not wanting to chance another run-in with the proprietor, he retreated to a safe distance.

The larger door must be the main entrance. What if dying was the only way to get inside? While he'd previously entertained such dark thoughts, at the moment, that wasn't something he was prepared to do.

Dog sat on the sidewalk out front and waited for someone to go inside so he might slip in behind them undetected. He needed to do something. Mama wasn't going to find herself. Once inside, he would see what's what.

Several people came and went through the small glass door. They ignored him. Why? Because he had no pedigree? At least he didn't smell anymore. One man glared and shook his head.

Humans can be so judgmental. It's not like he was a cat. He wasn't even a pup anymore. He was a dog. A little respect would be nice.

An hour passed before a woman and a small child exited heaven through the big front door. He paused to wrap his head around what he'd just seen. Heaven was supposed to be a one-way trip, wasn't it? If it was as good as Mama claimed, who would want to leave? This bothered him on several levels. If these people could just waltz out the front door of heaven, it seemed logical that others might, too. What if Mama was on her way back right now to find *him*?

No longer able to sit still, he paced in little circles, something he did when he got nervous. What if he'd come all this way for nothing?

The small one turned to Dog and pointed. "Mommy, look." She giggled.

What's so funny?

More giggling.

Dog smelled fear as the mother pulled her little girl close. He realized how scary he must have looked, chasing his tail in tighter and tighter circles like some rabid animal.

"I want to pet him," the girl said.

"That's not a good idea. He looks dangerous."

Dangerous? I'm two feet tall with my nose in the air.

"But he's so cute."

Wait. I'm cute? You want to pet me? Dog stopped. No one had ever said that before. His time on the street had taught him to be wary. But look at her, so small and cute, with curly blond hair that danced on her little shoulders when she walked. He took a step toward her then stopped. *No.* He'd thrown caution to the wind once, and it had earned him a swift kick in the ribs. He wouldn't let that happen again.

The girl walked toward him. His tail wanted to swing free, but he tucked it between his legs.

"Savannah!"

She ignored her mother's command and reached her hand out to pet him.

Dog took a step back. She followed and touched him gently. He wanted to run, but it felt SO good. She stroked the back of his neck. His breath sped up and his tail moved from side to side so quickly he thought it might fly off. He hadn't felt this good since before Mama left. Maybe this really *was* heaven.

He closed his eyes. *Oooh, yeah. Don't stop.*

Another girl joined their group from inside. She stood at heaven's door, looking down at a small black board in her hand. This one appeared to be older and not as friendly. She had darker hair, pulled back except for a few strands that hung on either side of her face.

The mother turned toward the older one. "What do you think you're doing?"

That earned her a huffy look and an eyeroll, followed by an exaggerated sigh.

"You're not going to school dressed like that."

The girl slipped the board into her pocket and folded her arms. "Yes I am."

"Where did you even get such skimpy clothes? I certainly didn't buy them."

"Dad gave me the money."

"Looks like I need to have a talk with your father."

"When you do, tell him I want to live with him." She blew at the strands of hair.

Dog sensed anger in their voices but didn't understand what they were saying. The little one was scratching behind his ears, so he didn't care. He licked her hand, then leaned in and soaked up the love that poured from her fingertips.

The woman chewed her bottom lip for a moment, then turned to the little one. "I told you to leave him alone." She focused her mean eyes on Dog. "Bad dog! Go away."

But he wasn't doing anything wrong, was he? How could something that felt so good be wrong? *Wait.* He remembered when Brian had called him that. Perhaps it was his name.

"Come on, Savannah, or you'll miss your bus."

She leaned in and whispered. "I'll be back after school. If you're still here, we can play."

Whatever school was, his friend Brian went there every day, and *he* came back. Dog had no reason not to believe this one would too.

Dog glanced at the woman. *What about that one over there?*

"That's my mommy. Don't worry about her," Savannah said and returned to the woman's side.

What did you say? Can you... can you hear me?

As they walked away, his new friend Savannah turned to the other one. "Bye, Chloe."

"Whatever."

Savannah shrugged, then turned to Dog and showed her teeth. His tail swung out of control again. He wanted to let out a playful bark and chase after her. She walked to the corner and waited with the big mean one.

Dog's mind had just been blown. Animals communicated with each other telepathically, but he'd never heard of a human who could do it. Is that what just happened? There may be hope for them yet.

Wait a minute. What if it had something to do with heaven? They'd all been in there. What if heaven opened their minds and made them more like dogs? Perhaps it only affected the little ones. He still had serious doubts about that big one.

The one she called Chloe walked away in the opposite direction.

He checked the corner. Savannah turned and waved. *Oh, boy! Is this a game?* He couldn't be sure; he hadn't played anything in such a long time. *Are they waiting for me? Do they want me to catch them?* He remained temporarily stuck in his analysis paralysis as a big yellow box rolled up to the corner and Savannah disappeared inside.

He would have been concerned if that box had not been full of other little ones laughing and playing. It looked like a big, yellow box of fun, and he wanted in. He considered a mad dash for the corner just as the door closed and the box rolled away. Savannah had said she would be back later. If she went to school every day like Brian did, maybe she'd take him with her next time.

Yikes! Cruella de Vil was headed his way. He turned and ran toward the bushes that fronted the building. Some might think him a coward, but in his defense, she appeared ten feet tall from where he sat. She bent down for a closer look. He held his breath, afraid he might end up in her crock-pot tonight.

"I know you're in there." She shook the branches. "Leave us alone and go back to wherever you came from."

After a few moments, she gave up and headed for the main door.

Dog waited. No way they'd let her back inside after that unpleasant display. When she pulled the door and it opened, he ran toward her. He caught up to her in stealth mode and ducked inside just before the heavy door closed behind him with a thud. He'd wanted to take a bite out of her heel but feared it would derail his mission.

He found himself in a large, mostly empty room with few places to hide. He ducked behind the only piece of furniture—a chair in the corner—and watched her stab a button on the wall with her finger. A door slid open in front of her, revealing some sort of large empty container. Cruella stepped inside and the door closed behind her.

Phew! He didn't know what just happened to her, but good riddance. Then he thought of Savannah. He had no way to know whether this was good news or bad, whether she was free from her evil captor, or she'd just lost her mama. Dog vowed to take care of his new friend if it turned out to be the latter.

Speaking of mamas, he needed to find his.

Chapter Eight

Dog was not impressed with heaven so far. He'd expected to find Mama and other dogs playing and eating bacon, but instead he sat alone in an empty, cavernous room after being threatened by one of its inhabitants. And who knew heaven was in such dire need of an interior decorator? He barked and listened to his voice echo around the empty chamber.

Where's Mama? What if this wasn't heaven at all? He searched for a way out and found only two doors—the one he came in and the one that swallowed up Cruella. He couldn't open either by himself, so he'd have to wait for someone to come along and let him out.

Savannah! She told him to wait for her. But for how long? In the meantime, he would look for Mama.

He toddled down the hall, cutting a wide path around the door that had swallowed the rude woman. Although he hadn't made up his mind about this place yet, he wanted to leave his mark in case he stayed. He lifted his leg next to a potted plant and gave it a squirt.

Satisfied with his work, he turned to find a giant human the size of a mail truck standing in his path. His white hair and dark skin were quite the opposite of the other humans Dog had met. Perhaps this one had gotten on the wrong side of a fire-breathing octopus.

The giant folded his arms across his mighty chest and looked down with mean eyes and a scrunched-up face from what seemed like twelve feet up. Dog got the feeling this would not end well for him.

"You little son of a…"

Dog's heart pounded, and he took a step backward.

"How did you get in here?"

The giant took a step forward, and Dog stepped back again. This continued until Dog's tail bumped up against the big wooden door he'd come in.

Yikes!

The giant leaned forward. Dog squeezed his eyes shut and pushed himself down onto the floor. Suddenly, the door gave way behind him. He opened his eyes just in time to see the giant rear back on one foot. Dog stumbled backward down the stairs to avoid the bottom of the giant's boot.

He picked himself up off the sidewalk and shook himself off. *Not cool! Dogs have feelings, you know.*

Mama never mentioned having to get past the palace guard. He wondered what else she might have left out.

"Bad dog!" The giant stabbed the air with his finger. "Don't let me catch you in here again!"

It was official. His name was Bad Dog. How did he not know that? Why hadn't Mama told him? He didn't care for the name at all.

Okay, okay, I get the point. Bad Dog shuffled off down the sidewalk.

He heard a growl and searched around with his nose in the air. No scent of other dogs. That's when he realized the noise came from his stomach. Time to look for something to eat. He wandered around the property until he smelled food, but it wasn't meat. He followed the scent around to the back of the building and found what must have been a garden. Mama had told him about exotic foods called vegetables that grew in gardens. He'd try anything at this point.

One problem. Fence.

He flashed back to Mama scraping the ground with her paws. Scraping and scraping until she'd dug a hole under the woman's fence big enough for them to crawl through.

After a few minutes of intense digging, he slithered through the hole and out the other side. He walked the neatly cultivated rows, inspecting his new produce department. Cucumbers and squash and beans, oh my. He started with a cucumber. The first bite hit his mouth like a wave crashing on the shore. *Hmm... not meat, but very refreshing.* The zucchini were so big, he only finished half. A few strawberries made a sweet little dessert.

He slithered back through the hole and walked around front to see if Savannah had returned yet but found no sign of her. He settled on a shady spot, far enough away from the giant, but close enough to see Savannah when she returned. His head heavy from walking all night, he rested it on his paws and drifted off to sleep.

Some time later, his eyes opened, and he jumped to his feet. *Oh, no! Did I miss her?* A sound came from behind the building, and he set off to investigate. He turned the corner and froze.

The giant looked smaller as he knelt inside the fence, his face scrunched up again. He held up the half-eaten zucchini. "What the..." He stood and looked around.

Bad Dog ducked back around the corner of the building. Rookie mistake leaving his leftovers behind. He hightailed it back out front to wait for Savannah. Afraid the giant might come looking for him, he walked down to the street corner.

His ears pricked up, and his tail moved. The yellow box approached. It stopped, and Savannah hopped off, showing all her teeth. "You waited."

They walked together. Bad Dog held his head high and strutted his stuff, hoping other dogs in the neighborhood might see him with his human and her teeth. They arrived at the front door, and Savannah reached for the handle.

An alarm went off in his head. *Danger! Danger!* He backpedaled a few steps.

"What's the matter?"

He stood his ground.

"I need to change into my play clothes. You can come with me. It's okay."

Not okay. He'd seen the bottom of the palace guard's boot once already, and that was enough. Even if he made it past the guard, he'd have to deal with Cruella de Vil.

"Mr. Baxter says no pets are allowed to live here, but you're just visiting. Besides, he usually spends the afternoon in his garden."

What about Cruella, I mean, your mama?

"My mom is at work. Chloe watches me until she gets home."

The one with the bad attitude and the skimpy clothes? She couldn't be trusted either.

Savannah shrugged and opened the door. "She's my sister. She's okay most of the time."

Wait! Did it just happen again, or am I losing my mind? Once is a fluke, twice is a coincidence. Third time is the charm. *I love you, Savannah Banana.*

Savannah bent down and hugged him. "I love you, too. Now, let's go inside."

Bad Dog's tail shifted into high gear. *Ho-lee cow!*

Chapter Nine

Jasmine Jacobs lived in apartment 2B with her cat, Luna. George had a no pet policy in the building, so Luna couldn't leave the apartment when he was around.

Most people in the building knew of Jasmine's psychic abilities, which she preferred to call her intuition. Her gentle and intuitive nature allowed her to tap into the energies surrounding an individual, as well as loved ones who had transitioned.

She'd become aware of her gift at a young age, living in a hippie commune in San Francisco during the seventies. Peace and love guided her formative years as she blossomed in the Age of Aquarius. She still looked the part, with pewter-colored hair that hung in wild curls and a colorful, seventies-style wardrobe.

Jasmine performed readings in her apartment to supplement her Social Security benefits. George had a policy about that, too, but he looked the other way because it helped pay her rent. When she heard about Dottie, Jasmine offered to help George communicate with her spirit. However, he never placed much faith in this so-called "hocus pocus" of hers, so he politely declined.

But Dottie had used Jasmine as a conduit to send messages to George. She'd told Jasmine of her disappointment with his recent behavior. While flattered that her passing left such a hole in his life, she wanted him to find happiness and live the rest of his life to the fullest. And she wanted Jasmine to tell him as much.

Jasmine knew George would be unreceptive, so she decided on a subtle approach until he opened his mind to the possibility. She knocked on his door with a casserole dish in hand.

"I heard you like tuna casserole."

George raised a suspicious eyebrow. "Dottie tell you that?"

Jasmine smiled. "I made it with peas."

His brow furrowed as he studied her. "That's how Dottie used to make it."

Jasmine had moved in three years ago, so she'd never met Dottie. She offered another smile and a knowing nod as she handed him the dish. She would find a way to make a believer out of him.

"You didn't have to."

She kind of did. She felt her gift came with an obligation to respect the wishes of the spirits who communicated with her.

"Thank you." He smiled an out-of-practice smile. "I'll put it to good use."

This wasn't the first time she'd cooked for him or left him the perfect little present on his birthday. He surely must have wondered how she knew so much about him.

George Baxter wasn't her only project in the building. There had been others, and more to come. She'd been guided to move into this building for reasons that were, at the time, unknown.

Savannah entered the building with a small dog in tow.

"Who have we got here?"

She froze like a deer in headlights. "You're not going to tell Mr. Baxter, are you?"

"What he doesn't know won't hurt him."

"I found him outside."

Jasmine bent down to pet the little dog. "I think he found you, honey."

"We're going outside to play after I get changed."

Jasmine returned to her apartment. Luna watched Bird TV, ignoring her as cats do unless they want something. She stared out the window for hours from her perch on the back of the sofa, keeping track of all the birds in the yard, unless she was preoccupied in one of her frequent catnaps. Occasionally, she amused herself by scaling the carpeted, multi-level cat castle that occupied one corner of the living room.

"I saw Savannah in the hall with a little dog."

Luna continued to stare out the window. *Whatever.*

"This wasn't just any dog. I have a good feeling about him. He's special."

I'm special.

"Of course you are, dear."

• • • ❂ • ❂ • • • •

Bad Dog had watched with suspicious eyes as the colorful woman walked away. She smelled human, but with a different vibe, like she knew him, or at least why he'd ended up there. He also picked up another scent. She smelled like a cat. This place got stranger by the minute.

Bad Dog's heart pounded while they waited in front of the door that had swallowed up Cruella. *I'm not going in there.*

Savannah bent down and whispered, "It's okay. It's just an elevator. That's how we get upstairs."

Maybe that's how YOU get upstairs.

The door opened, and she stepped inside the box. He sniffed the air and found nothing sinister.

"Are you coming?"

He hesitated.

Savannah patted her thigh. "Come on, boy. Hurry."

Her voice had a sudden urgency. What should he do? He couldn't let her go alone. What if he never saw her again? The door began to close. *Make a decision!* He leapt inside just before the heavy metal doors could chop off the end of his tail.

The box moved, and he steadied himself. What had he done? He looked up at Savannah and sniffed. No fear. Okay, maybe he overreacted.

When the elevator stopped and the door opened again, he ran out ahead of her, grateful for the solid ground beneath his feet. But where was he?

She passed him and stood in front of an open door. "Are you coming?"

He followed her inside. Is this where she lived? It sure beat a cardboard box, or even Brian's underground room. There were obstacles everywhere, and he navigated around them, sniffing as he went. The soft carpet released new and unusual scents with every step. Warm air filled the room, but he found no octopus.

"This is my room," Savannah said as she led him through another door.

A menagerie of colored animals congregated near her bed. Strange that he hadn't picked up their scents. He crept closer and sniffed the air. Something was wrong. He growled.

"What? You don't like my stuffed animals?"

What are they stuffed with?

"I don't know. They're not real. They're my play friends."

I thought I was your play friend.

"You're my NEW play friend."

This concerned him a little. Did the others start out that way before they got stuffed? He kept an eye on the other animals as he retreated to the far side of the room.

"I have to change before we go out to play."

He sat in the corner and watched her peel off her skin. She didn't seem too concerned, so he kept quiet. She replaced it with different colored skin. Apparently, he had a lot to learn about humans.

He glanced at the stuffed animals on the way out of the room. None of them had moved. Savannah stopped in front of another door and knocked. The door opened a crack and part of Chloe's face appeared.

"I'm going outside to play."

Chloe glanced at the dog. "What's he doing in here? Mom's gonna kill you."

"I don't care. He's my friend."

Chloe's eye—he only saw one of them—rolled around in its socket.

"Anyway, Mom doesn't have to know."

"Whatever."

"We'll be out front."

The door closed, and she led him into another room.

"I need a snack before we play."

He tilted his head. *Snack?*

Savannah opened a big box with a light inside. Cold air mixed with delicious scents crawled across the floor and swirled round his feet. His nose told him the box contained a mouthwatering collection of food items. His tail cut the air like a metronome on steroids, and he moved closer for a better look.

The door nearly snapped off his nose as Savannah walked to the other side of the room with her arms full. He followed, then jumped up as high as he could to see what she had.

"Be patient. I'm making us a snack."

There's that word again. The smell of cheese and almost-bacon reached his nose, and he knew *snack* was a good thing.

She put everything in a bag, and they left the apartment.

Bad Dog stopped when he reached the hall. *Wait. What am I doing?* He wanted to spend time with his new friend and her snacks, but he came here to find Mama.

I can't play right now.

Savannah turned around and gave him a curious look. "Why not?"

I need to find Mama.

"Where is she?"

He hung his head. *She's supposed to be here. Where are all the dogs?*

"There are no dogs here. It's against the rules."

That's a stupid rule.

"I know."

I don't understand. I thought all dogs go to heaven when they die.

"That's a different heaven."

Wait. There's more than one heaven?

She nodded.

The sign, the bacon—he'd been sure this was the right place. But if there were no dogs, and no Mama, he must have been mistaken. Now what?

"Let's go have a snack, and I'll help you look for your mama."

Snack? That sounded like a plan.

The elevator delivered them to the first floor without incident, and he followed her to a shady spot under a tree in the side yard. Saliva dripped from Bad Dog's mouth as he listened to the rustle of the paper bag, almost giddy with anticipation. The snack didn't disappoint. A big slice of something she called ham, wrapped around a cylinder of cheese. She'd made him two, with a cookie-thingy for dessert.

When they finished, he caught Savannah staring at him. He met her gaze, and she showed her teeth for longer than usual.

What? Do I have food in my teeth? He ran his tongue around the inside of his mouth.

"No, silly. I'm smiling. It means I'm happy."

Is that what that is?

Eventually, Bad Dog rested his head on his paws while Savannah stroked his back. This must be how the other half spent their afternoons. *I love you, Savannah Banana.* His eyes were heavy, and he soon fell asleep.

He awoke to a human voice.

"Savannah," a woman called from in front of the building.

"Mama's home." She gave him a quick hug. "Go hide!"

What about helping me find Mama?

She turned the corner of the building and disappeared.

He stared at the side of the building that he had thought was heaven. A black cat stared back from a second-story window. It looked more and more like Savannah had been right.

Still hungry, he headed around back toward the produce department. The breeze brought with it the smell of something burning. Unlike the wildfires he'd smelled from miles away on his journey here, this one had a sweeter aroma that was not at all unpleasant.

He peered around the corner of the building. The giant who had chased him out of the building earlier sat on the patio. He didn't look as big and threatening as the last time, until Bad Dog noticed the burning stick in his mouth. Perhaps it was some kind of weapon used to torture small animals.

Chapter Ten

George wiped the sweat from his forehead, removed the cigar from his mouth, and took another big gulp from a beer can. He stared at his garden and cursed the no-good critter that had burrowed its way under the fence to dine on his vegetables. The smell of a good cigar had a way of relaxing him when he became tense.

He had an idea how to stop the critter but carting two wheel-barrows full of bricks had driven him to the brink of heat exhaustion. A cold beverage and a break were needed to cool him off both mentally and physically.

Dinner time approached, but he didn't plan to stop until the garden perimeter had been fortified. "No four-legged son of a biscuit is gonna make a fool out of George Baxter."

He finished his beer, hitched up his trousers, and went back to work. He filled in the hole, then trimmed the grass that grew along the bottom of the fence. Next, he laid down a course of bricks along the perimeter to discourage any more digging.

George felt someone watching as he worked his way down one side of the fence. He turned around to find the dog who'd broken into his building lying in the grass watching him. "Not you again."

The dog took a step backward.

George sized up the mutt and compared it to the hole he'd just filled. "You did this, didn't you?" He took the cigar butt from his mouth and flicked it in the dog's direction. "Go on, get outta here."

The dog ran, and George resumed his work. He finished one side of the garden and began the next. A bark startled him from behind. He closed his eyes and took a deep breath before he turned around. Sure enough, the mutt had returned. George didn't care for animals of any kind, except maybe horses. Dottie loved horses.

The barking continued until George raised his shovel and took a step. "Don't make me come over there."

George had won. Not only did the barking stop, the dog ran away. But before he laid another brick, the barking started again. This time, the dog grabbed George's pant leg from behind and pulled, causing him to lose his balance and fall backwards. He lay on the ground, his head full of thoughts about what he would do to that damn dog, until he heard a rattling sound. An enormous snake sat at the edge of the garden, coiled and ready to strike.

Feet and hands churning the ground, George scrambled to a safe distance. He grabbed his shovel and swung it at the snake, cutting it in half. He blew out a long breath and muttered, "I never saw him coming." He turned to the dog. "It looks like I owe you an apology. You might have just saved my life."

George stared for a moment at the brave little dog before he spoke again. "Thank you. Now, get out of here. I have work to do."

The dog didn't move.

"Suit yourself." George set his shovel down and went back to work.

The dog watched, and George felt his stare.

"You can go now."

Apparently, the dog had other ideas.

"What do you want?" George had a chip on his shoulder, but he wasn't a monster. "You look hungry. I've got something you might like better than those vegetables." He held up a finger. "Wait here."

He grabbed another beer and a package of hot dogs from the fridge and returned to his chair in the yard. The dog approached cautiously as George held one of the hot dogs in the air.

"Want a hot dog?"

The dog tilted his head.

"It's okay. I won't bite." He laughed at the irony.

Before he knew it, the dog had snatched the meat from his hand and gobbled it up.

"I guess you were hungry," he said and pulled another from the package.

After George watched him devour two more hot dogs, he turned on the hose and let him drink as much as he wanted.

He noticed the dog had no collar. "What am I going to do with you?"

The furry little stray looked up at him with big, sad eyes.

George shook his head. "That won't work on me." Truth is, it worked a little. "Scram. It's getting late, and I have work to do."

The dog hung around and watched from a distance. When George finished his work, he picked a ripe cucumber and latched the gate.

"I'll make you a deal," he called to the dog. "You stay out of my garden, and you can have this." He tossed the cucumber toward the dog.

George threw his tools in the back of an old pickup truck parked near the garden. He'd bought the F-150 new back in 1975 and kept it in good running order, even though his poor eyesight prevented him from driving it.

With dinner in the microwave, George set the table for two. Halfway through his meal, he gazed at Dottie's empty chair. "The darnedest thing happened today. A little dog pulled me away from a rattler. Probably saved my life." He paused, as if listening to her reply. "Of course I thanked him. He looked hungry, so I gave him a few hot dogs." George chuckled. "He gobbled them up so fast it would have made your head spin."

He didn't tell her he'd almost clobbered the defenseless little mutt with a shovel. It hadn't been one of his finer moments.

. . . . ● . ● . . . .

Bad Dog gnawed on a cucumber under the big maple tree in the side yard while the cat watched from its perch in the window. He wondered how the cat got in there. Cats were sneaky and, in his experience, not to be trusted. Still, it couldn't hurt to have another ally on the inside. He wagged his tail, hoping the cat would see that he was a friend. The cat looked at him indifferently, then turned away without any kind of acknowledgment.

Never mind the cat, he had a decision to make, but not until he finished eating. He took his time, postponing the inevitable.

The day had been a roller coaster of emotions. He'd finally found heaven, or so he thought, and then been booted out. On a positive note, he'd made a friend, and eaten more in one day than he had in the past week.

If he stayed, Savannah had promised to help him look for Mama. Given his track record, he could certainly use the help. However, it appeared that Mama wasn't there. Perhaps he needed to cut his losses and look elsewhere.

After some deliberation, he decided to stay. He loved Savannah. Even if Cruella disapproved, he could be her secret friend. A little voice in the back of his head told him it wasn't a practical plan for the future. He needed security and a proper home. Another voice told him to chill out and take it one day at a time. It couldn't hurt to let the girl help look for Mama.

The night temperatures were still warm enough to sleep outside. So, he found a comfy spot behind the maple tree where the cat couldn't spy on him and settled in for the night.

In the morning, he stayed out of sight as he watched hot dog man sweep the sidewalk in front of the building. Later, Cruella walked Savannah to the corner while Chloe strolled by in the other direction. The older one looked up briefly from the little black board in her hand and waved to Bad Dog. His tail swung, but he resisted the urge to follow her. They weren't there yet in their trust relationship.

Bad Dog alternated between napping and investigating the area around Savannah's building. On one foray into the surrounding neighborhoods, his nose picked up the scent of dogs. No bacon, but many different dogs. Could he have stumbled upon the real heaven?

His ears stood up, and he picked up his pace when he heard happy dogs barking. The joyful noise grew louder. Eventually, he spotted a grassy space set back from the road and surrounded by a metal fence. Within its borders were all manner of dogs running and playing with each other. He looked for Mama. This might be heaven, despite the lack of any signs.

Perhaps the sign had been stolen and placed on the building with no dogs, just to trick him into going inside and being kicked. Given his experience with humans so far, it was not beyond the realm of possibility.

Happy dogs as far as the eye could see. There were some humans inside this place, as well. Perhaps the few good humans who loved and cared for dogs were allowed entry. Most dogs needed someone to feed them and pick up their poop.

Bad Dog ran toward this heaven. He put his paws up on the fence and watched the dogs play games he'd never seen before. His tail wagged out of control, and he barked, hoping someone might hear him and let him in, but everyone appeared to be busy.

A small black dog, with a head too large for its body, heard him and toddled over to where he waited. Bad Dog pushed his nose through the fence and the other dog licked it. His tongue smelled sweet, like he'd just eaten a treat. He must be a good dog.

Is this heaven? Bad Dog asked.

The other dog tilted his head. *I'm not sure. I think it's called Dog Park. At least that's what Lily, she's my human, says whenever we get into the car to come here.*

Can I come in?

I'm pretty sure you need a human. Where's yours?

A woman called to them. "Come back here, Max."

That's me. Gotta go. Nice meeting you. Come Back Here Max turned and ran toward the woman.

Bad Dog watched him run off to his human, who petted him and gave him another treat. He was clearly a good dog, who Bad Dog wanted to get to know better. Unfortunately, they hadn't had a chance to sniff butts, what with the fence and all.

Bad Dog didn't have a human. Perhaps if he couldn't find Mama, finding a human would be the next best thing. As much as he'd liked talking with Come Back Here Max, he was somewhat relieved that he didn't have to admit to not having his own human.

Chapter Eleven

Lying around outside heaven, or the dog park, or whatever that place was, annoyed Bad Dog after a while. He wasn't the jealous type, but watching all those dogs play when he couldn't join in wasn't fair. He tried to ignore everything and take a nap, but a bunch of noisy, happy dogs wouldn't allow it. He hung his head as he walked back to the building where Savannah lived.

When he got there, he took some time to retrace his steps back to the tracks, giving the garden a wide berth to avoid any temptation. He'd dined on a slightly used breakfast sandwich outside the coffee shop earlier, but his stomach reminded him that was four hours ago.

He reached the tracks and turned around to check the sign again. Still there. This must be a cruel joke. It didn't feel like heaven, but neither did the other place. Mama wouldn't have been able to get in there without a human, which neither of them had. So, where was this elusive heaven? Did it even exist? Perhaps mamas told their pups such things so they wouldn't be afraid of death?

As he stood there thinking, a giant snake roared by and scared the bejeezus out of him. His legs didn't stop moving until he reached the hot dog man's back yard. He stopped to catch his breath and lick his paws that had been scratched by the brambles. That had been a close one, but he couldn't die yet. Mama told him every dog had a purpose. He was still looking for his.

When Savannah returned home from school, the two went upstairs to have another snack. She introduced him to peanut butter, which tasted... AMAZING. He wondered how something that good had eluded him for so long.

Chloe walked into the kitchen. "What are you doing?"

"This dog is lost, and I'm going to help him look for his mama."

"You mean his owner."

"No, silly. I mean his mama. She's a dog."

"He doesn't have a collar," Chloe said.

"That's because he's lost."

Chloe rolled her eyes at her sister, then turned to the dog. "He looks thirsty."

Bad Dog lowered his head and blinked several times, which he'd learned had a positive effect on humans.

"I'll get him some water."

Bad Dog wagged his tail enthusiastically as he watched her fill up a bowl in the sink. She set it on the floor in front of him and watched him lap at it.

"So, what should we call him?"

"I'm going to call him Dog," Savannah said, "until we find out his real name."

A nickname. Short. Easy to say. A tad generic, but I like it better than Bad Dog.

Chloe nodded her agreement. "Maybe his mama has a collar, and we can find out who they belong to."

Dog hesitated to tell them Mama had no collar. He didn't want to burst their bubble or give them any reason not to help him. *Thanks for the water.*

"That's why we have to find her."

"Can I come?"

Savannah turned to Dog.

Sure. We can use all the help we can get. The ability to communicate telepathically came in handy with a mouth full of peanut butter.

"Okay," she told her sister.

Chloe bent down and scratched behind his ears. "You're a cute one, aren't you?"

He leaned in. This one sure ran hot and cold. He welcomed the attention, even if it might only be temporary.

"I hope when we find your mama, she treats you better than mine treats me."

Savannah frowned. "That's not very nice."

"Well, it's true. You're the one who gets all the attention around here."

Girls! Let's not forget why we're here.

"We're going to go now, and we don't need your help."

What? I'm pretty sure we do.

"Wait. I'm sorry." Chloe glanced at Dog, then back at Savannah. "I really want to help."

Savannah hesitated.

Do I get a vote? Because I vote yes.

"Fine. Let's go." Savannah led the way.

They checked the basement and all the common areas first. Then they planned to knock on every door and ask if anyone had seen another dog in the building. They searched every nook and cranny in that basement but found no dogs.

George met them at the basement door. "What were you girls doing in the basement?" Then he spotted the dog behind them. "Was that dog down there?"

"Uh, yes, but he was with us," Chloe said.

George looked at them with squinted eyes. "What do you mean, *with us*?"

"Well, you see..."

Savannah interrupted. "He lost his mama, and we're helping him look for her."

"Is that so?" He folded his arms across his chest. "He's not supposed to be in here."

"He said you only told him to stay out of the garden," Savannah replied.

Chloe and George looked at her in unison, then at Dog, then back at Savannah.

"Really?" George said. "The dog told you that?"

Savannah nodded.

The heavy smell of emptiness surrounded this man. He'd suffered the loss of his family. Dog felt a connection and raised his big, sad eyes.

George shook his head and pointed at the dog. "I told you that won't work on me."

"We just need to look around for her." Savannah put her hands together. "Pleeeeeze?"

After some hesitation and a big shrug, he said, "Okay. You can show him around, then show him the door."

"Thank you."

Off they went.

"That was George Baxter. He owns the building."

Chloe stopped. "What's the matter with you? I know who George is."

"I was talking to Dog."

This earned Savannah another eyeroll.

Dog studied Chloe and wondered if her googly eyes indicated a medical condition that required treatment. More importantly, the hot dog man had a name. George. George the Giant.

After searching the common areas on the first floor, they took the elevator to the third floor and worked their way down. The second and third floors each had five apartments. George lived in the only apartment on the first floor. The rest of the floor included the lobby, a lounge, and a coffee shop.

The first door they knocked on, apartment 3C, belonged to Sam Nguyen.

"So sorry. I go work and come home. I not see dog."

They thanked him and moved on.

"He talks funny," Savannah said after he closed the door.

"Don't say that. He's from Vietnam. He probably thinks *you* talk funny."

"Why is he here?"

"He lives here. I think he works in a restaurant downtown."

"Did you hear that, Dog?"

Dogs hear everything.

"He hasn't seen her." She lowered her voice. "He talks funny because he's from Vietnam."

Chloe watched her sister squat next to the dog and whisper in his ear. "You know he can't understand you, right?"

Savannah pushed out her chin. "That's what YOU think."

Each door they knocked on produced more of the same. No one had seen any dogs in or around the building. Dog often smelled fear when the doors opened. Like most humans he'd met in his travels, present company excluded, they weren't friendly and kept to themselves. He wanted to meet them all and get to know them. They all lived in the same place, like one big pack. He desperately wanted to belong to a pack again.

Chloe provided some background information that she'd gained from Ruby, the resident gossip in 3E. Ruby, a larg-er-than-life Texan, made it a habit to not only know everyone's business, but to disseminate it freely and without provocation. If you looked up "busybody" in the dictionary, you would find her picture.

Tom in 3B had lost his son and eventually divorced. He wore a sad face most of the time and kept to himself. Marilyn in 3A, also divorced, spent her time interviewing potential replacements for her ex-husband. Chloe thought Marilyn and Tom should hook up, but said Marilyn needed something first. Pretty sure she called it a makeover.

On the second floor, an older woman, Rita, lived in 2D and took care of her sick husband, John. When she opened her door, a mixture of sadness and cookies escaped on the air.

"They used to own a bakery," Chloe said. "Rita still bakes sometimes in her apartment and makes the whole floor smell like heaven."

That explains the cookies. Wait. Did she say heaven?

Abigail in 2A, a singer in a bar downtown, dreamed of moving to Nashville and becoming the next Carrie Underwood.

"She plays guitar and sings real nice. Sometimes, I sit outside her door and listen."

Perhaps I can join you next time. Does she take requests?

When Dog heard Mike in 2C was a retired police officer, he wondered if he'd been the one who took Mama.

A cop? Does he have a dog?

Savannah shook her head. "Remember? No pets allowed in the building."

He planned to keep his distance from that one, nevertheless.

With apartment 2E empty, the only one they hadn't checked was 2B. Was Mama even in the building? 2B or not 2B, that was the question.

Jasmine, the eccentric old woman living there, wore tie-dye clothes and loud jewelry and knew things about everyone that she couldn't possibly know.

"Some people say she's a witch. There's a rumor going around that she has a black cat, but I've never actually seen it."

"Me neither," Savannah added. "Pets aren't allowed in the building."

I'm aware.

The scent of cat assaulted Dog's nose when Jasmine opened her door. This must be where the nosy cat in the window lived.

"Hello, girls. What a pleasant surprise." The seven bracelets on her arm jangled as she pointed to Dog. "Is this your dog?"

"No, but we were wondering if you've seen his mama."

She bent down to Dog's level and looked at him with sparkling blue eyes that could see into his soul. "What's the missing dog's name?"

Uh... Lola.

"We don't know her name," Chloe replied.

Jasmine stood. "It's Lola."

Savannah nodded. Chloe frowned.

Dog blinked back his surprise. *How did you do that?*

Jasmine studied Savannah for a moment. "I wish I'd seen her, girls, but I can tell you she's not in the building."

"How do you know?" Chloe asked.

"Thank you," Savannah said before Chloe asked any more questions. "If you see her, please let us know."

The girls looked at each other, then turned and ran, leaving Dog alone for a moment with Jasmine.

You ARE a witch.

Jasmine winked, and Dog took off after the girls. He caught them at the elevator door. *Did that just happen?* Never in the history of the world had a grown human been able to understand a dog, at least as far as he knew.

Given everything he'd just learned about the inhabitants of the building, he had to say they were a strange bunch. Everyone needs a sense of belonging, whether it's with family, friends, or community. That's not something that can be found stuck within their little apartments. They needed to get out. Meet some people. Sniff some butts.

The place sounded more like the Heartbreak Hotel than heaven, and Dog's heart sank a little lower. Clearly, Mama had left the building—that is, if she had ever been there in the first place.

Chapter Twelve

It had been a long, disappointing day, and Dog's stomach growled like an angry Doberman. He sat under the maple tree with Savannah and Chloe as he wondered where to go from there. Hunger always made a situation feel worse, but he didn't see how this one could be any better with food.

Savannah stroked his back. "I'm sorry we couldn't find her."

I don't want to be alone.

"You're not alone."

"You have us," Chloe added. "I wonder why he thinks his mama is in our building. Wait. How did you know her name was Lola?"

Dog heard Mama's name and picked his head up off his paws. His tail moved back and forth.

"He told me."

"That's impossible."

"Look how he perked up when you said her name."

Chloe turned to Dog. "Lola, Lola, Lola."

Dog stood up and his tail moved faster. *Where? Did you see her? Which way did she go?*

"That's mean."

"I wish *my* mama would disappear," Chloe said under her breath.

Tell her to take that back. That's the worst thing that could ever happen to her. I know.

"Don't say that."

"It's the truth."

Dog paced in tight circles.

Savannah glanced at Dog, then looked at her sister. "Now look what you did."

Chloe watched Dog for a moment, then laughed. "It's just a stupid dog."

"He's smarter than you'll ever be."

"You're a spoiled little brat."

"Am not."

Dog stopped circling. *Girls! Girls! Let's not waste time fighting with each other. I had five brothers and sisters that were taken away before I got to know them. I'd cut off my tail to have them here with me right now. And you can be sure we wouldn't be fighting and calling names.*

Savannah wrapped her arms around Dog while Chloe glared.

Tell her not to be so angry.

"Please don't be mad."

"I'm not mad."

Does her face know that?

Savannah giggled.

"What did he say?"

"He said he lost his brothers and sisters and would give any-thing to have them back."

Chloe's expression softened, and she tilted her head. "You can really understand him?"

"Yes, but he won't talk to us anymore if we don't stop fight-ing."

I couldn't have said it better myself.

"And... he wants to see us hug."

Nice touch.

"Now?"

"Right now."

Chloe paused while she studied the dog, then rolled her eyes. "Fine."

The two leaned in for a hug. Dog rested his head on his paws once again and watched. Now that they had settled this matter, he needed to find food and a place to sleep.

The girls agreed to come back after dinner with some food. Dog stayed put and waited. And waited. Like most dogs, this one had a poor sense of time. The girls finally returned as promised, with a variety of smuggled chow which Dog made disappear like a magician.

Chloe watched him eat. "How come he only talks to you?"

Savannah shrugged.

"Do you think he'll talk to me?"

"I don't know. Ask him."

When he finished eating, she leaned in close to Dog's face. "Dog, will you please tell me something?"

Were the brussels sprouts your idea? Because I'm not a fan.

Savannah giggled.

Chloe scrunched up her face. "I didn't hear anything. What did he say?"

"He doesn't like brussels sprouts."

They further discussed his plight, but this time without the name-calling. Unable to communicate herself, Chloe listened to her little sister explain how Dog ended up in their building.

"You need to tell him he won't find Lola here, or anywhere else."

"You can't hear him, but he can hear you."

"This town is named Heaven, but it's not the place people, or dogs, go when they die. He'll probably see her someday, but not while he's alive."

Dog's worst nightmare had become real, and he hung his head. Savannah squeezed him, and her compassion comforted him, but it didn't stop the pain.

"Maybe we can keep him," Savannah said, her eyes filling with tears.

Chloe shook her head. "That'll never happen. Mom doesn't like dogs."

Savannah stood, and Dog watched her wander off toward the back yard. He turned to see if Chloe knew what had just happened. She caught his stare and shrugged.

Savannah returned a few minutes later with a handful of wildflowers and laid them down in front of Dog. "These are for you, so you won't feel so sad."

He sniffed them for a moment. The sentiment warmed his heart. *Thanks, Savannah Banana.*

Chloe rolled her eyes. "What's a dog supposed to do with flowers?"

"Mom says they cheer her up."

"This dog isn't Mom, is he?"

Lighten up, sister. For your information, it was very thoughtful. Something you should work on.

They sat in silence as the sky grew dark, and a light rain fell. They walked Dog over to George's truck, and Chloe hoisted him up into the bed. She made some room in one corner and pulled a tarp over the spot to protect him from the rain.

"You'll be okay here for the night. We'll figure something else out tomorrow."

Savannah hugged her sister around the waist before they both returned to their warm, dry apartment.

Dog had survived much colder temperatures, but the rain made it difficult to sleep. Fortunately, the tarp kept him reasonably dry.

When morning finally arrived, he jumped down onto the wet grass. He'd survived the night, but not without a bad feeling about what the new day might bring. He foraged outside the coffee shop for something to eat, knocking over a trash can and sampling its contents.

Dog heard a noise behind him. *Yikes!* A man in gray stood within four feet, holding a pole with a loop at the end. *Where did he come from?* He slipped the loop over Dog's head and tightened it. Dog tried to escape. First left, then right. He bucked up and down, but that only made the loop tighter. He could barely breathe as the man dragged him through the grass.

He heard a scream when they reached the front of the building. *Double yikes!* Savannah watched them from the sidewalk.

"Nooooo! Let him go." She struggled to escape her mother's grip.

Dog looked away, embarrassed that he'd put himself in this situation. He was apparently a bad dog again for something, but he didn't know what.

Cruella dragged Savannah down the sidewalk in the opposite direction.

The man pushed Dog into the back of a van and slipped off the loop. He slammed the door as Dog gasped for air inside the cage. When everything moved, he steadied himself. He watched his building shrink in the distance out the back door. Savannah cried on her corner. He wished the poor girl hadn't witnessed his violent abduction. After being thrown from side to side a few times, he pushed himself down onto the floor.

The truck stopped and the man in gray opened the door. He slipped the noose around Dog's neck and led him into a brick building. Dog went peacefully to avoid more pain from the choking hazard around his neck. Another man hoisted him up onto a cold steel table and poked and prodded him. Resistance seemed futile.

"No tags or microchips," he said to the man with the pole. "Put him in with the other strays."

Pole man dragged him, paws scratching against the cold, unforgiving floor, into a dreadful room that reeked of fear and sadness. The harsh lights that buzzed overhead like a hive of bees provided an eerie backdrop for the clamor of whines and barks that filled the air.

Keys jangled as a door opened on a small cage in the middle of a long row of small cages. A dirty blanket and a water bowl were the only furnishings. The door closed behind him with a sickening metallic clank.

A German Shepard in the adjoining cell pushed his nose through the cage as far as possible and sniffed. *Welcome to hell.*

Dog took a step back and stared, too frightened to speak. What was this terrible place and why was he here? None of the puzzle pieces fit, with the possible exception of Savannah and Chloe, who he may never see again. How could Mama have been so wrong?

Don't get too comfy. If your owner doesn't show up in a couple of days to claim you, they ship you off to the county.

What happens there?

You don't want to know.

Dog didn't have an owner. He was doomed.

Chapter Thirteen

George turned the dirt between the garden rows in the warm afternoon sun. He stopped every couple of feet to get down on one knee and pull his magnifying glass out of his back pocket to ensure the plants he uprooted were, in fact, weeds. He refused to admit getting old, even as his eyes became a serious problem.

Savannah ran around the corner of the building and hooked her fingers through the fence.

"Mr. Baxter, something terrible has happened."

George stood. "Did someone get hurt?"

"They took the dog away."

"Okay, calm down. Who took what dog?"

"He doesn't actually have a name, but he's been hanging around here for a few days." She stopped to catch her breath. "A wicked man with a big stick put him in a truck and drove away."

George leaned on his rake. "I see." He knew the dog she spoke of. "Someone probably called the dogcatcher."

She frowned. "Who would do that?"

He would have if he'd thought of it. "I don't know."

"We have to help him."

"It's not our dog. I don't think there's anything we can do."

She hung her head and pushed out her bottom lip.

George glanced up at the sun in a cloudless sky and wiped his forehead with the back of his hand. "Why don't I meet you on the front steps with a nice cold glass of lemonade, and we can talk about it.”

She nodded and disappeared around the building.

“Lemonade?” he muttered. “Where did that come from?” He looked up to the heavens like he had a pretty good idea.

They sipped their drinks in an awkward silence. George spoke first.

“Are you feeling any better?”

“Not really.”

Chloe opened the front door enough to stick her head out. “What are you doing?”

“Just taking a little break,” George said. “Want some lemonade?”

“Sure.” She sat next to them, and George handed her a drink.

He’d anticipated the sister stopping by, so he’d made three drinks. Must be all those years living with Dottie were rubbing off on him.

“Did you see what happened this morning?” he asked Chloe.

“You mean about the dog?”

George nodded.

“They took him away in a truck marked *Animal Control*.”

“What does that mean?” Savannah asked.

“It means that he’s at the dog pound.”

She looked up at George with fearful eyes. “We need to go get him.”

“Like I said, it’s not our dog.”

“But he could be.”

Chloe shook her head. “Mom says no pets.”

“There’s got to be something we can do.” Savannah folded her arms, and her chest deflated.

A voice in George’s head spoke. *Isn’t that the saddest thing you’ve ever seen?*

“Yes, but...” George realized he’d said it out loud.

"But what?" Savannah asked.

Both girls waited.

When he didn't finish, Chloe said, "My friend Jason used to volunteer at the pound. He said it's a terrible place. If a dog's owner doesn't claim them within seventy-two hours, they put them down."

"Really?" The less he knew, the better.

"What does that mean?" Savannah asked, her voice brittle.

"It means they kill them," Chloe said.

Savannah cried.

George wished he'd stayed in the garden. "There, there. Don't cry, Angela."

Chloe glanced around, confused. "Who's Angela?"

"Angela?"

"Yeah, you just called Savannah Angela."

"Uh... it's... I meant Savannah."

Chloe continued. "Miss Jasmine said the dog saved your life."

Miss Jasmine needs to keep her mouth shut. "I admit, that dog did save me from a snakebite."

"Then you need to go get him. You owe him that much."

Savannah raised her big, sad eyes, just like the dog had done. It worked.

"I guess it won't hurt to take a ride down there and see what's what."

The group hug nearly toppled him over.

. . . . . • . • . . .

The old truck fired up on the second try. This was a bad idea, but what choice did he have? He still had a valid license, and no one had told him not to drive. He could see the other cars on the road, he just couldn't read the signs.

Before Dottie died, he'd promised her he would see the eye doctor—a promise he never kept.

Three strays had been brought in that day, but only one matched the description George gave them at the pound. A clerk behind the desk summoned a volunteer to escort George into the kennel to identify the dog. The dogs clamored for attention when he walked through the door. They stopped halfway down the aisle, and the volunteer pointed to one of the cages.

"That's the one," George said.

The dog must have recognized his voice, because he jumped up, wagging his tail and scratching at the cage door.

"He looks happy to see you."

George blew out a breath. "That makes one of us."

The volunteer nodded and escorted him back.

"So, how does this work?" George inquired when they returned to the front desk.

"I'll need to see proof of rabies vaccination and a valid license before I can release the animal."

George had neither. "Let's say, hypothetically, that I have neither of those things. What then?"

"I would say, hypothetically, that you need to fill out a license application while we take the dog out back and give him his shot."

In the meantime, the volunteer brought the dog up to the counter. George stared into a pair of sad eyes, similar to those he'd seen on Savannah's face an hour ago.

"And how much, hypothetically, would something like that cost?"

"One hundred and eighty dollars."

George blinked back his surprise. "That much, huh?"

The clerk nodded. "Would you like an application?"

George had no choice. He couldn't face the girls if he returned without the dog. No one wanted to disappoint a child. He glanced at the frightened little mutt. "Yes, please."

The clerk pulled a piece of paper from a tray and clicked his pen. "What's the dog's name?"

"I'm sorry. What?"

"The dog's name."

"Yes... of course."

He didn't know the dog's name. Should he make one up right then and there? He studied her, but he drew a blank. The dog's tail wagged under George's stare. What would Dottie do? He thought of her favorite television show. That's it.

George leaned against the counter. "Gracie."

"Gracie?"

"Yes. The dog's name."

The clerk glanced at the dog, who was clearly male, then back at George with a confused look. "You're sure?"

George placed both hands on the counter and leaned forward. "You think I don't know my own dog's name?"

"Oooookay. Gracie it is." He wrote it on the paper.

The volunteer took Gracie out back while the clerk helped George fill out the paperwork. George slid his credit card across the counter and blew out a big breath while he waited for his receipt. He hadn't planned to buy a dog today.

"I know this was your idea, Dot," he muttered. "I hope you thought it through."

· · · · · ● · ● · · · ·

Ouch! Dog sat on the cold steel table again while a man in a white coat jabbed him with a needle. His mind raced. *Why is George here? How did he find me?* None of this made sense.

A second man entered the room with something in his hand. When Gracie looked away, he slipped it around his neck from behind and tightened it. *Yikes!* He hadn't seen that coming. He stifled the urge to resist for fear of being choked again. But the man's hands were empty—no loop and no pole.

He pawed at the collar around his neck. *What is this?* Something dangled below his neck. He twisted his head to get a better look, but that didn't work.

The man in the white coat helped him off the table and led him back to the front of the building where George waited.

"You're all set," the clerk said.

George nodded, then turned to Gracie. "I guess we can go home now."

Home? He liked the sound of that, but what did it mean? Last time he checked, he had no home. Wherever his destination, it would surely be better than the hell he'd been rescued from.

I'm going home. I'm going home. Gracie sang a happy song as he followed George across the parking lot.

When George opened the truck door, Gracie scampered up onto the front seat.

"Oh, no you don't." He shook his head. "You ride in the back."

Gracie hung his head and raised his sad eyes.

"I love you, Dot, but what have you gotten me into this time?" George climbed in and turned to Gracie, who had planted himself in the middle of the bench seat. He pointed to the passenger side. "That's your side over there."

That's me over there? I get the window seat? Gracie wagged, slid over, and gazed through the glass.

Watch out for dogs, he said as George drove away. He didn't want any other pups to lose their mamas.

When the truck pulled into the driveway, Savannah and Chloe jumped up from the steps. They shouted and waved and danced around. It looked like fun. He barked out the window at them, and they danced even more. He couldn't wait to join them.

Is this what George meant when he said home? Gracie's tail pounded the seat.

Chapter Fourteen

The girls followed the truck down the driveway, waving their arms and squealing. Gracie watched with sheer joy. He bobbed and weaved, his tail pounding every surface.

George tried to stifle a smile. "Settle down until I turn the truck off."

Settle down? Are you watching this?

The girls opened the door, dragged Gracie out, and showered him with hugs and kisses. Gracie nearly wet himself from the excitement. He'd never felt such love and attention, but it didn't change the fact that George had been the one who'd rescued him.

When George approached, Gracie tore himself away from the girls and stood at his feet.

Thanks, man. I owe you one.

George couldn't understand, but Gracie needed to say it. He barked a couple of times to make it official.

"Is he your dog now?" Savannah asked George.

He pulled a copy of the license application from his pocket. "This paper says so, but—"

Chloe grinned. "I guess pets are allowed in the building now."

George's face twisted like he hadn't thought this one through.

"What are you going to name him?"

"He's a she, and her name is Gracie. The name reminds me of my wife."

Savannah squatted and gave Gracie the once-over. She stood and turned to George. "Mr. Baxter, I think he—"

Chloe gave her a nudge and a keep-your-mouth-shut glare. "I think that's a nice name."

"I'd better get her inside and make us some dinner."

"Can we play with him..." Savannah glanced at her sister. "Uh, HER, anytime we want?"

Gracie tilted his head, waiting for a reply.

"I hope so," George said. "I'm too old to play much anymore."

· · · · · ● · ● · · · ·

Gracie followed his new human inside. He strutted down the hall beside him like he'd just inherited the building. *Stayin' Alive* by the Bee Gees played somewhere in the background.

Inside the apartment, Gracie sniffed around, getting the lay of the land. *Not a bad place. Plenty of room for both of us.* He tried to play it cool with his new human. He'd never had a home, and he didn't want to jinx it.

"Gracie."

Gracie continued to investigate, sniffing everything in sight.

"Gracie."

He stopped. *Oh. That's me.* He padded over to where George sat and looked up at him. He wanted to say something to George about the name. It was better than Dog, but it didn't fit. He checked his private parts, which on a dog weren't very private. *Yep, still there.* He finally got a name of his own, and this is what he had to live with. What about Rex, or Buddy, or Max?

"That's a good girl. Now sit."

Good girl? This would take some getting used to. Gracie tilted his head and stared. He didn't know what George meant by *sit.*

"Come on, Gracie, sit."

Still nothing.

George leaned over and pushed Gracie's butt into the carpet. "Sit," he said again.

It made more sense now, but he wanted to be sure. He stood. "Sit."

He sat.

"Good girl."

Gracie puffed out his chest, his head bobbing as he moved it from side to side. *Check it out. I'm sitting. That's right. I can sit.*

He stopped bragging when he remembered Mama had told him that humans generally handed out treats after you performed for them. He waited a moment, eyes wide and aimed at George. *Nothing?* Apparently, he had some training of his own to do.

George opened a big food box like the one he'd seen in Savannah's kitchen. A light went on and cold air spilled out. He retrieved two packages and placed them in another, smaller box. George pushed some buttons and the box hummed. He filled a mixing bowl with water and placed it on the floor. "That's for you."

Thanks for the water, but I'm hungry, too.

A bell rang and the humming stopped. Gracie watched George carefully remove the steaming packages. George had a cold box AND a hot box. There was a lot to process here. He hoped he wasn't in over his head.

What's that smell?

"Dinner's ready," George announced. He blew on the packages, then set one on the floor in front of Gracie. "There you go."

Some of the finest scents he'd ever smelled tickled his nose. *Meat and gravy and potatoes, oh my.* He stuck his face into the plastic tray and didn't stop until he'd licked it clean.

He watched George work on his tray at the table. *Why hasn't he tried to sniff my butt? I've made it available to him. How will he ever get to know me?* Must be a human thing. He noticed they kept their butts covered all the time, which made getting to know each other nearly impossible.

While George cleaned up in the kitchen, Gracie wandered into the living room and jumped up on the giant leather recliner. *Now, this is what I'm talking about.* As he settled in, George stood in front of the chair with his hands on his hips. He didn't look happy.

What?

George snapped his fingers and pointed at the floor.

Gracie slunk down onto the carpet. *I guess beggars can't be choosers.*

"This is MY chair. Got it?" George flopped down into the big chair. "Looks like we need to set some ground rules."

Gracie stared up at him from the floor.

"Without rules, there's chaos."

Chaos. Got it.

"Rule number one. MY home is not YOUR bathroom. You do your business outside."

Gracie had looked forward to marking his new territory. He put those plans on hold.

Got it.

"Rule number two. This is MY chair. You can sit on the couch if you must, but I prefer you stay on the floor."

Sounds like this one had some wiggle room. Roger that.

"Rule number three. I best not find you chewing on any of my stuff."

Gracie glanced at the slippers on the floor next to the chair. They looked tasty. He removed them from his to-do list.

"Rule number four..."

How many rules are there? I don't know if I can remember more than three.

"No farting."

Seriously? Come on, George, don't you think that one's a little harsh? Dogs fart. We can't help it.

George paused. "That's all for now."

For now? Did that mean there would be more? Living on the street, there were no rules. He went wherever he wanted and did whatever he felt like, which included farting. He'd learned to think only of himself. Apparently, that would have to change.

George picked up a black stick from the table next to his chair. When he squeezed it, a window opened on the wall in front of him. Gracie stared at the humans on the other side of the glass. They talked and moved around like they didn't know they were being watched.

"Let's just sit and watch some TV."

Gracie looked from George to the window full of people. *TV? Okay, George, but I'm a big dog now. You don't have to spell.*

Gracie watched George stare at the TV for a moment before making himself comfortable on the carpet and doing the same.

· · · · ● · ● · · · ·

One of the last things on George's mind when he awoke that morning was bringing a dog home to live with him. In fact, it hovered just below seeing a flock of pigs fly by, and just above hell freezing over. As such, he realized he was ill-equipped to handle his new roommate.

George stared at the empty couch where Dottie would sit every evening. Time to make his nightly run to the kitchen. He pulled a fresh six-pack from the fridge and packed it in a small cooler with some ice, then grabbed a bag of cheese popcorn from the cupboard. Gracie's stare met him when he turned around. "What are you looking at?" He pointed to the water bowl on the floor. "You want a drink? It's over there."

Gracie shuffled over to the bowl. When he'd had his fill, he returned to his spot on the carpet. George opened the first can and took a long drink. He didn't want to dull the memories, just the pain that accompanied them. When he opened the bag of popcorn,

Gracie stood and stared with a pair of big I'm-still-hungry eyes. George tossed a piece in his direction, and Gracie snatched it out of the air.

This kept George amused until he'd finished the first beer. "That's enough," he said as he closed the bag. "Go lay down." He popped open another can. *Gunsmoke* had just started.

George woke to the flickering light of the TV in an otherwise dark room. Gracie lay still on the floor at his feet. As he turned on the light and turned off the TV, he suddenly realized he hadn't given any thought to where the dog would sleep. The alcohol-induced fog that shrouded his brain made it difficult to apply any logic to the situation. With any luck, he could sneak into his bedroom and let Gracie sleep right there on the carpet.

Two empty cans hit the floor when he climbed out of his chair, and Gracie stirred. Before George could say *go back to sleep*, Gracie jumped to his feet.

"Shhh! Go back to sleep."

Gracie looked up at him and barked.

"Come on, gimme a break here."

Another bark.

A deep breath kept George from saying something inappropriate. Then it hit him. "You need to go to the bathroom, I mean, outside." His expression softened when he thought about what he might have found when he woke up the next morning. "Good dog. Let's do this quickly. I'm tired."

George probably should have taken the dog out in the woods behind the building, in case he needed to drop a deuce, but he wasn't in the mood for a midnight stroll. "Number one only."

He led Gracie outside and waited while the dog wandered aimlessly, doing everything except what he'd been brought out there to do.

"Come on, Gracie, I need to get some sleep."

George looked up at the stars. "I hope you're watching this, Dot." He paused and a frown wrinkled his face. "It's not funny."

Shortly after George's second warning, Gracie decided on a spot and lifted his leg.

Back inside, George refilled the water bowl and laid a couple of blankets down in the corner of the living room. "Time for bed."

After a couple of good sniffs, Gracie curled up on the blankets.

George retired to his room and climbed into his own bed. Just before he drifted off to sleep, the bed shook. Earthquake? He sat up to find Gracie sprawled out on Dottie's side of the bed.

George's patience was wearing thin. "Rule number five. Stay off the bed."

Chapter Fifteen

The next morning, a knock at the door roused Gracie from his makeshift bed. *Who could that be at this hour?* He hadn't had breakfast yet. There must be a rule about that.

When he neared the door, he smelled his two new friends. The scent of a third, unwanted guest necessitated a loud bark. George shooed him away and paused in front of the door. He didn't get many visitors unless something broke or someone needed a few extra days to pay the rent.

When George opened the door, it blocked Gracie's view. He peeked around the door to find Cruella De Vil in the hall with Chloe and a big, round puffy thing with feet.

Yikes! What's SHE doing here?

"I'm sorry to bother you, but the girls wanted to deliver a little welcome gift to your new houseguest."

Gracie eyed her suspiciously. He didn't understand what was happening. Savannah peeked over the top of the not-so-little gift, and he realized she held it in front of her, hiding everything but her feet.

"Come on in," George said.

What? Gracie backpedaled. *The little ones can stay, but the big one needs to go.*

"This is Gracie." He gestured toward the dog. "Gracie, you know the girls, and this is their mother, Mrs. Miller."

"You can call me Michelle," she said to George, then turned her attention to the dog.

Gracie shrunk a little and waited for a lecture, or for her to cast a spell.

"We met out front the other day. I didn't realize it was your dog." She reached her hand out, and Gracie shrunk a little more. He expected it to smell like blood or dead animals. Soap was all he could detect.

"You were right, girls, he's a cutie," she said as she gently scratched under his chin.

The old double standard. When he was a stray, he was a savage beast that wouldn't think twice about eating her babies. Now that he's got a collar and a place to stay, he's a cutie.

He hated to admit it, but she had a nice touch. Maybe they could get along after all. George seemed to like her. He did, however, fail to notice her use of a male pronoun. Perhaps his eyes weren't the only thing going bad. *Oh, well.*

Savannah dropped the round, puffy thing in front of Gracie. "Here, it's for you."

Mrs. Miller smiled. "Actually, it's for both of you."

George placed a hand on his forehead. "I don't know what to say, except you didn't have to do that."

"We kind of did. The girls haven't stopped talking about Mr. Baxter's new dog. They dragged me out first thing on a Saturday morning to buy it and insisted on paying for it out of their allowance."

"That was very kind of you, girls."

Gracie circled the strange item, sniffing it from every angle. *What is this thing?*

"It's a dog bed, silly." Savannah picked him up and set him down in the middle of the bed.

Gracie's legs stiffened. He'd never stood on anything so soft and feared he might fall over.

"Sit," she said.

Gracie knew that one. He sat in the middle of the big, soft circle. It made him want to lie down. He rested his head on his paws and looked up at the small audience.

"He likes it." Savannah clapped.

"It certainly looks that way." George smiled. It was the first time Gracie had seen his teeth since he'd arrived in heaven, or whatever this place was. "Do you think you can help me find a good spot for it?"

"Sure," Chloe said.

Savannah nodded.

"Someplace in the living room would be good."

"Come on, Gracie," Savannah said, and the two ran off.

Chloe picked up the bed and followed.

Gracie hadn't tried running in the apartment yet. *This is fun!*

They found the perfect spot under the window, and George nodded his approval. Gracie's tail swished from side to side, and he performed a combination of twirls and hops that would make a Russian ballerina jealous.

"What's happening?" George asked.

Savannah's eyes sparkled. "That's his happy dance."

He thanked them all again for the thoughtful gift.

"Can Gracie come out and play with us?"

How could he refuse? "Sure. You can play outside after we get back from the market."

He glanced at Mrs. Miller, who nodded her approval.

After they left, George poured a cup of coffee, added a shot of Baileys, and sat down with the newspaper and his magnifying glass. "Let's see who died yesterday."

George's trip to the market, like everything else, it seemed, had changed. Gracie walked along by his side instead of Dottie and watched as George ponied up an extra ten bucks to have his groceries delivered. The twenty-pound bag of dog food was not something either one could lug home over their shoulder.

When they returned, George left Gracie outside with the girls. The yard was full of vibrant scents and the promise of adventure. He rolled in the fresh grass of the fall growing season. The leaves gave off a specific scent as they slowly changed colors, and he closed his eyes and breathed it in. The girls ran, and he chased, then they switched roles. Their high-pitched voices filled him with pure delight.

Time didn't matter until the shadows grew long and Mrs. Miller's voice called. "Time for dinner, girls."

They promised Gracie they would pick up where they left off tomorrow and dropped him off at home.

Gracie fidgeted as day turned to dusk and George prepared for another evening of beer, popcorn, and classic TV. Gracie's dinner had not settled properly, and he anticipated a gastrointestinal event of considerable magnitude. *Yikes! Rule number four.* In his defense, it was an unfair rule.

He settled into his bed as his collar tightened and his eyes bulged. This was about to happen. If he could hold it until the end of *Jeopardy!,* perhaps George would leave the room for a few minutes to take care of his own business.

He clenched his butt cheeks. The room spun and he began to hallucinate. Ken Jennings read the last answer on the board. "This canine misfit was banished for breaking rule number four on only his second day in captivity." A contestant buzzed in. "Who is Gracie?" The crowd cheered. Gracie had no choice but to ease up on his butt cheeks and relieve some of the pressure.

George scrunched up his face and looked over at Gracie. "I thought we had an understanding."

It came on suddenly. There was nothing I could do. Gracie lowered his head and raised his eyes. *I'm sorry.*

"You need to take that outside."

Gracie rose and George followed him to the door.

"You know what you have without rules, don't you?"

I know, I know. Chaos.

George pointed to a spot past the garden and into the woods and waited. Gracie wanted to warn him that this one might take a while. The people he'd seen walking their dogs always picked up the poop in little bags and brought it home with them, which he thought was ridiculous. George had not brought any bags. Apparently, what happened in the woods, stayed in the woods.

After Gracie concluded his business, they returned to their nightly ritual.

He wandered around the apartment while George sank into his chair and popped the top on another beer can. With his stomach suddenly empty, he searched for a way to fill it. He sniffed out something sweet and followed the scent into the kitchen. Unable to open the cabinets himself, he'd nearly given up when he spotted the brightly colored box sitting near the edge of the table. A well-orchestrated swipe brought it to the floor with a smack.

"What's going on in there?"

Busted. He took it into the living room and deposited it at George's feet.

"What have you got there?"

Gracie nudged it a little closer, and George picked it up.

"You found my Jujubes." He shook his head. "Nothing gets past you, does it? You know, they're not good for dogs."

Gracie hung his head and looked up with sad eyes.

"I guess one wouldn't hurt." He tossed it into the air, and Gracie caught it in his mouth. George held up the package and stared at it with his head tilted. "I've been eating these things since I was a kid. In the army, they called me Juju, because I always kept a box in my back pocket."

Thanks, Juju. A little rough on the teeth, but tasty.

"That's it." He set the box on the table next to his chair. "Now, shush. I'm watching my show."

Chapter Sixteen

In the morning, Gracie opened one eye when he heard a noise in the apartment. George had risen earlier and was rattling around in the kitchen. The eye soon closed, and Gracie settled back into the softness of his new bed. He'd had the best sleep of his entire life and didn't want to move. *Go figure, a bed just for dogs. How thoughtful. There might be hope for humans, after all.*

Gracie's head popped up, and he thrust his nose high. *Wait. I know that smell. George has bacon?*

Sure enough, George stood in the kitchen holding a pan full of bacon over an open flame.

How could this not be heaven? Two weeks ago, he slept in the street and ate other people's garbage.

"Mornin' Gracie," George said as paws clicked on the kitchen floor.

Gracie had decided to let the name thing slide. George had been willing to take him in and give him a home when nobody else would. That, and he had no way to tell him he'd made a mistake.

"I made us some breakfast. I gotta warn you, I'm a pretty good cook when I wanna be." He wore a humble expression, but Gracie sensed his pride. "You like bacon?"

Somebody pinch me. Do I like bacon? If I was made of bacon, I'd eat myself to death. He did a little happy dance.

"I'll take that as a yes."

After breakfast, George sat at the table and read the newspaper while Gracie sniffed around the apartment. He slipped into the bedroom when George wasn't looking. The only other time he'd been in that room, it had been dark, and George had banished him from the bed. He could live with rule number five, now that he had his own comfy place to sleep.

He picked up the scent of another human and followed it to the closet door. He scratched at the door and tried to push it open, but it held tight, so he moved on.

A picture of George and two females stood on the little table by the bed—one about George's size and the other smaller, like Chloe. He wondered why he hadn't seen them before now. Maybe one of them was the invisible Dottie he talked to all the time. Gracie had never seen her. Perhaps she was an imaginary friend. Or maybe he kept her in the closet.

It suddenly occurred to him that George may have lost her. Mama was gone, but Gracie still talked to her from time to time.

Curious about the other one, he carefully removed the picture and carried it to the kitchen in his teeth. George did not look happy when he saw him coming.

"Gimme that." He wiped it off and set it on the table.

Gracie felt a rule number six coming.

"Who told you to go in there and touch my stuff?"

Head hung, Gracie raised his sad eyes.

"Don't look at me like that."

Yikes! If this look stops working, I'm in trouble. He kept it up anyway.

George picked up the photo. "You probably want to know who these people are in the picture." He sighed. "If we're going to live together, I suppose you should know a little about me."

He pointed at the bigger one. "That one's my Dottie. We fell in love and were married for forty-two years before the cancer took her from me." He wiped the liquid that suddenly dripped from his eyes. "I can still feel her presence sometimes and hear her voice." He held a cloth up to his face and made a loud honking sound.

I feel you, George. They had something in common, and he wanted to help with his pain. Mama had said sometimes the best thing you can do to help someone in pain is just to be there.

George stuffed the cloth in his pocket and pointed to the smaller one. "That's my daughter, Angela." He paused and his eyes filled up but nothing leaked out. "I really messed up with her. She'll be forty this year. We'd always had a strained relationship. She'd come around from time to time, but only to see her mother." He paused again. "We haven't spoken since Dottie's funeral."

Gracie couldn't have had a bigger lump in his throat if he'd swallowed a grapefruit. He shuffled over to George's chair and lay down at his feet. George picked up his paper again while a deafening silence hung in the room.

After an appropriate amount of time had passed, Gracie wandered into the living room. The sun went missing from the sky and left the apartment gray and lifeless. Sadness and boredom stripped him of his energy, and he curled up in his bed.

A knock at the door woke him from a sound sleep. George sat in his chair, eyes closed, and making strange sucking noises. Several empty cans littered the floor around where he sat. Gracie barked, and George's eyes opened.

Another knock, and Gracie ran to the door.

George moved much slower. "I'm coming."

Mrs. Miller reeked of fear as she stood in the hall. "Savannah is missing, and I wondered if she might be here playing with Gracie."

"I'm sorry, but I haven't seen her. We've been alone all afternoon."

A true statement. Even though downing a few brewskies and passing out in his chair is also an accurate account.

"I got nervous when she didn't come home for supper. I wouldn't even have let her out alone if I didn't think she was on her way here to play with the dog."

So, this is my fault? If he hadn't seen the softer side of this woman yesterday, he would have assumed she'd cooked Savannah and eaten her for dinner, then tried to blame it on *the dog.*

Dinner? Wait. What time is it, anyway?

George glanced at the clock on the wall. Gracie did the same, not that it did him any good. When he looked back at Mrs. Miller, he noticed her eyes had sprung a leak.

"George, I need your help. She's never wandered off like this."

He took a deep breath as he ran his hand back over the top of his head. "Okay. We'll help you look for her."

"I haven't met some of the other tenants. Do you think one of them could have—"

"Let's not go there yet. She's probably playing somewhere and lost track of time. Where's her sister?"

"She's with her father. They're on their way over here."

Gracie paced in tight circles. *This isn't good. She could be in danger. I can't lose her, too. We need to find her.*

"What's the matter with your dog?"

"She does that when she gets nervous."

"Oh, God. I've heard dogs can sense things we can't. This isn't a good sign."

George held up his hands. "Let's stay calm. I'll organize a search party. We'll get the other tenants to help." He looked down at Gracie. "You coming with us, or you gonna stay here and wear a hole through to the basement?"

Wild horses couldn't keep him away. He wasn't sure what that meant, but he'd heard it was a thing. His nose worked better than all of theirs put together. They needed him. Savannah Banana needed him. Dinner would have to wait.

They rode the elevator up to the Millers' apartment. George suggested they search the place from top to bottom to make sure Savannah hadn't crawled behind the couch or into a closet and fallen asleep. Gracie would sniff her out if she had.

George didn't realize that Savannah's scent was everywhere in the apartment. Scents fade over time, so it would be a matter of where her scent was the strongest.

Gracie sniffed the air, filtering out Chloe and Mrs. Miller. He followed his nose into Savannah's bedroom, but his search came up empty. Chloe and her father arrived and pitched in. Savannah was not in the apartment.

The search party moved into the hall and knocked on doors. No one had seen Savannah. Marilyn in 3A and Tom in 3B offered to help look for her.

Ruby in 3E opened her door. She stood there in her cowboy boots and colorful, flowing dress that did an admirable job of camouflaging her ample figure. A few tendrils of her wild, curly auburn hair had broken free from a messy bun and hung loose on the side of her face.

She placed her hands on her hips. "What's going on?"

"Savannah is missing," George said. "Would you like to help us look for her?"

"Wild horses couldn't keep me away."

Gracie looked at everyone. *Did you hear that? It IS a thing.*

Ruby grabbed her oversized purse, locked her door, and joined the posse.

No one answered at Sam's door.

"I saw Sam leave for work this morning around eight." Tom turned the doorknob and found it locked.

"I had breakfast with Savannah at nine," Mrs. Miller said, "so she can't be in there."

Jasmine joined them, and they knocked on Mike's door. Retired detective Mike McGuire cast an imposing figure, with salt-and-pepper hair and a chest the size of a barrel. He wore regular clothes, not the blue uniform that Gracie expected. A pair of wire-rimmed glasses rested on a slightly crooked nose. Behind the lenses were a pair of piercing blue eyes that could penetrate the deepest of mysteries. He looked like the guy you wanted on your side when things went sideways, but Gracie wasn't entirely convinced. He slipped inside for a quick look around.

Gracie followed his nose, looking for Mama. *Coffee... and glazed donuts. Some habits die hard.* Framed certificates and medals adorned the living room wall. He weaved in and out of piles of newspapers and crossword puzzle books but found no sign of Mama. His search turned up nothing suspicious, not even the big stick that policemen often carried.

Mike joined the posse, and they moved on. No one on the second floor had seen Savannah.

Chloe and her dad headed for the basement while the others congregated in the lounge. The tenants talked among themselves, some of them for the first time. The mood in the room took a turn for the worse when the basement search came up empty.

A man wearing blue, with a big stick hanging off his belt, entered the room and spoke with Mike.

What is HE doing here? Gracie ducked behind the upholstered chair where Jasmine sat.

"What's the matter, Gracie?" Chloe asked, her head wedged between the chair and the wall.

A reply at this point would be pointless without Savannah to translate.

"He doesn't like policemen," Jasmine offered.

"Why not?"

"I'm not sure. Something to do with his Mama."

"He seems okay around Mr. McGuire."

"Maybe it's the uniform."

Chloe removed Gracie from his hiding place, sat down cross-legged on the floor, and set him in her lap. "It's okay. The policeman won't hurt you. He's here to help."

That's what they want you to think.

George addressed the crowd. "Officer Edwards has told me there is no waiting period for missing children under the age of 18, so Savannah's name and information will be entered into the FBI's National Crime Information Center Missing Person File immediately."

The crowd murmured, and Mrs. Miller wrung her hands. Mr. Miller placed his arm around her shoulders.

"Officer Edwards is here to help us search for her." He paused. "It appears that Savannah is not in the building, so we'll expand our search outside." The policeman pointed at Gracie, who buried his head in Chloe's lap. "That dog might be able to help us find her."

Jasmine reached down and pulled Gracie up into the chair. She looked directly into his eyes. "Time to step up, my little friend. Savannah is in trouble. She needs you. It's almost dark, and it's starting to rain."

My nose doesn't work so well in the rain.

"You can find her. I know you can."

Apparently, he'd been mistaken about her ability to understand him. He scanned the room and felt the weight of everyone's stare. *My nose doesn't work in the rain.*

"I heard you the first time," Jasmine said. "But trust me, you can do this. It's one of the reasons you're here."

He wasn't sure, but that sounded like a purpose.

The weight of the world had been deposited on the shoulders of the little dog with the awkward name from the other side of the tracks. He'd never felt so important and so afraid at the same time. Too much pressure for one dog.

They sent Chloe upstairs to get something of Savannah's for Gracie to sniff.

She returned with a stuffed penguin and held it in front of Gracie. "This is her favorite. She sleeps with it every night."

Seriously? A penguin? Not a dog? He gave it a couple of good sniffs, anyway.

George picked up Gracie and led everyone outside. They spread out, calling Savannah's name.

Rain pelted Gracie's face as George set him down.

"Go find her."

Gracie sniffed the air, then put his nose down into the wet grass. The water diluted everything. He wanted to go back inside and wait out the storm, but that wasn't an option this time. Savannah was his friend. Friends were supposed to take care of each other, but she went missing on his watch. *Bad dog!*

It was up to him to find her. *Man up, Gracie. You can do this. It's just a little rain.*

He kept moving and sniffing.

How can a day that started out so well end so badly?

Chapter Seventeen

This wasn't where Gracie thought he would be at this point in his life. He was too young to be on his own with such a heavy burden. Mama wasn't supposed to leave him alone without nurturing or adult supervision. It had become painfully obvious that he was no closer to finding her now than when he'd started looking.

But feeling sorry for himself wouldn't help him find Savannah. He needed to suck it up, put her first, and carry on. She was out there somewhere, feeling lost and alone. He knew the feeling well and wouldn't wish it on his worst enemy, let alone his best friend.

He sniffed around the edge of the woods. While the smell of wildflowers threatened to overpower her scent, it brought back a memory. Savannah had picked wildflowers for him when he'd felt sad about Mama. Perhaps she'd wandered into the woods to pick flowers for someone.

Were the flowers for him? Could he be responsible for this fiasco? It hit him like a kick in the ribs. If something bad happened to her, he would never forgive himself. He switched his nose into high gear. Wild horses couldn't keep him from finding her now.

The woods, dark and wet, surrounded him as he forged ahead. She had to be in there somewhere. He felt it in his bones. Her scent became stronger, and he charged after it, barking for the others to follow.

He moved deeper into the woods and left the footpath behind as her scent grew stronger. Brambles tore at his legs, but the pain only strengthened his resolve. He barked to let the others know he was close.

I'm coming, Savannah Banana! Where are you? He stopped to listen.

"Over here."

Her voice sounded weak, but he'd heard enough to lock in her location. He ran as fast as the terrain would allow toward an enormous oak tree.

Over where?

"In the tree."

He looked up, confused. The lowest branch hung at least ten feet above the ground. No way she could have reached it. He had to trust his nose. He put his head down and followed it around the giant tree.

"Gracie!"

He raised his eyes. Savannah clutched a handful of wildflowers as she shivered inside the rotted-out base of the tree.

Savannah Banana, you're alive! He smelled the flowers. *Are those for me?*

"No. They're for my mom. She was sad, so I came out to pick some flowers. I was looking for just the right ones, and I guess I went too far into the woods."

He barked three times to signal the others, then pressed his body against hers to keep her warm.

Chloe and her dad were the first to arrive. He picked Savannah up and held her tight. The others arrived a few moments later. They rubbed her back and voiced their relief as Gracie watched from the sidelines. He was left behind while the crowd headed back home.

Mike bent down, and Gracie flinched. He scratched behind Gracie's ears. "You saved her, Gracie. Good dog."

Relief and a little pride washed over him. He was a good dog again. The others should have included him in their celebration, but all that mattered was Savannah's safety. And Mike seemed like a decent guy, despite his chosen profession.

When Gracie reached the building, he found George waiting by the door. "Good job, Gracie."

Thanks, George. It was nothing.

The room erupted with applause when he walked in. All eyes were on him, and he stood a little taller.

Chloe ran to him and threw her arms around his neck. "Thank you for saving my little sister. You're a hero."

Hero? He'd been called many things before, but never a hero. *I was just helping a friend in need.* He tilted his head. Maybe that's what heroes do.

"If your mama was here, she would be so proud."

But she wasn't there, and he sagged a bit. Then the strangest thing happened. He spotted Mama in the crowd, standing next to Jasmine. She held her head high, and he heard her say, *That's my boy.*

Mama? This really was heaven, and he'd found her, but reaching hands and lots of teeth surrounded him. Dreadful memories of his siblings being kidnapped flooded his mind, and he closed his eyes and pressed himself against the floor. He feared being taken away by strangers to some unfamiliar place. But these hands didn't grab and pull, they caressed and scratched like loving hands. Gracie relaxed into them.

When he opened his eyes again, Mama had gone. He stared at the spot where she'd stood a moment ago. When he looked at Jasmine, she nodded, like she understood what had just happened. She was a strange woman.

· · · · **·** · **·** · · · ·

The next day, Gracie had the run of the building. He cruised up and down the halls as *Stayin' Alive* played somewhere in the background. He'd become an overnight celebrity. Everyone knew his name and had heard of his heroics. They treated him differently.

Something else happened as a result of the previous day's events. They treated each other differently, too. People who were strangers the day before greeted each other in the halls. Some even stopped to chat. Rumor has it, 3B asked 3A out for coffee.

There he is now.

Tom smiled. "Hello, Gracie."

Way to go, Tommy. If you ever need a wingman...

Tom left the building as Rita walked in. They chatted for a moment before Rita stopped and pressed the elevator button.

A smile flickered on Rita's lips when she noticed Gracie.

Hey, Rita. Missed you at the party last night. Keep on smilin'. It looks good on you.

When the door opened, he hesitated then followed her inside. She pushed the button for the second floor, and the doors closed.

I'd appreciate it if you could push 3 for me.

The doors opened again, and she stepped off.

Oh, well. It was worth a try. Give John my best.

Chloe had told him that John's cancer took a turn for the worst last week. Gracie made a note to stop in and see him sometime soon.

He stared at the button with the number three printed on it. He hadn't thought this one through. As he considered a jump to slap at the button, the elevator moved upward.

The door opened on the third floor, and he found himself face to face with Ruby. Anything you might say to Ruby had the same effect as issuing a press release. Fortunately, she couldn't understand him.

She stepped into the elevator. "Hello, Gracie."

He gave her a courtesy tail wag.

"I hear you're the talk of the building."

I hear you're the talk-er.

The door would close any second and trap him in the elevator with her. *Gotta bounce.* He jumped off just before that happened.

He found Savannah's door and waited outside.

"Hi, Gracie," Chloe said when she opened the door. "If you're looking for Savannah, she's still asleep. She's not going to school today."

Gracie hung his head.

"Maybe you can see her later." She closed the door. "I have to go. Do you want to ride down with me?"

Gracie followed her into the elevator. She pushed the button marked with a 1. Gracie barked twice.

"What do you want?"

He barked twice again.

Chloe's eyes widened. "You want to get off on the second floor?"

Gracie nodded.

She pushed the button and smiled. "I'm sorry I called you stupid the other day."

Apology accepted.

On the second floor, he stopped at Jasmine's door and scratched. He made a mental note to complain to the ACLU or the SPCA or some other letters about installing doorbells down lower. Ditto for elevator buttons.

After a few more scratches and a well-timed bark, Jasmine opened the door.

We need to talk.

Chapter Eighteen

"Come on in, dear." Jasmine smiled and stepped aside.

The place smelled like something burning, but not in a bad way. Probably to hide the cat smell. Or maybe she'd put the cat in the oven. Witches eat cats, don't they? Or is it children they eat? He sniffed the air. If she had a cat in the oven, it would smell much worse.

Cats like to pounce on unsuspecting victims, so he checked over both shoulders.

"I knew you were coming, so I locked her in the bedroom."

See? There you go again. That's what I want to talk to you about.

"Is this about your mama?"

How did you know that?

"Contrary to popular belief, I am not, nor have I ever been, a witch."

Good to know. Now, back to Mama.

"You saw her last night, I could tell."

Where did she go?

"She's still here."

Gracie's eyes darted back and forth. *Tell me you didn't lock her in with the cat.*

"She's not here like you and me. She's here in spirit."

And by spirit, you mean dead?

"I'm afraid so, but that doesn't mean she's not still with us."

Chloe had told him as much, but it still hurt. His legs grew weak, and he sat. *She spoke to me last night. She said she was proud.*

"Sometimes, if a spirit's emotion is strong enough, it can bleed into the physical world. Like it did last night."

So, this really isn't heaven, is it?

"It's complicated. The short answer is yes... and no."

His brain hurt. *If you're not a witch, what are you?*

She smiled. "I'm just a woman who can communicate with the other side."

The other side of what?

"The other side of... life, I guess."

Now we're guessing? He stood and walked around, resisting the urge to pace in little circles, which apparently freaked humans out. *Is that where Mama is? Is that the real heaven?*

"You can call it that, I suppose. It's the heaven that most people think of when a loved one dies. But this could be heaven, too."

He pictured the sign out back.

"Or across the street, or across the country. Just about any-where can be heaven, if you let it."

He stopped. *Okay. Now you've lost me. Let's circle back to Mama.*

"Your mama's memory and her love will always be with you. You have the power to keep her alive in your mind and in your heart."

A warmth started in Gracie's chest and spread throughout his body.

Jasmine nodded. "Just like that. That's what heaven feels like."

Can I talk to her?

"Sure. You may not always hear her respond. Sometimes it's just a feeling you get, but she's always listening."

Will I ever see her again?

"Eventually, you'll cross over and be with her."

She had a way to make everything sound better than it really was. He knew that was a nice way to say he would die. *Will I see her again while I'm, you know, still here?*

"I don't know. Last night was special. Perhaps there will be other special times."

Gracie sat and scratched an itch on the back of his neck while he pondered everything she'd just said. *Who else do you talk to?*

"I know where you're going with this."

Of course you do.

"I talk to Dottie often."

What does she say? He tilted his head. *Or is that some kind of HIPAA violation?*

A smile flickered on Jasmine's lips before her expression turned serious. "She's worried about George."

So am I. He drinks too much and passes out in front of the TV. He sighed. *But I still love the guy.*

"So does she. She asks me to pass on messages to him, but he resists my attempts every time." Jasmine paused, as if listening to something. "She wants to know if you'll help her."

Who wants to know? Dottie?

Jasmine nodded.

She's here?

Another nod.

He stood. *Hey, Dottie, Gracie here.*

"She knows who you are."

Oh, yeah. Okay. I'm not sure I can help, but I'll give it a try.

"She says she's disappointed that he stopped writing. He wrote such beautiful stories."

Are we talking about the same George?

"She was his muse. When she died, he stopped writing, but he has another story in him that needs to be told. He just doesn't know it yet."

That may be, but what can I do?

"Be his muse."

I'm not even sure what that means, let alone how to do it.

"He's in a dark place. He needs you to help him find the light."

He swallowed hard. *How am I supposed to do that?* Saving Savannah felt like a walk in the park compared to what she'd just asked of him.

"You have a big heart. Share some of that love with him. Can you do that for him? For me?"

I'll do my best.

"Thank you. There's one more thing..."

His stomach inched its way farther up his throat. He had a hard time wrapping his head around the muse thing. Now she wanted to add something else?

"She says Angela can help."

The same Angela that he hasn't spoken to for seven years? That's the Angela that's supposed to help?

"She's the key, but only you can turn it and open the lock."

Cute metaphor, but... ARE YOU INSANE? Gracie looked at Jasmine. *How about I meet that cat of yours?*

She blinked back her surprise.

Didn't see that one coming, did you? As long as we're tossing around impossible outcomes, what's one more?

Jasmine disappeared down the hall and returned a few moments later with Luna at her feet. "Luna, Gracie. Gracie, Luna."

Luna was as black as the devil's boots, with shifty green eyes. The two walked slowly around each other, eyes locked.

Gracie spoke first. *So, you're the illegal cat I've been hearing about.*

Not anymore.

You're welcome.

Sorry, cats never say thank you. Oops! They never say sorry, either.

Why am I not surprised?

"Luna and I will help you with George, but you two need to get along."

Luna hopped up onto the back of the sofa and stared out the window. *Surely you jest*, she said without turning around.

. . . . . ● . ● . . . .

Gracie took the stairs down to the first floor. A pounding noise echoed up the stairwell. When he reached the hall, he found George kneeling in front of the apartment door. All manner of tools surrounded him on the floor.

"What do you think?" George said when he saw Gracie.

He didn't know what to think. A hole had been cut in the bottom half of the door and covered up with a flap. *What's going on, George?*

"Your own private entrance." He gestured toward the square portal. "It's a doggy door."

Gracie tilted his head. *For me?*

George pushed the center of the flap, and it opened inward, creating a passage into the living room.

First a comfy bed and now my own door? You're spoiling me.

"Go on. Try it."

Does it come with an instruction manual?

"Go ahead. Just walk right through it."

Gracie poked at the flap with his nose then cautiously put one front foot inside and then the other. George gave his butt a shove, and Gracie landed in the living room.

"You won't need me to take you outside anymore to do your business. You can go by yourself. I installed another one of these in the back door so you can get outside."

Gracie poked his head back through the flap. *Great idea, George.*

"Good girl. Come on out the same way you went in."

He stepped back into the hall. *I can see how this might come in handy. You think you can install one on everyone's door?*

Gracie hopped into the apartment through the new door, then hopped back out. He did this a few times while George watched.

George flashed a proud grin. Gracie put his paws on George's chest and gave him a big thank-you lick on the cheek.

"You're welcome," he said, and his teeth made another appearance.

Chapter Nineteen

Gracie thought of George as a good man who'd been through some real emotional doo-doo. His big heart would make an appearance from time to time before returning to wherever it was he'd hidden it. Gracie made it his mission to find it and free it from captivity. It's what Dottie had asked him to do. That sounded like a legitimate purpose.

Time to check on Savannah Banana. He scratched at her door. When it didn't open, he barked.

Mrs. Miller opened the door, and he took a step back. He considered a dash between her legs, but he didn't remember which room was Savannah's. He turned to run back downstairs to safety.

"Wait."

Gracie stopped.

"She's been asking for you."

She has? Aww.

She led Gracie into Savannah's room. Savannah's eyes lit up the moment she saw him. She patted the bed next to her, and Gracie checked with Mrs. Miller. She shrugged her shoulders and nodded.

Who are you and what have you done with Cruella? He jumped up on the big, soft bed next to Savannah.

She hugged him so hard, he nearly passed out.

"You're my favorite dog in the whole wide world."

Right back at you, sister… except for the dog part.

Her expression fell. "I wish you were *my* dog."

We're best friends.

"It's not the same." Her eyes drifted for a moment. "Maybe Mr. Baxter would let you live here. We can put your bed right over there." She waved her hand toward an empty spot next to her dresser.

He had to admit, it looked like a great spot. *What about your mama?*

"She's not a dog person. But I think she likes you. After all, I might not be here if it wasn't for you."

Gracie tilted his head. Dog person? He didn't know that was a thing. Was he a person dog? It appeared he hadn't gotten any closer to figuring out humans.

George and I are pretty tight. I don't think he'd go for that. Besides, I think he's my purpose.

"Maybe I'm your purpose. You saved me from the woods. I could have been eaten by a coyote, or something."

Hmm. I never thought of it like that. He paused to scratch his neck.

They spent the next hour together until Mrs. Miller appeared in the doorway to announce the end of their party. Savannah needed to rest, and Gracie needed to leave.

After the appropriate number of hugs and goodbyes, Mrs. Miller escorted Gracie into the hall. As he wandered toward the stairs, Luna startled him from behind.

Gracie's heart raced. *Didn't Jasmine ever tell you not to sneak up on someone like that?*

She might have, but it's what cats do. We can't help it.

What are you doing out here?

I'm feeling a little frisky since the pet ban was lifted.

He'd never seen her outside her apartment. *Where's your master?*

Silly dog. Luna held up her chin. *In my home, I'm the master.*

Cats!

Let's get going, she said. *We have work to do.*

We do?

Don't you remember? Jasmine said we need to help George, so let's go help.

How?

She shrugged her little cat shoulders. *We'll find something. Are you coming, or aren't you?* She headed for the stairs.

With George busy in the garden, it wouldn't hurt if they looked around. But he couldn't allow her to go in there without supervision. He caught up with her and took the lead.

Luna followed him downstairs and watched him step through the door. *What just happened?*

Gracie poked his head back through. *What's the matter?*

Nothing, I—

It's a doggy door. He knew something that her majesty didn't?

I know what it is, it's just that... I'm a cat.

Nice recovery. *It works for cats, too.*

Inside, Luna prowled around. *This place isn't terrible.*

He beamed with pride as he showed her his bed. When she took a step toward it, he cut her off. *Dogs only.*

She moved on without incident. *What's this?* She jumped up on George's chair.

Yikes! Get down here. He paced in circles. *Rule number two. Rule number two.*

You need to chill. She hopped up onto the arm of the chair. *Where I come from, there are no rules.*

Chaos. That's what THIS is. George says without rules you have chaos.

You're more of a hot dog than a chili dog. She hopped down. *See what I did there?*

Gracie stopped. *Yeah. You're a regular comedian.*

Before he could say anything else, she disappeared into George's bedroom. *Yikes!* This was a bad idea.

When he caught up with her, he found her prancing around on the bed. *Rule number five! Rule number five!*

He startled her, and she made a scared-cat jump onto the nightstand, knocking something over the edge. It shattered on the floor with a sickening sound.

They stared at the pieces.

What is it? Luna asked.

It's broken, that's what it is. He didn't have to know exactly what it was to know they were in trouble. Correction: HE was in trouble. He would have to take the hit. Even if he had some way to tell him, George wouldn't believe a cat had come in and done this unless he'd caught her red-handed.

You'd better get out of here before George gets back.

She looked from Gracie to the mess on the floor, then back. *What about—*

I'll take care of it. Just go!

He didn't have to tell her twice. She left the room like she'd been shot out of a cannon.

A thank you would have been nice, he called after her. *Oh, I forgot, cats never say thank you.*

Gracie didn't know what to do. He could push everything under the bed and hope George wouldn't miss it. Who was he kidding? It sat right there on the nightstand for who knows how long. Then it magically disappeared? George would notice, and the cover-up would make things worse. This was bad. Really bad.

He would have to face this head on. George seemed like a reasonable human, one of the better ones he'd met, in fact. And Gracie's big, sad eyes hadn't failed him yet.

The apartment door opened and closed. *Showtime!*

"Gracie. I have something for you."

He panicked. *I'm afraid I have something for you, too, but you're not going to like it.* He picked up the biggest piece in his mouth and walked into the lion's den.

"There you are," George set a basket of vegetables on the table. His expression fell as Gracie approached.

Gracie set the broken piece on the floor and lowered his head, blinking.

George picked it up and examined it, then hobbled off toward the bedroom faster than Gracie had ever seen him move. He waved his arms and shouted words that Gracie probably wouldn't understand until he was much older. Except for *bad dog.* He knew that one.

George fell to his knees. His eyes leaked as he sifted through the pieces. "What have you done?"

Gracie tried to comfort the man. *I'm sorry, George. It'll be okay. You can buy another one.* He wagged his tail, hoping George would understand that it was an accident. It wasn't even his fault.

No reaction.

He nuzzled George's leg to let him know he was there if he needed him.

George pushed him away. "Bad dog!"

We're back to that? He'd thought they were making progress.

George's shoulders slumped and his mean expression softened. He turned to Gracie with softer eyes. "This was one of the first gifts Dottie ever gave me. She knew how much I liked trains, so on the one-year anniversary of the day we met, she bought me this clock that looks like a locomotive engine. The alarm sounds like a train whistle."

So, that's what I hear every morning. It's a little scary, don't you think? He looked down at the carnage. *I'm sorry, George. Maybe if I had opposable thumbs, I could fix it, but—*

"It reminded me of her every morning when I woke up." The muscles in his neck tensed. He took a deep breath and let it out slowly. "But that's not going to happen anymore, is it?"

George's tone told Gracie he was in the proverbial doghouse. He never understood that saying. Like a doghouse was a bad thing.

"I tried to make this work, but I'm too old for this kind of aggravation."

They were way past the doghouse stage now. He turned on the sad eyes, but George gazed up at the ceiling.

"I tried, Dot, I really did."

We can still make this work.

George grabbed Gracie by the collar. "Let's go, troublemaker."

Let's not overreact. What would Dottie do?

Gracie planted his feet and pulled back, but George overpowered him. He dragged him across the floor, all four legs slipping and sliding as they went out the door and into the hall. George opened the building's back door and tossed him outside.

Come on, man. You don't really want to do this.

The door slammed shut.

Not cool! After a moment, Gracie glanced at the doggy door. *You realize I can get back inside.*

Crickets.

He stared at the back of the building. *So, THAT just happened.* He wasn't sure what to do next.

The irony of the big welcome sign was not lost on him. He'd just been thrown out of heaven for the second time... for something he didn't even do. He needed a good lawyer.

Chapter Twenty

Gracie paced in circles in the grass behind the building. His stomach reminded him it would be dinnertime soon.

If only he could talk to George and explain what happened. The whole thing had been the cat's fault. Was this any way to treat a hero? Savannah could have been eaten by a coyote. Then how would George feel?

One day they're hoisting you up on their shoulders, and the next you're shunned. The punishment didn't fit the crime. People can't stay mad at dogs forever, can they?

He stopped pacing before he drilled a hole in the ground he couldn't get out of. He needed to find some food. The logical first place to look would be the trash cans near the coffee shop door. He remembered what happened the last time he tried that, but desperate times called for desperate measures. He went around front and saw a closed sign in the window, then came back to check the cans.

He'd get something to eat, then go back inside the building. George still needed him, whether he knew it or not. Gracie would not give up on him yet. Besides, he still had friends in the building, a building that felt more and more like something he'd never had before. A home.

The coast looked clear. All the dogcatchers were probably home having dinner with the devil. Exercising a good deal more caution than the last time, he raided the cans outside the coffee shop, grateful for humans' ability to carelessly waste good food. The scraps quieted his noisy stomach, and he returned to the building to figure out the night's sleeping arrangements.

Savannah would take him in a heartbeat, but he didn't want to press his luck with Mrs. Miller. Jasmine might be a safe port in a storm, but he needed some time before he could even look at that cat again. He was running out of options.

Sleep came in fits and starts on the third-floor landing. Gracie missed his comfy bed. In the morning, a short man with squinty eyes startled him, and Gracie pushed himself into the corner.

"Hello, dog. You must be one who save little girl. We not met. My name Sam."

Gracie stood. *So, you're Sam. My name is, uh, Gracie, but you probably can't understand me.*

He held out his hand, which smelled like nuts and some kind of herbs he didn't recognize. Gracie licked it.

"You did good with little girl." A broad smile crossed his face. "I not eat you."

What? Gracie took a step backward.

"Ha ha. I kidding."

Gracie relaxed. *You got me, Sammy. The girls didn't tell me you were such a funny guy.*

Sam patted him on the head. "Gotta go work. I bring you something from restaurant. Doggy bag. Ha ha."

Everyone's a comedian.

Sam said goodbye and walked away. The man was an enigma—all smiles and jokes on the outside, but a deep longing inside. He might have fooled the others, but dogs can sense what humans feel inside. Sam was searching for something. Gracie knew that feeling all too well.

If Sam kept his word, Gracie wouldn't be eating from a trash can again tonight. Right now, he'd give anything for one of

George's bacon and egg breakfasts. He should have known that was too good to last.

He wandered the neighborhood in search of food with no luck, until an old woman called to him from her front porch. The whole *desperate times* thing convinced him to climb up there with her.

"What a cute little doggy," she said from her rocking chair.

He wished he could say the same about her and her ratty bathrobe that smelled like coffee and vomit. She had too much skin, which made her face look like it had melted, and her hair looked like she'd just rolled around in a pile of leaves, but he didn't smell any leaves.

"I'll go get you some water." She stood and waddled across the porch.

Got any bacon?

She disappeared inside, and he reclined on the floor. A squirrel that must not have seen him on the porch ran across the front yard. When it reached the sidewalk, it turned and met his gaze. It froze for a second, then glanced at one of the massive trees that lined the street, then back at Gracie with a bet-you-can't-catch-me look. It wasn't worth getting up to give chase. He'd never caught one before and probably never would.

Dogs are notoriously bad with time, but it seemed like the woman had been in the house for the better part of the day. He barked.

She called from inside. "Who's out there?"

He barked again.

She appeared in the doorway. "What a cute little doggy."

Thanks, but...

"You look thirsty. I'll get you some water." She disappeared again.

What's happening? His throat was parched, but this might be another one of her fake-outs. He stood and pushed his nose up to the screen. *Maybe I should come in and supervise.*

She returned within a reasonable amount of time, but she appeared to walk backwards. He wondered if she'd just lost the few marbles she had left. She pushed the door open with her butt and turned around with a tray in her hands. She bent to place it on a small table, showing him her butt again.

Gracie tilted his head. *Does she want me to sniff it?* He hesitated.

She set a bowl of water in front of him, and he lapped at it, spilling some onto the floor. She set a bowl of kibble beside it. He dove into the kibble like a kamikaze.

"I used to have a dog. His name was Ralph, but he passed."

Sorry for your loss. Given how stale the kibble tasted, old Ralphie must have departed around the turn of the century. But Gracie needed food, and beggars can't be choosers. It had to be better than eating cat food at Jasmine's place.

When he finished, he lay down next to the lady's chair to keep her company. Spending a little time with her seemed like the least he could do to repay her kindness. She went on about her kids and how nobody comes to visit anymore. Gracie felt her loneliness and nuzzled her leg. When she digressed into the medical stuff, his eyes became heavy, and he drifted off to sleep.

The playful sounds of children woke him when Savannah's yellow box drove by. He jumped up, gave the lady a couple of farewell barks, and ran down the street toward the corner.

"Gracie, Gracie, Gracie." Savannah knelt and threw her arms around his neck.

He nuzzled her neck and sniffed her hair. The world seemed right again, if only for a little while. They went up to her apartment to swap her skin and get a snack, and then went outside to play.

She taught him a new game called *fetch*. She would throw a stick and expect him to retrieve it. He understood the word fetch to be a human shorthand for "go get the stick." He chased it down and returned with it in his mouth, presenting it proudly, head held high and eyes shining with pride.

However, instead of a "good dog" or a pat on the head, she would throw it again. She was far too young to have lost her marbles like the old lady down the street, so he figured her behavior was within the rules of the game. This wasn't the kind of game he'd had in mind. It didn't turn out so bad once he got the hang of it.

The afternoon was all fun and games until Savannah's mother called her in for dinner. They said goodbye and Gracie wandered up to the third-floor landing. All that fetching had worn him out, and he closed his eyes.

The smell of food woke him some time later. Sam climbed the stairs and smiled when he noticed Gracie looking down at him. "I have something for you."

Gracie's ears perked up at the words, delivered in Sam's curious yet endearing tone. His nose twitched with anticipation at the delightful medley of complex fragrances.

Sam held out a little white box with a wire handle. Gracie closed his eyes and indulged in the warm, spicy aroma. He sucked in as much air as his lungs would hold, then followed Sam.

"I hear your name Gracie. That funny name for male dog."

Yeah, tell me about it. What have you got in that little white box? His tail whipped up the air in the hall.

"I also hear you lose mama."

If you're trying to distract me, it's not working. Do I smell duck?

Sam unlocked the door, and Gracie followed him into his apartment. He opened the box and set it on the floor. Gracie attacked it—a feast of exotic delights that made his tail wag with uncontrollable enthusiasm.

"Me and mama lucky to be alive." Sam stepped back and watched. "Well, she dead now, but we were saved by American soldier in Vietnam many years ago. We never get to thank him. When we come to America, we look and look and look. His name Juju. No last name. Impossible to find. Mama die a few years back, but I still look."

Gracie stopped. *Wait. Did you say Juju? Like the candy?*

"I suppose I never find. Make me sad."

Nah. What are the chances? Couldn't be... could it? Gracie finished eating and pushed the box around the room trying to lick the inside.

"Good dog. We friends now." He held out his hand, palm up. "We shake."

What do you mean? Gracie tilted his head. *Your hand is empty.*

"We shake. Like friends." Sam grabbed Gracie's front paw with his other hand.

Gracie flinched and took a step backwards. *Not cool, man! What kind of freak show is this?*

"I not hurt. We shake."

Okay, but only because you fed me. The food was excellent, by the way. He played along, allowing Sam to pick up his front paw and place it in his open hand.

Gracie paused. *Okay. Now what?*

"See? This called shaking hands. We friends now." He let go of Gracie's paw and immediately held out his hand again.

Gracie placed his paw in Sam's hand, causing Sam to show Gracie all of his crooked teeth.

Shaking hands. Interesting concept. Perhaps it's the human version of butt sniffing.

Chapter Twenty-One

Gracie spent another night on the landing. He'd slept in worse places. The concrete floor reminded him of Brian's basement, but not as cold. On the bright side, he had a full belly, and he'd made a new friend. They even shook on it.

His sleeping arrangements needed to change. Too proud to beg, he planned to look for somewhere nearby to spend the nights and visit his friends during the day.

The sound of footsteps on the stairs interrupted his thoughts. Stay or run?

Before he had time to react, Jasmine reached the landing, followed by her cat, whose name he'd erased from his memory banks.

"Luna told me I'd find you here. She said you were in trouble."

She didn't happen to elaborate on the kind of trouble, did she?

"No, just that you needed our help."

Gracie glanced at Luna, who shrugged her stupid little cat shoulders.

"You're going to stay with us until we get this sorted out."

It's not so bad up here.

"Nonsense. Now, let's go." She took a step sideways and gestured down the stairs. "After you."

He hesitated, but finally gave in and descended the stairs. He was a fugitive now and knew Jasmine to be skilled at hiding illegal pets. Jasmine followed him to her apartment while what's-her-name brought up the rear.

"I have extra bowls, so I'll get you some water," Jasmine said. "We'll figure out the menu later."

No cat food, please.

"Luna wouldn't hear of it. She can be a little stingy with her things."

I prefer to call it protective, Luna said from her perch.

"I plan to have chicken tonight. You can eat with me."

A real home-cooked meal. *I'm looking forward to it.*

"Make yourself at home. I'll fix you someplace to sleep later." She disappeared into the kitchen.

Gracie sniffed around the living room, puzzled by all the calming, otherworldly scents he encountered. He figured a good aromatherapy plan was a prerequisite for living with a cat.

His nose led him into another room full of comfortable cushions and adorned with mystical artwork and rich tapestries. Colorful gemstones were arranged strategically around the room.

So, this is where the magic happens?

"That's my reading room," Jasmine said.

He thrust his nose in the air. *Is that patchouli?*

"You have a good nose."

I'm a dog. He paused. *Fun fact: a dog's sense of smell is one hundred thousand times better than humans.*

"That much, huh?"

She didn't say the room was off limits, but he chose not to push his luck. He wandered some more, staying clear of the carpeted, climbing thingy in the corner. He didn't want any cat trouble on his first day.

Moving on, he detected a faint but unpleasant smell. It grew stronger as he approached a plastic box in another corner of the room. Curiosity moved him forward despite the odor.

Luna jumped down from the sofa and cut him off.

What's that thing? Gracie asked.

It's a litter box.

Littering is against the law.

Luna rolled her little cat eyes. *Not this kind.* She climbed in and did her business right there in the apartment.

No way! You can do that inside? I have to go in the woods. He wagged his tail. *Where can I get one of those?*

Luna shook her head. *Cats only.*

• • • ● • ● • • •

After a dinner he thoroughly enjoyed, Gracie found a spot to recline in the living room. Jasmine finished cleaning the kitchen, then sat cross-legged on the floor next to him.

"You look sad. Was dinner okay?"

Dinner was superb.

"It's George, isn't it?"

I thought I did everything right. I loved him, and I thought he loved me. He threw me out for something I didn't even do.

Luna, who'd been eavesdropping, slipped quietly out of the room.

It's not fair. Fairness didn't seem to hold the same importance for humans as it did for dogs.

"I know." She stroked his back. "Sometimes people see what they want to see. George didn't want to see someone to love. That would be a betrayal of his wife. So, to protect himself, he saw you only as a troublemaker, someone unworthy of his love."

Do YOU think I'm worthy?

"Of course I do. And George will too, but it might take some time and a little healing."

I'm worried about him.

"George is battling demons from long ago. They caused damage to his family and created chaos."

Chaos? Apparently, the reason for all his rules.

"He's full of regret. And with Dottie gone, he's lost his way in this world." She paused, and her eyes drifted. "But you're a good dog."

He didn't understand the demons part but wagged for good dog.

Luna returned to make annoying scratching noises as she scaled the thingy in the corner. Gracie cringed. This would take some getting used to, but he had little choice. He could stay there or somewhere down the road.

I appreciate your help, but I can't stay here forever.

Luna arched her back in a languid stretch. *You got that straight.*

"Luna. Behave."

Just sayin'...

"I'll work on George. He'll come around."

What if he doesn't? Gracie asked.

"I'm sure Dottie will lend a hand. In the meantime, I've become skilled at concealing pets from the management."

Luna glanced at them. *We had a bird for a while.* She turned back to the window. *It was delicious.*

"Luna!" Jasmine looked at Gracie. "Don't pay any attention to her."

Not a problem.

"It's late. Let's figure out where you're going to sleep tonight."

Jasmine did an admirable job of making Gracie comfortable—a couple of soft blankets far away from the cat's quarters. But it seemed a shame to have a perfectly good dog bed sit empty one floor below them.

In the morning, Gracie ate breakfast with Jasmine while the cat slept in. A sense of lawlessness permeated the apartment. The cat seemed to do whatever she wanted whenever she wanted without rebuke. Were there no rules here? Without rules, there's chaos.

For some inexplicable reason, Jasmine didn't eat bacon, so they dined on toast and jam. They ate in relative silence, and Gracie suspected she had something on her mind.

Everything okay?

"I'm not sure. I had a dream about John. He may have transitioned overnight."

Transitioned?

"Passed. Moved on from this plane to the next."

I didn't think John was in any condition to fly.

"He went to heaven."

They have flights to heaven? I had to walk.

"No, Gracie, he died."

Why didn't you just say that? Humans wasted a lot of words.

"We need to do something for Rita."

Mama said when someone is sad, they just want people to be there with them.

"Then that's what we'll do."

Ruby met them in the hall when they opened the door. "Did you hear about John?"

"Not officially," Jasmine replied. "What happened?"

"Cancer finally took him last night." She sighed. "Poor Rita."

"We're going over there now to offer our condolences."

"She's not home. She went down to the funeral home to make arrangements."

"Okay, we'll have to catch up with her later."

Ruby raised an eyebrow. "Isn't that George's dog?"

"Uh... I'm dog-sitting." She paused. "We need to go. Bye, now."

That was close.

"She knows George threw you out. I heard it in her voice when she asked. Now she knows where you're staying. We might as well have written it in a note and slipped it under his door."

What do we do now?

"I'll handle George. Right now, I need to talk to the other tenants to see if anyone would be interested in attending a little get-together in John's honor. You're going to lay low in the apartment."

Will I be able to go to the party?

"I haven't decided yet."

Jasmine returned with good news. Everyone she'd spoken to had expressed interest in attending. After lunch, they called on Rita.

"May I help you?"

"I'm Jasmine from across the hall."

"I know who you are. And this must be Gracie."

"Yes, I'm dog-sitting for George." Her expression fell. "I'm very sorry for your loss."

"Thank you, dear."

"The reason I'm here, well, I'd like to plan a little get-together in the building to say goodbye to John."

"We've lived here a long time, but we hardly know any of the other tenants."

"That doesn't matter. I'd like to think we can all rally together for a friend in need."

"That's very kind of you, but... do you really think they would come?"

"It's unfortunate, but tragedy is often the thing that brings people together." She paused. "I've already spoken to some of the tenants, and every one of them said they would attend."

"Really?" Rita fought back a tear. "I think John would like that."

"Then it's settled. I'll take care of everything."

"When do you plan to hold this... event?"

"How does Saturday sound? We can use the lounge downstairs."

"Perfect. John should be back by then. I'd love to bring him."

Didn't see that coming.

Jasmine's cheeks flushed, and she twisted her hands. "Oh. I'm sorry. I... I thought..."

Despite the grief that hung heavy in the air, a flicker of a smile crossed Rita's lips. "I should clarify. John is being cremated tomorrow. I'll have his ashes here on Saturday."

"That's perfect."

Yes. We wouldn't want him to miss his own party.

"Can I bring anything?"

"Just yourself. And, of course, John." She nodded. "I'll let you know when I have more details."

"We need to get to work," Jasmine said on the way back to her apartment.

I'll clear my calendar.

Chapter Twenty-Two

Gracie wanted to do more, but without opposable thumbs or a speaking voice, his options were limited. That, and he needed to fly under George's radar for the time being. While George worked in the garden, Gracie accompanied Chloe and Savannah as they hung fliers around the building. Jasmine arranged for snacks and bottled water for the event. Rita baked a tray of cookies for her own husband's funeral. *Who does that?*

Saturday afternoon rolled around, and the room filled up.

Ho-lee cow! Look at all the people.

Rita arrived with John and wiped away tears at the sight of the large turnout. She set his urn down in the place of honor that the girls had prepared. One by one the other tenants greeted her and offered their condolences. They asked questions and let her reminisce.

Gracie made himself available for petting and scratching to anyone who was so inclined, but did it in such a way that it wouldn't steal too much attention away from the guest of honor. This was Gracie's first real party, and he thoroughly enjoyed the attention. Jasmine said it would be okay to call it a party because they were celebrating John's life rather than mourning his death. He wished someone had thrown a party for Mama, but they were alone at the time of her death. He had lots of friends now, which he was sure would make Mama happy.

Gracie watched everyone talk and get to know each other. Tom and Marilyn played it cool, but even a dog could see something was going on there. He remembered what Sam had said about the soldier named Juju, and he hoped he might find a reason to speak with George. Gracie's fugitive status made it impossible for him to facilitate that conversation.

Gracie kept a low profile, picking up scraps to ensure the floor stayed clean. He steered clear of George, but inevitably their paths collided.

"I thought I told you to leave," George said when he saw Gracie.

Come on, George. Can't we work this out?

George reached for Gracie's collar, but the dog slipped away and crawled under a chair.

Not cool, George. This is a party.

Jasmine witnessed the fracas and hurried over to run interference. "Really George? Now's not the time."

"How did that dog get in here?"

"Probably through the dog door you installed."

"I guess we don't need that anymore. I'll have to remove it."

Jasmine folded her arms. "Maybe I'll adopt him."

He raised a doubting eyebrow.

"Unless you've decided you want him back."

George hesitated.

Gracie watched from under the chair. *Tell her, George. Tell her I can come home.*

Sam had also been watching the two argue. "I want dog if she not take."

Jasmine grinned. "It seems Gracie's become quite popular around here."

"I might have to reinstate my no-pet policy."

"Can we talk about this later?" Jasmine whispered.

"There's nothing to talk about, except maybe that cat you've been hiding."

Jasmine let out a big huff and walked away.

It's no wonder George's daughter doesn't talk to him. Gracie hung his head. He might need to make some longer-term plans.

· · · · · ● · ● · ● · · · ·

When the party was over, Jasmine followed George down the hall to his apartment.

"Why are you being so stubborn?"

"Excuse me?"

"Gracie is your dog, George. They're like children. You don't just decide one day to turn your back on them."

George jabbed an index finger toward her face. "You leave my daughter out of this."

Jasmine was caught off guard by his reaction but decided not to pursue it. "You did a wonderful thing when you gave Gracie a home."

"We both knew it was a temporary arrangement."

"Really?" She pointed at his door. "That dog door says otherwise."

George squeezed the back of his neck as he shook his head. "That was a mistake. I guess I got caught up in the moment."

"Dogs will do that to you." She paused. "Dottie said not to worry about the clock. She never liked it anyway."

"What?

"That's what this is about, isn't it?"

"Who told you that?" He didn't wait for an answer. "She bought it for me. She loved that—"

"She loved you. She bought it because she knew it would make you happy."

"Wait a minute. How do you know all this?"

"That's what I've been trying to tell you, George. Dottie speaks to me from time to time."

George opened his mouth, but no words came out.

"She's still here because she wants to make sure you don't waste the rest of your life mourning her."

"She said that?"

"She wants you to write again."

"I wouldn't know what to write." He hung his head. "I don't have any ideas anymore."

"I think you sent your inspiration packing. He left through that hole in your door."

"The dog?" He waved a dismissing hand. "He's been nothing but trouble."

"You know that's not true. That's grumpy old George talking." Her bracelets jangled on her wrist as she placed her hands on her hips. "You've changed since that stray dog wandered into your life. We all have. He's here for a reason."

He raised a sarcastic eyebrow. "I suppose Dottie sent him?"

"That would be my guess."

He folded his arms across his chest. "Tell me again why you're here?"

"I hoped you'd reconsider letting Gracie come home. That dog has done more for this building in the last week, than…"

George took a half step toward her and puffed out his chest. "Than what? Than I've done in the last seven years?"

"I wasn't going to say that, but the fact that you did tells me something." Her hands were on her hips again. "What about Savannah?"

An awkward silence descended between them.

"I'll think about it."

· · · · ● · ● · · ● · · ·

On Monday, Gracie and Savannah planned to have a snack and play fetch after school. Chloe joined them in the yard.

"What's that?" Savannah asked.

"It's a rope."

"What are you going to do with it?"

"It's for Gracie."

Gracie didn't like the sound of that. Bad dogs got tied up. Did George put her up to this? He couldn't think of anything he'd done wrong since the clock incident.

"We're going for a walk, and we need a leash."

"Where are we going?"

"To the dog park."

Gracie's ears perked up. *Dog park? You mean THE dog park? Where I met my new friend Come Back Here Max? Oh, boy! I must be a good dog again.*

"Now?"

"Yep. Mom said it was okay, but we can only stay for an hour."

What about the snack?

"We were going to have a snack."

"We'll have it when we get back."

Chloe tied the rope around Gracie's collar, and he led the way down the street. He was on a mission. No time to stop and sniff every little tidbit along the way. After a couple of blocks, he could smell the dogs and hear the joyful noise. He picked up his pace, and the girls walked faster to keep up.

When they reached the fence, Chloe opened the gate, and they walked right in, just like that. He couldn't wait to find Come Back Here Max and show him his humans. That, and chase him, and catch him, and bite his neck.

Chloe untied the rope, and Gracie took off. *See you later.*

"We'll be right over here," Savannah called after him.

There were many dogs of different shapes and sizes running free and having the time of their lives. Except one old black and brown one whose ears dragged on the ground. He looked sad and didn't run.

Gracie stopped to sniff a few butts and ask if anyone had seen his friend. All at once, someone jumped on his back and knocked him over. They rolled in the grass, and Gracie recognized that oversized head, and pinned him to the ground. He licked his face and chewed his neck. After that, he let him up and they performed the ritual butt sniffing to see what other information they could gather.

Gracie led him over to show off his humans. Come Back Here Max's human saw them and joined the party. She said her dog's name was Max, which must have been a nickname. Gracie preferred the more informal name.

Soon they were off again, running through the grass and trying to catch each other's tails. When they stopped for a breather, Max introduced him to some of the regulars. Gracie asked about the one with the big ears. Max said he was just old. But they went over to say hi, anyway.

After that, Chloe came over and said it was time to go. Gracie was having too much fun to leave. However, he reluctantly said his goodbyes when Savannah reminded him of the snacks they'd left at home.

Back in the yard, Savannah opened her paper sack and passed out the food.

Gracie worked on his ham and cheese stick and thought about Rita, whom he hadn't checked in on yet that day.

Poor Rita. I wish we could do something for her.

Savannah took a bite of her sandwich. Her eyes drifted. "We should do something nice for Rita."

"On TV, when someone dies, everyone brings food," Chloe said.

What if we bring her some vegetables from George's garden?

Savannah frowned. "Wouldn't that be like stealing?"

Chloe scrunched up her face. "Stealing what?"

George told me, since his wife died, he throws most of it out, anyway. Mama used to say it wasn't stealing if you take something that someone is throwing away.

Savannah relayed the message.

Chloe looked at Gracie and smiled. "I think I would have liked your mama."

"What are we going to carry it in?"

"I'll go get a bag." Chloe stood. "I'll be right back."

She returned with a large paper sack. But before they put their plan into motion, George approached from the opposite direction. He spotted them and stopped before entering the building.

Gracie gained his feet, ready to run if George came any closer. George stared for a moment, then shook his head and continued into the building.

"That was close," Savannah said.

Gracie wondered why George didn't chase him off like at the party.

"How will we get the vegetables now?" Savannah asked.

Chloe rose to her feet. "You guys go pick the vegetables. I'll make sure George stays in his apartment. If he comes out, I'll run out and warn you."

Sounds like a plan.

Savannah stood. "Okay. Let's do it."

Their plan went off without a hitch, and they knocked on Rita's door. She invited them in.

"Come sit with me for a minute." When they were all seated, she opened the bag. "These are beautiful vegetables. Are they from George's garden?"

No answer.

"Thank you, girls. You're so sweet."

Despite Rita's outward appearance, Gracie sensed a profound loneliness.

"Gracie helped, too." Savannah reached down and patted his head.

Gracie's tail stirred up the air in the apartment. *It was kind of my idea.*

"He's quite a wonderful dog, isn't he?"

Someone should tell George.

Savannah giggled.

Gracie's curious nature had him wandering around the apartment. He didn't care for her decorating style, especially the plastic covers on all the furniture. The smell of cookies taunted him from the kitchen, but he thought it might be rude to track them down and help himself. John's scent was still everywhere, and he didn't know if the man might be watching from his jar on the coffee table.

After ten minutes, Chloe stood. "We should go now. Come on, Gracie."

He lay down at Rita's feet. *You guys go. I've got it from here.*

"Maybe he can stay a little while longer." Rita reached down and stroked his back. "I'll send him home before dinner."

The girls looked at each other and shrugged.

After they left, Rita scratched behind his ears. "You're a good dog, aren't you?"

Gracie felt the lonely ache inside her melt away a little with every scratch, and he realized he could provide something she needed.

The warm feeling grew in his chest again, and they sat together for an hour before Rita dozed off. He was a good dog.

Chapter Twenty-Three

A week passed since Jasmine had confronted George outside his apartment. He'd always thought of her as a nutjob, but in the past month, she'd said some things that gnawed at him. And that dog. What if she was right about Gracie?

He glanced at the bag of dog food as he fried up some bacon for breakfast. Three strips instead of six. At least he'd saved some money on groceries since Gracie's been gone.

"Don't you start," he said to an empty room.

His daily conversations with Dottie had not been going well lately. He'd been drinking more, and the whole Gracie thing had them on opposite sides of a contentious debate.

That morning, she didn't mention Gracie. She did, however, suggest he check in on Rita. He decided not to fight it.

"George. Please come in," Rita said when she opened the door.

"I can't stay long, I just..." He noticed Gracie on the floor next to her chair. "I... I just wanted to see if you needed anything."

"I'm fine, but I want to thank you for the vegetables."

George frowned.

"And for letting me borrow Gracie. John's passing has been difficult, as you might imagine, but Gracie's company has helped."

George studied Gracie for a moment before turning back to Rita. "Is that so?"

"Oh yes. He scratches on my door every morning. I let him in, and he keeps me company. Sometimes we just sit in silence and sometimes I talk to him. Of course, he never replies, but I can tell he's an excellent listener." She smiled briefly before her expression fell. "I hope I haven't been monopolizing his time."

"Not at all." George rubbed his chin. "I'm glad you have someone like Gracie to help you through this."

"Everyone in the building has been so nice. John needed my full attention these last two years, so I guess I haven't been very sociable. But they treat me like an old friend now, thanks to Gracie."

"Gracie?"

"Yes. I hear the party was the dog's idea."

George understood she was getting on in years, but... "I see." Best not to argue with them when they start to lose their minds.

"I have such wonderful neighbors. Mike offered to pick up groceries. Sam brought me dinner from the restaurant a couple of nights. And Ruby, bless her soul, checks in on me and keeps me informed on what's happening in the building."

"That's nice."

"It's really just gossip, but it's a wonderful distraction."

"It sounds like you're being well taken care of." He paused. "If there's anything you need, don't hesitate to call."

"That's sweet of you, George. Thank you."

On the way back to his apartment, George thought about the way he'd handled the Gracie incident. Perhaps he'd over-reacted. He hated to admit it, but Gracie had been a pleasant distraction from his own grief.

He shook his head. Dottie had sent him up there. She knew exactly what would happen. "Well played, my dear."

Upon his return from the market, George put the groceries away, changed his clothes, and tended the garden. He wondered about the vegetables Rita had mentioned, and why she thought they were from him. He had the crazy notion that Gracie had somehow been involved. But that was impossible, wasn't it?

George put a lot of time and money into the garden but ate very little of the harvest. For the past few years, his vegetables had mostly rotted on the vine at the end of the season. He realized how that must have made Dottie feel. Perhaps he should resurrect the free produce stand that Dot used to set up in the lobby.

A cardinal landed atop one of the fence posts, looked at George for a moment, then flew off.

• • • • • • • • • •

Gracie had been a fugitive for two weeks, but he'd finally seen a crack in George's armor. He wasn't fooling anyone at John's party, especially Jasmine. She let him have it afterwards. That day at Rita's couldn't have gone any better if Gracie had written the script himself. If George hadn't left there with a heart full of regret, someone had better check his pulse.

Now's the time to make my move. Gracie waited in the bushes out front until George left for his daily trip to the market. When George reached the corner, he set out after him. He'd had no experience tailing anyone, so he wasn't sure how much distance to keep between himself and the subject. However, he knew enough to always have a plan in case the subject got spooked and turned around. He learned that from *The Rockford Files,* one of the old detective shows he watched with George.

George moved slowly with his cane, obviously unaware he was being followed. Gracie debated whether to catch up to him and walk alongside like nothing had changed, or to wait outside the store and surprise him. After some deliberation, he chose the latter and kept his distance.

Unfortunately, Gracie's nose distracted him, and he didn't see that George had stopped outside the market. Sniffing along with his head down, he almost bumped into him.

"For your information, I don't need a chaperone," George said. "I've been making this trip myself for years."

Gracie tucked his tail between his legs and hunkered down. He raised his eyes slightly to ask if George could ever forgive him.

George stared for a moment then opened the door. He shook his head. "What am I going to do with you?" A little bell jingled as he walked inside.

Well, that could have gone a lot worse.

Gracie debated whether to stay or go, but George seemed different. He hadn't chased him away, so Gracie waited. And waited. *Is he still in there? Did he slip out the back door?* They'd seen that on *The Rockford Files*, as well. He let out a sigh of relief when George stepped outside carrying a large paper sack.

"You are persistent, I'll give you that."

Wild horses couldn't drag me away.

"You can walk with me this time instead of tailing me like a PI."

He wondered why George had begun to spell his words. *T-H-A-N-K-S.* A new game, perhaps? It was a good sign.

George said little on the way home, and Gracie worried about what might happen when they got there. In a surprise move, George sat on the front step and set his bag down next to him.

"Come over here. I have a surprise for you."

For me? Another unexpected move. Gracie hesitated. George had been a wild card since the clock incident. This entire trip might have been a setup. He didn't care to see the bottom of George's boot again, so he kept his distance.

"Come over here. I won't bite."

Gracie crept closer, ready to bolt at the first sign of aggression. "Sit."

Gracie obliged.

George reached into his bag and pulled out a long, slim package. He tore open one end and peeled back the wrapper. "You ever have a Slim Jim?"

A pleasing aroma wafted through the air and Gracie breathed it in. *I really hope you're not messing with me, George.*

George held it out in front of Gracie, who took another big sniff.

Some kind of meat stick? He bit off a piece. *Ho-lee cow! That's good.* He looked up at George, who peeled back more of the wrapper. *What's going on here?*

"You like it?"

Does a fat dog fart?

He held it out again, and Gracie snatched it, leaving George with the empty wrapper.

"I guess that's my answer."

The man had obviously heard the saying about a dog's heart and his stomach.

George reached over and stroked the top of Gracie's head. "I'm not very good at apologies, but I guess I owe you one." He hesitated a moment. "I may have overreacted when I sent you away. Seeing how everyone in the building loves you made me feel like I might have been focused on the wrong thing."

You're on the right track now. Keep going.

"I'm sorry, and I'd like it if you would come back home."

I accept your apology and would like to offer one of my own. None of this would have happened if I hadn't brought that damn cat into the apartment. We were only trying to help, but I promise, no more cats. I'm sorry, George.

"What do you think?"

Gracie stuck his nose in the bag, looking for more. Cold cuts, bread, a cigar, and a couple of boxes of Jujubes.

"Sorry, there's no more. Maybe next trip." George waved his hand, and Gracie stepped back. "So, you think you might come home?"

Gracie held out his paw like Sam had taught him.

George took it with a surprised expression. "Where'd you learn that?"

As if on cue, Sam walked out of the building. Gracie took advantage of the opportunity and knocked over the bag, spilling George's groceries onto the sidewalk.

"Gracie! What did you do that for?"

Sam rushed to help. He squatted and returned the contents to the bag one at a time until he noticed the Jujubes. He stopped and stared, then slowly picked up a box. An eerie silence filled the air until he turned to George. "These for you?"

George nodded. "I know I shouldn't eat them, but I've been doing it since I was a kid. In the army, they nicknamed me Juju because I always kept a box in my back pocket."

"Wait." His eyes widened. "You name Juju?"

"That's what they called me."

Gracie's tail wagged. *Yes, yes, that's Juju.*

Sam sat back on the step like a gust of wind had blown him over. A mixture of emotions washed over his face.

Go on, Sammy. Ask him. Ask him.

Sam regained his composure. "You fight war in Vietnam?"

George straightened up. "I did. First Infantry Division." He turned to Sam. "You north or south?"

"I live in south." His voice cracked. "I was little boy. I think you save me and my mama."

Attaboy. I knew it!

After blinking back his surprise, George studied Sam. "I pulled a little boy and his mother from a burning hut near Da Nang and helped them get to safety."

Sam stood. "That me. That me." He lunged at George and threw a big hug around his neck. "*Ngợi khen Chúa*. Praise God. I look for you my whole life."

You're welcome.

George loosened Sam's grip. "What are the chances?"

"We live in same building all this time and not know. I wish Mama still alive to see."

Gracie's shoulders slumped a little, reminded of his own mama. *I feel you, Sammy.*

"This is incredible," George said. "Let me get these groceries inside, and I'll make us some coffee. We've got a lot of catching up to do."

"I call work. Tell them I'm late today."

Gracie held his head high as he followed them inside.

Chapter Twenty-Four

For the next hour, Sam and George swapped stories about the war and their lives before and after. Sam excused himself after his second cup of coffee and left for work. They promised to pick it up again later.

"Did you hear that, Gracie?" George said after Sam left.

Dogs hear everything.

"Sam and me, we go way back. Turns out I saved him and his mother over fifty years ago. He called me a hero."

Looks like we have something in common.

"I just did what any decent human being would do."

I know. Like rescuing a stray dog who was lost and alone.

"And to think we met up again after all these years because of Jujubes."

Technically, yes, but there's more to the story.

"Funny thing." He scratched his head. "If you didn't knock over that bag of groceries, all of this might never have happened."

Might?

"I gotta thank you. I hated that war. No one appreciated the hell we went through to serve our country. They made us feel dirty when we returned home, like we did something wrong."

He grabbed Gracie with both hands and scratched affectionately behind his ears. "But now, because of you, I feel like something positive came out of it. Like what I did made a difference in someone's life."

You're welcome. Don't stop scratching.

"If I didn't know better, I'd think you knocked that bag over on purpose."

On purpose... I guess that's a good way to put it.

"But that's crazy, right? You're just a dog."

Just a dog?

"Well, anyway, it's good to have you back."

Gracie licked his hand. *Good to be back, George.*

"This calls for a special treat tonight. What do you say I grill a couple of nice, juicy, bacon cheeseburgers?"

I say... you just blew my mind. Cheese AND bacon on a burger? Sounds delish. What are you having?

It had been a productive morning, and Gracie's dog bed called his name from the other room.

If you don't mind, I think I'll take a nap before dinner.

He circled his bed, looking for the perfect spot, then curled up in the pillowy softness for the first time in two weeks. How had he gotten by without it for that long? Then he remembered the year he spent living on the streets. *I must be getting soft.*

With his head resting on his paws, he tried to replay the morning's events, but visions of cheeseburgers danced in his head. You know, like that song? Or was it a poem? Either way, it made it difficult to concentrate on anything else. Eventually, he drifted off to sleep.

When he awoke sometime later, he held up his nose and checked for bacon. Nothing. Must not be dinnertime yet. He found himself alone in the house, so he pushed through the doggy door and wandered up to Savannah's. Chloe answered after a couple of scratches.

She looked up from her little black board. "Hey, Gracie. Come on in. Savannah is in her room watching TV."

He padded down the hall to her room. *Hey, Savannah Banana. Guess what?*

She ran and gave him a hug. "I haven't seen you around lately. Where have you been?"

Here and there, you know, doing dog stuff. I've got good news. I moved back in with George.

"That's awesome. What happened?"

I guess he missed me. He asked me to come back. No harm, no foul.

"I'm so happy for you. And for me. I thought you might have to go away."

It was touch and go there for a while. You got any snacks?

"We'll get something to eat after this show."

Who is that big dog?

"That's Scooby-Doo. He can talk."

I see that. He's a lucky dog... except for his name.

"He's not so lucky. He's always getting into trouble."

And the way he talks. Is that how humans think we would sound? Rut-ro. Rime Rooby-Roo, and Rime in rouble. Frankly, I'm a little insulted.

When the show ended, they grabbed a snack and headed outside to play.

They played fetch and a new game called *bet you can't catch me*. Savannah knew a lot of games for such a little one. He chased her around the yard until he smelled food and ran around to the back of the building. George stood on the patio, which was what he called the old concrete station platform. A black box made sizzling noises and flames leapt into the air when he opened it.

The wind carried clouds of smoke in Gracie's direction, and he filled his lungs.

"Dinner's almost ready."

George didn't have to tell him twice. He glanced over his shoulder at Savannah. *Later, Gator.* He dove through the doggy door and ran down the hall. Another leap and he landed inside the apartment. It smelled like bacon, and he trembled with anticipation.

George arrived a few minutes later and prepared them both a plate. His plate went on the table and Gracie's on the floor. They attacked their food.

"It's not a race," George said, pausing to watch the carnage.

Gracie won anyway, and his eyes asked for more.

"Sorry, that's all there is. You go on, now. I need to have a chat with Dottie. You know, tell her about my day."

Back to his bed for a dessert nap.

Later, during *Jeopardy!*, Gracie heard a noise at the door. His ears perked up, and he went to check it out.

"What's the matter?" George said as Gracie passed his chair.

I heard something.

George rose from his chair and followed.

Ho-lee cow! Is it Christmas already?

A rawhide chew toy in the shape of a gigantic bone sat on the carpet in front of the door. Gracie had seen something like it before, but only dreamed of ever owning one. He assumed it was for him.

George scratched his head as he watched Gracie do his happy dance. "Looks like you have a secret admirer." He opened the door and looked down the hall. "I wonder who it could be."

Gracie stopped to sniff the toy. *Sam. It smells like Sam.*

"I guess we'll never know."

By the time he closed the door, Gracie had dragged his prize into the living room. George returned to his chair, and Gracie worked on his new toy most of the evening.

Instead of *Gunsmoke* or *Bonanza,* George watched a bunch of men with colored caps chase a ball around. It appeared to be some form of fetch for humans but using a little white ball and a stick. One of them would hit the ball with the stick, and the others would all try to fetch it, which was ridiculous. They divided into teams and kept score. George liked the team from San Francisco. He called them giants, but they didn't look any bigger than the other team.

Something strange happened that night. George only drank two cans of beer with his popcorn. At the end of the game, he turned to Gracie. "Say goodnight, Gracie."

Unsure how to respond, Gracie let out a playful bark, which seemed to satisfy George, who nodded and walked into his bedroom rather than sleep in his chair.

Gracie laid his head down next to his big, fat rawhide bone. All in all, it had been a very good day.

Chapter Twenty-Five

Gracie awoke the next morning to an empty apartment. He barked. No reply. George must be sweeping the walk out front, or in his garden, or maybe an early trip to the market. *Nothing to smell in the kitchen. Where's breakfast?* Not a good sign. *Maybe he's still asleep or... or... dead.*

Please don't die on me, George. He ran to George's bedroom. Empty. He let out the breath he'd been holding.

George had told Gracie that he was on probation. He didn't know what that meant, but he didn't like the sound of it. What if it meant he could live in the apartment, but George had to leave? *Yikes!*

Gracie's mind led him down a rabbit hole while he paced in tighter and tighter circles. *What would I do? Who will feed me? I need you, George. Wait.* He stopped. *George needs me, too. I didn't do anything wrong last night, did I? I'm a good dog.* His heart pounded in his chest. *Get a grip, Gracie. Breathe.*

He needed to check the usual spots and talk to the usual suspects. Someone must have seen him. His stomach reminded him he needed food. But if he didn't find George, he might starve.

He dove headfirst through the doggy door and somersaulted into the hall. Where to check first? He ran to the front door. Nothing out there. He ran to the back door. George wasn't in his garden.

Gracie teetered at the edge of the rabbit hole. *Keep it together, man. There are still a few more places to look.*

He scratched a little too hard on Rita's door.

"Why, hello, Gracie."

Sorry about the door. Have you seen George? He squirted through her legs and made a quick circuit around the apartment. No George. *Gotta bounce. Catch you later.* He ducked back out the door before she had time to close it and ran down the hall to Jasmine's. He took a deep breath and scratched. The door opened.

Have you seen George this morning? I can't find him, and I'm worried.

Luna stopped weaving her way around Jasmine's legs. *Wait. Let me get this straight. You lost your human? Isn't it the dog that usually gets lost?* She shook her condescending little head.

"I haven't seen him, but he must be around here somewhere. Do you want me to help look?"

Thanks, but no. I'm going to run down to the market and look for him there.

"Good luck. Keep me posted."

Luna snickered. *Yes, please keep us posted.*

Gracie flew out the back door and ran down the street toward the market. By the time he reached his destination, he'd nearly run out of gas. He sat in front of the store, panting. If he waited around for George to come out, and he wasn't in there, he'd be wasting precious time.

He hid under a produce rack outside until a customer came by, then slipped in behind her. There must have been a butcher shop in the back—the smell of meat was everywhere. Given the present condition of his stomach, he had difficulty concentrating. He needed to get some food or get outside... or both.

He moved quickly up one aisle and down the next, looking for George. Convinced he wasn't there, he grabbed a cookie from a bottom shelf and headed for the door.

The man behind the counter waved his fist. "Hey! Get back here with that."

Put it on George Baxter's tab. He slipped out the door and didn't stop running until he'd gone a safe distance. He sat under a bench and tore open the package. *Bonus!* There were two cookies inside. He gobbled them up. He'd be no good to anyone on an empty stomach.

Okay. Back to work. By the time he reached The Station, he was parched. He returned to his apartment to check his water bowl and found it full. *That's strange.* Perhaps George had returned from wherever he'd gone. He barked and waited. Nothing. He lapped up the water and continued his search.

Options were dwindling. He ran back into the hall. His heart jumped when he noticed the basement door open a crack. He nudged the door and found the light on, so he barked.

"Is that you, Gracie?"

Gracie felt conflicted—relieved to find George alive, but upset that he'd wandered off without telling him where he was going.

No, it's the other dog who lives in the building.

Obviously, George needed to work on his communication skills.

Gracie had trouble navigating the old wooden stairs, but eventually his feet hit solid ground. George was leaning over a tall wooden box that resembled the produce rack outside the market.

What are you doing down here? And what happened to breakfast?

"Hey, Gracie. Sorry I left so early, but I needed to see if we still had Dottie's old produce stand. We used to set it up in the lobby with a FREE sign. The tenants loved it."

That's nice. By the way, I charged breakfast to your account at the market.

George took a step back. "Well, here it is. What do you think?"

It looks empty. Where are all the veggies?

"Mike is on his way down to help me carry it upstairs."

Good choice. Mike looked fit for his age, like he could carry that thing upstairs with one arm tied behind his back. Must be all the exercise he got lifting donuts on the job.

"I'm starved. How about you?"

You really have to ask?

"After we get this upstairs, I'll make us some breakfast. I can fill up the stand later."

"Hello," Mike called from the top of the stairs.

"Just in time. Come on down."

Mike seemed like a pretty nice guy, but Gracie kept his distance.

It didn't take long to get the empty stand upstairs and situated in the lobby. Of course, Gracie supervised the operation. Mike did all the heavy lifting. Literally.

Ten minutes later, the apartment smelled like bacon, and all seemed right with the world again. After breakfast, a certain doggy bed in the living room called his name.

"Okay. You take a nap. I'm going to the market."

Yikes! You might want to avoid the guy behind the counter. He's having a bad day.

Gracie awoke to the sound of bags folding and groceries being put away. He stayed in his bed.

"Jack said he saw you in the market this morning."

Gracie pushed himself down farther into the soft bed. *I have one of those familiar faces. I get that kind of thing all the time.*

"He said you made off with a cookie."

Two, actually. I told him you'd take care of it.

"You've never gone down there alone. I'm guessing you were looking for me. You were sleeping when I left this morning. I would have left you a note, but, you know."

A note would have been better than nothing. I could have had Jasmine translate. Anyway, I forgive you. What's for lunch?

"I'm going out back to pick vegetables. Care to join me?"

Gracie wagged his tail and followed.

In the garden, Gracie tried to help by wrapping his mouth around a cucumber and shaking his head until the vine snapped. He walked it over to George, who inspected it.

"It's full of teeth marks. I'll do the picking from now on." He tossed it into the corner.

Gracie followed and made himself comfortable. No sense wasting a perfectly good snack. While he ate, he watched George load up a wagon full of produce.

"These are for the tenants," he said to Gracie when he'd finished.

As opposed to those of us who are just dogs?

Chapter Twenty-Six

Luna slipped out through the doggy door and strolled to the edge of the patio as Gracie watched from under the maple tree. She looked left and right, like she was about to cross a busy street.

You look like you've never been outside.

Maybe I haven't. She took a tentative step into the grass, then jumped back onto the patio.

Seriously? It's grass. It won't bite you.

I didn't expect it to feel like that.

Don't be such a pussy.

The least you can do is not make fun of me when I'm trying to help you.

Sorry. He paused. *Dogs use that word, you know. Thank you, too. You should try it.*

Luna walked toward Gracie like she was trying on a pair of shoes that were two sizes too small. Gracie stifled a laugh. She hopped up on one of the wide roots when she reached the tree.

Gracie walked over to where she had perched. *You were saying something about helping me?*

Jasmine wants to see you. She has an idea.

That's it? You tap-danced all the way over here to tell me that? You could have just told me from the patio.

I'm trying to be discreet.

You know we can't talk, right? No one can hear us.

Gracie walked over to the patio. The cat stayed put.

You coming?

In a minute, she said, trying to act aloof.

It didn't fool Gracie, who chuckled as he continued on to Jasmine's apartment.

Your cat says you want to see me. By the way, you should let her out once in a while. She's stuck in a tree out there.

Jasmine dropped what she was doing and hurried to the window. "You let her climb a tree?"

Climb? Are you kidding? She's sitting on a root. I think she's afraid of the grass.

"And you left her out there?"

What was I supposed to do, carry her home on my back?

"Poor Luna."

You can get her later. What's your idea?

She picked up a folded newspaper and held it in front of him. "I came across this while I was reading the paper."

Uh... you're going to have to read it to me. That print is way too small.

"Sorry." She forced a smile. "I forgot you're just a dog."

Not you, too. He paused. *Oh, I get it. You're sore at me for leaving your cat in a tree.*

"The local bookstore, Paperback Paradise, is sponsoring a writing contest."

Gracie tilted his head. *But I can't write. I'm just a dog. Remember?*

"It's not for you, silly. I thought George should enter."

I see. George, the writer, in a writing contest. Brilliant idea.

"Dottie said she wanted him to write again. This might be just the push he needs to get started."

Wonderful, but he thinks you're a witch, or some kind of nutjob. How are you going to convince him to enter the contest?

"I'm not." A mischievous smile crossed her lips. "You are."

Me? But I'm just a—

"A dog. I'm aware. All you have to do is take this paper to George and make sure he reads it."

So, you think he's going to read it and say, 'A writing contest? That's brilliant. Thanks, Gracie, I'm going to sign up right now.'

"There's a five-thousand-dollar prize."

Ho-lee cow!

She handed him the folded newspaper. "Just make sure he reads it. Entering this contest could change his life."

Gracie didn't see how that was possible, but he agreed to try. *Okay, I can give him the paper, but I can't make him enter the contest. I'm a dog, remember?*

"A very resourceful dog. You'll think of something."

Gracie returned to the apartment to find George reading the paper with his magnifying glass. He dropped the newspaper from Jasmine at George's feet.

"I already have the paper."

Not this one. Gracie barked.

"Go play with something."

Come on, man, just pick up the paper. Gracie nudged it a little closer and barked again.

"If you need to go outside, just go."

Oh, for crying out loud. He picked up the paper in his teeth and looked up at George with those sad eyes.

George studied him for a moment, then took the paper. "What's all the fuss about?"

Just read it, okay?

George passed his magnifying glass back and forth over the folded paper. "A writing contest? Is that what you wanted me to see?" He paused. "Wait a minute. You're a dog, you can't read." He walked to the door, opened it, and looked down the empty hall.

"Who put you up to this?" He shook his head. "It had to be that Jasmine." He returned to his seat at the table. "I used to write, back in the day. Published three books. Dottie said they were the best she'd ever read. Of course, she didn't read much."

He scanned the article again. "I gave it up when she passed. Just didn't have it in me after that." He set the paper down. "Thanks, but no thanks. Besides, I can't see well enough anymore to type."

It's just a short story. Maybe that's what you need to get back in the groove.

"What would I even write about?"

Oh, I don't know... a dog, maybe?

George took a long sip of coffee and returned to his newspaper.

It could change your life... or so I'm told.

Gracie shuffled into the living room, feeling like a failure. He hated letting anyone down, even if they might be a witch. He'd had one little job to do. Sure, it was a stretch for a dog, but Jasmine seemed to think he was no ordinary dog, and something inside him wanted to believe her.

He circled his bed, then climbed in and rested his head on his front paws. He needed time to think.

Chapter Twenty-Seven

After dinner, Gracie spotted the newspaper that Jasmine had given him atop a pile of papers headed for the recycle bin. *Not this one.* He plucked it from the pile and deposited it on George's chair. Later, when George found it, he called Gracie over.

Play it cool, dawg. *Yo, Georgie, what's up?*

"Did you put this here?"

Gracie assumed it was a rhetorical question, since dogs can't talk.

"I thought this matter was closed."

Well, think again. I know you can do this, but you're gonna have to put on your big-boy pants, fire up that old laptop, and pound out a story.

George held the paper out in front of him. "Go put this back on the pile in the kitchen."

That wasn't going to happen. On his way to the kitchen, Gracie took a detour into the bathroom and deposited it on top of the magazine pile next to the big, ceramic water bowl. He took a long drink before returning to the living room.

Gracie reclined in his bed, watching George in his chair. *How could he be so stubborn?* This might be too much for one dog to handle. He needed help.

Gracie rose and walked nonchalantly past George's chair. Once he made it through the doggy door, he ran up the stairs to Jasmine's place.

Houston, we have a problem.

"What's the matter?"

He didn't take the bait.

"I have an idea," she said after a few moments of silence. "I know the owner of the bookstore, and he knows George. He likes to support local authors. I'll call him and see if he'll talk to George about the contest."

Hmmm. Not bad, but the way I see it, we still have two problems. First, his eyes are bad. He can't type while he's holding that giant magnifying glass. Second, he says he doesn't know what to write about. Seems all his inspiration left with Dottie.

"I'll take care of the first problem. You need to work on the second."

Let me get this straight. All I need to do is inspire a grieving old man to fire up his laptop after seven years and write a prize-winning story? Where's the challenge in that? I mean... ARE YOU INSANE?

"You're a resourceful dog. You'll think of something."

You keep telling me that.

"Dottie says George would rather fall on his face than admit he's getting old and needs glasses. She tried more than once to take him in for an exam. The old fool always had an excuse."

So, what are you going to do?

"Tomorrow, I'm going down to the dollar store and buy him a pair of cheap reading glasses." She pointed at Gracie. "And you're going to deliver them."

Gracie agreed to the new assignment and returned to his bed, where he settled in to watch another game of fetch with George. His giants, who still didn't look any bigger than the other team, were playing a bunch of mariners from Seattle. At one point, George attempted to explain the rules, but it was too much for Gracie to process. However, he did learn the name of the game—baseball.

Once again, George limited his beer intake to two cans and spent the night in his bed rather than the chair.

· · · · ● · ● · · · ·

George's phone rang after breakfast. *I'm not one to eavesdrop… Wait. Who am I kidding?* Gracie crept a little closer. Hearing only one side of a conversation proved frustrating. *Put it on speaker, George.*

It must have been the guy from the bookstore, because George gave him all the same excuses. Finally, George said he'd think about it. In Gracie's experience, that translated to a big fat NO. After George hung up, he sat and stared at nothing for much longer than usual. Gracie hoped he was giving it some thought, or maybe listening to Dottie give him an earful.

Gracie ran upstairs to tell Jasmine. True to her word, she held up a pair of glasses.

"These should take the place of his magnifying glass. He has bigger problems with his eyes, but this will at least allow him to use his computer again."

Luna walked by languidly and grinned like it had been her idea.

Jasmine slipped the glasses into a bag and handed it to Gracie.

Gracie returned to the apartment and found George at the table with his coffee and paper. He walked up to him with the bag in his mouth.

"What do you have this time?"

You can thank me later.

George held up the glasses. "What are these for?"

Do I have to spell it out for you? Just try them on. He lowered his head to avoid George's glare. *If you're really out there, Dottie, now would be a good time for a little help.*

"I know you didn't do this by yourself."

Can't get anything past you, can I?

"Did that woman upstairs put you up to this?"

If you're referring to Jasmine, yes, she put me up to it. It's for your own good.

"She's a witch, you know."

She's no more a witch than you're a fairy godmother. Just try on the glasses.

"It would be nice if people minded their own business around here."

That's your take away from this? Thirteen people call this building home. Granted, one of them is a pile of ashes living in a jar on Rita's coffee table. But until two weeks ago, all they did was mind their own business. They couldn't tell you the names of their neighbors. Look at them now, talking and getting together. And just between you and me, I think Tom and Marilyn are hooking up.

George slipped the glasses over his nose and picked up his paper. "Hmmm. I can read the paper with these."

See, George—no pun intended—Jasmine is trying to help. She cares about you. We all do.

"I see what you're trying to do here. Now that my hands are free, you think I can type again. Maybe enter that contest, right?" He removed the glasses and studied them in his hand. "You forgot something. My muse is gone. I have no inspiration, nothing to write about." He set them on the table. "You can't just go to the store and buy one of them."

You're probably right. Otherwise, I'm sure Jasmine would have picked one up when she bought the glasses. But I'm going to find a way. I'm like the third dog on the ramp to Noah's ark and it's startin' to rain.

Chapter Twenty-Eight

The next morning, Gracie paced around the apartment while George read the paper with his new glasses. Who says you can't teach an old human new tricks? Jasmine had done her part, with a little help, of course. Now, the weight of the entire operation sat squarely on his shoulders. He needed a good roll in the grass to clear his head.

He stopped for a drink on the way out, then found a nice warm spot in the sun and dropped. He rolled and rolled until he couldn't roll anymore. His eyelids became heavy as he lay in the warm grass.

Mama came to him in a dream. She assured him they would be together someday, but in the meantime, she felt proud of what he'd accomplished so far. She reminded him that dogs are tenacious. It was a big word, but Mama said it meant they never give up. Once a dog sets his mind to something, wild horses couldn't stop him.

He pushed everything out of the way and focused his mind on George winning the contest. This was followed immediately by an image of Gracie walking down the aisle in Pet Stop Warehouse alongside George and his pocketful of prize money.

"Gracie, Gracie, Gracie!"

What? Where am I? Gracie lifted his head to see Savannah running across the grass. *What are you doing home so early?*

"It's Saturday, silly."

He tilted his head. *What's Saturday?*

"That means I don't have to go to school."

Bonus! Grateful for his power nap, he jumped up, ready to play.

For the rest of the afternoon, they played *fetch* and *bet you can't catch me*, and another game whose name eluded him.

Gracie returned home a little before dinnertime to the smell of Vietnamese food. Several of those little white containers with the wire handles sat unopened on the table.

Honey, I'm home. I hope that's dinner I'm smelling.

He found George and Sam talking in the living room over a couple of beers. Gracie settled into his bed under the window and perked up his ears. He found their conversation fascinating and lost track of time.

He'd been so engrossed in listening to George and Sam tell their stories, he'd forgotten about dinner. *What?* That had never happened before.

He hatched an idea. A big idea. A bigger than big idea.

First, he ran into the bathroom and grabbed the folded newspaper from the pile next to the big water bowl. Then, he searched the kitchen. *Come on, George. Where'd you hide them this time?* He looked everywhere. Twice.

Another brilliant idea popped out of that big brain of his. He stepped on the foot pedal at the bottom of the trash can. The top opened, and he stuck his head inside. He'd seen George do it a hundred times, except for the head part. He'd even tried it himself a few times when George wasn't around.

Score! He pulled an empty box of Jujubes from the can and dropped it on the floor on top of the paper, then scooped them both up into his mouth.

"What's that?" George said when Gracie deposited them on the floor in front of his chair.

Sam leaned over to get a better look. "Maybe he want you eat candy."

"No... The box is empty." George shook his head. "I'm pretty sure it has something to do with that damn writing contest."

"At bookstore? I hear about that. Big bucks. You write books. You should enter contest."

George threw up his hands. "Don't you start, too."

Gracie noticed that George's gaze never left the box and newspaper. *Come on, George. I can see your wheels turning. This is my best shot; number one on the hint parade. You can do this. Writing contest, Jujubes, your new friend Sam. Put 'em all together.*

"I'm sorry, Sam. It's just that this is the third time that someone has told me I should enter this contest."

Fourth, if you count dogs.

"Let me ask you something," George said, breaking an awkward silence. "Would you be okay with me writing some of this down?"

Sam's eyes widened. "You write book about us?"

"More like a short story."

Attaboy, George.

"For contest? I'm honored."

"I'm not saying that's what I'm going to do, but if I did, I wanted to make sure you were on board."

Of course he's on board. Why wouldn't he be on board?

"I haven't written anything in a long time, but you have to admit, it's an interesting story."

Interesting? You might be looking at a Pulitzer.

"I agree. Very interesting."

"Okay, Sam. I'll let you know what I decide. If I do this..."

He means WHEN he does this.

"I might need help filling in some of the details."

"No worries. I glad to help."

The two shook hands, and Sam left. Ordinarily, Gracie would have taken time out to revel in his accomplishment, but it was WAY past dinnertime and his stomach had other ideas.

George heated the Vietnamese takeout, and they dined like two tourists on their first night in Saigon.

After dinner, Gracie went for a walk. *Stayin' Alive* played as he strutted through the hall on his way up to Jasmine's. She opened the door, and he ran inside.

I did it! I did it!

Luna turned. *Let me guess. You found Waldo?*

Gracie glanced at her, immune to her sarcasm, then looked at Jasmine. *Guess what dog persuaded George to enter the contest?*

Jasmine smiled while Luna rolled her arrogant little eyes.

Me... I'm that dog.

"How did you manage to convince him so quickly?"

Just the best idea ever. He explained how everything went down.

With the contest deadline three weeks away, Gracie needed to help George stay on track. He returned to the apartment to find George unpacking a clunky metal object and setting it up on his desk. He watched him roll a piece of paper into the thing and begin poking at it. Each poke produced a clicking sound. Then a bell rang, and Gracie jumped. George continued poking. More clicking and another bell. Gracie covered his ears. *Stop it, George.*

But George kept on clicking. Gracie barked, and he stopped. "What's the matter, girl?"

Gracie put his paws over his ears again.

"You don't like the sound of the typewriter?"

About as much as I like eating poop. Wait... the typewriter thing is worse.

"My laptop is on the fritz, and I want to jot down some ideas before I forget them. I know this old typewriter isn't as efficient, but it's all I've got."

That's how you're going to write your story? Yikes! What have I done?

This new wrinkle needed to be ironed out, or Gracie would be looking for another place to spend the next three weeks. He hated to admit it, but he needed Luna right about now. Cats were experts at pushing things off tables and counters with little or no remorse. Gracie could never intentionally destroy any of George's stuff, no matter how annoying it might be.

Chapter Twenty-Nine

The next day, Jasmine intervened. After Gracie briefed her on the unexpected typewriter development, she had a little *come-to-Jesus* talk with George. She explained that the contest only accepted electronic submissions, so the typewriter had to go. He described his laptop problems, and she offered to drive it to the repair shop for him.

George accepted her offer and asked if she would take Gracie while he attended to an appointment he'd made.

On the way out of the building, they crossed paths with a stranger coming in. He nodded politely as he held the door for them, then stepped inside. The man appeared to be in his mid-forties, wearing a baseball cap and denim jacket. Thick stubble covered the bottom half of his face, and he wore a patch of hair between his nose and lip.

Jasmine shuddered as they walked toward her car. "Have you ever seen that man before?"

I don't think so. Why?

"I got a bad vibe, the moment I saw him."

Gracie wasn't sure what that word meant, but it didn't sound good. He'd also picked up on something—a darkness in the man's soul that he didn't understand. Perhaps that was the vibe she spoke of.

"He's like a big ball of negative energy. I hope he's not George's appointment."

Should we warn him?

"I think we better try."

They went back inside and knocked on George's door. The man with the stubble sat at George's kitchen table.

"That was fast." He glanced at the laptop under her arm. "Was there a problem?"

"Can I talk to you in private?"

George glanced at Stubble, then back to Jasmine. "Now's not a good time."

"It's important."

Gracie slipped inside. Jasmine was right. Something didn't smell right. A darkness swirled around this stranger, the kind that threatened to pull you in if you got too close. Gracie barked.

"Gracie!" George pointed to the door. "Outside."

I wouldn't stay if you paid me. He ran out the door, and George followed him into the hall.

"Who's that inside?" Jasmine asked.

George looked at her through squinted eyes. "Not that it's any of your business, but he's here about the vacant apartment."

"Don't do it."

"What?"

"I got a bad vibe when I saw him. He's trouble."

"So when he sues me for discrimination, I can use the *bad vibe* defense?"

"Trust me, George, there's something evil about that man."

"Look, Jasmine, I don't mind you telling me from time to time what Dottie may or may not have said, but this is a little more serious." He waved his hand. "Now, please go drop off the laptop like you offered and let me take care of business in MY building."

Gracie barked again. George glared at him, and he lowered his head.

Jasmine chewed her bottom lip as George closed the door.

We tried. I just hope Stubble didn't hear any of that, or you just painted a target on your back.

"Let's go."

Gracie experienced sensory overload when they walked into the big-box electronics store. He bounced along, head and tail swinging in every direction as he followed Jasmine to the back of the store where they fix stuff. The kid behind the counter called a friend over when he saw George's laptop. They examined it like a fossil that had just been unearthed at an archaeological dig.

"What do you want us to do with it?"

"The owner says it's slow and freezes up. Can you fix it?"

They inspected it again. "We'll give it a try. You can pick it up on Wednesday."

They returned home and found George sweeping the sidewalk. "Can they fix it?" he asked.

"It'll be ready on Wednesday." She hesitated. "How did your appointment go?"

"His name is Bradley, and he'll be moving into 2E tomorrow."

"I hoped you wouldn't say that."

"Now look here, Jasmine—"

She held up her hands. "I get it. Your building, your rules. Don't say I didn't warn you."

George folded his arms and leaned on the end of his broom. He looked at Gracie like the dog might have something to add.

What SHE said.

. . . .

Gracie lay sunning himself on the patio when Ruby pulled up a chair. Since their conversations only went one way, she wasn't a threat to him. Whatever he said to her was strictly confidential, while anything she said—not so much.

Hello, Ruby. What's the scuttlebutt today?

She closed her eyes and leaned her head back, undoubtedly enjoying the warmth of the sun on her face.

Granted, he was just a dog, but this silence couldn't last long. It was Ruby, after all. He waited a few moments. *Three...two...one...*

"So, did you hear a new tenant moved in today?" Ruby said. "I ran into him in the hall. He seemed nice enough. He didn't have much stuff, which I thought was odd. How does a man in his forties not have a truckload of personal belongings?"

I hear most serial killers travel light.

"Anyway, you didn't hear it from me, but Tom and Marilyn had another sleepover last night. Things are moving fast with those two. He jumped on her like a duck on a June bug."

She opened her eyes and looked down at Gracie. "Look at me. I'm talking to a dog." She chuckled. "Sometimes, I can be dumber than a watermelon."

He wagged his tail.

"If I were you, I'd be careful around that Chinaman in 3C. I heard they serve dog at that restaurant."

Sam is Vietnamese, and I've eaten food from his restaurant. It was delicious. You should try it. He turned to leave, then stopped. *There was no dog. I would know a dog if I ate one.*

He wandered up to Jasmine's.

"Anything new?" she asked.

Well, let's see, Tom and Marilyn are getting pretty cozy. He stopped. *What am I doing? I'm sorry. I ran into Ruby earlier.*

"That's okay. I already picked up on that vibe."

She was like a vibe magnet, if there was such a thing. He wondered if HE had a vibe.

What are we going to do about Stubble?

"His name is Bradley Wolfe."

Whatever.

Luna climbed down from her perch and slunk over to where they stood. *He might be a serial killer. The kind that only kills dogs.* She grinned like the Cheshire Cat.

Yikes!

"Luna!" Jasmine turned to Gracie. "Relax, there's no such thing."

He probably deserved that for his snarky remark to Ruby. But in his defense, Ruby didn't understand dog.

"Let's Google him."

Is that legal?

"Yes, it's quite legal. It just means we're going to look up his information online."

Jasmine sat at her desk and turned on her computer. Gracie jumped up on her lap and his eyes widened at the mysterious lights and moving images. A new game. He assumed he was supposed to catch them. But when he tried, Jasmine pulled him back.

"You can stay up here and help, but you need to keep your paws off the keyboard."

He wanted to help, so he sat quietly. *I'm helping*, he said when he caught Luna's stare. Her eyes were green with envy, and he grinned like the Cheshire Dog, if there even was such a thing.

Luna returned to her Bird TV, turning in his direction occasionally to give him the stink eye.

"When we passed that man on the way out of the building, I sensed he isn't from around here," Jasmine said, "But I don't know where to look."

He wore a Seattle Mariners baseball cap, if that helps.

"Really? How do you know that?"

I saw it on his head.

"No, I mean, how did you know it was Seattle?"

Sometimes, George and I watch baseball together. Two nights ago, his giants played the Seattle Mariners.

Jasmine stroked his head with a gentle hand. "You make a pretty good sleuth."

Gracie didn't know what that meant, but he knew the word good, as in good dog. He wagged his tail.

Luna left the room.

All they had was a name, but even that was suspect. The initial search turned up nothing useful. The only two hits were a sixty-two-year-old English professor at Columbia University in New York and a mailman in Florida who died in 1997.

Bradley was a ghost, which made his being there even more threatening.

I'll need to watch him like a hawk until we can figure out what he's doing here.

"I can help you, but we need to keep your sidekick, Savannah, out of this as much as possible. All I need is a few minutes with him to see what other information I can gather. He lives next door, so I hear him coming and going. I'll make it a point to run into him in the hall and chat him up. That's something you can't do."

Okay, I guess you got me there.

· · · · ● · ● · · · ·

After dinner, Gracie settled in for a snooze. His eyes opened an hour later to an empty apartment. He checked the usual places and found George sitting in a chair on the back patio.

"Hey, Gracie. Come on over."

Gracie sat next to his chair, and George stroked his back. An attempt at distraction perhaps? Gracie kept his eyes fixed on the burning stick in George's mouth.

"I got a little overwhelmed, so I came out here to clear my head." He removed the stick and held it in his hand.

Gracie scuttled backwards to put more distance between them, his gaze never leaving the fiery tip.

"What's the matter?" He glanced at the smoking stick in his hand. "You don't like my cigar?"

Cigar, huh? I like it in your mouth. In fact, it smells pretty good. Better than burnt dog hair.

"Maybe you don't like the fire. It's perfectly safe." He stuck it back in his mouth and waved Gracie over. "Come on back here."

Gracie returned to his spot, and George resumed his petting.

"I can't believe I'm about to say this to a dog, but your idea for my story was a good one. But it's made me think about everything that's happened over the years, and that's brought back some painful memories."

Don't give up, George. You've got to push through it.

"I still miss her, you know."

Of course you do. And that's okay. You'll always miss her. I miss her, and I didn't even know her.

"I wasn't always the best husband or father. That damn war really messed me up. I know that's no excuse." He took a long puff of his cigar. "If I could do it all over again, things would be different."

That's something we don't get to do. Our situations are different, you and me, but I know what it feels like to lose someone who was my whole world. Dogs have feelings, too.

George stopped petting Gracie and stared off into the distance.

I'm sorry, George. Perhaps that story wasn't such a good idea. But maybe it will force you to loosen your grip on the past and move on with your life. I know you're no spring chicken, but we can still have some good years together.

The two sat in silence, watching the sun set over the treetops.

I can be your best friend, you know, like that saying, and your confidant, your wingman, maybe even your muse, whatever that is. But you have to take responsibility for your own life. Nobody can do that for you.

Gracie didn't know where all this was coming from. *I know you can't understand any of this, but maybe I needed to hear it as much as you.*

George took another puff of his cigar and shook his head. "I had some emotional issues after the war, but Dottie knew what she was getting herself into. Angela didn't have a choice. Things got worse, and I drank too much. I wasn't there for her when she needed me. Dottie did a pretty good job of holding things together while she was alive."

Gracie felt George's profound sadness and nuzzled his leg. George dropped his free hand and stroked the back of the dog's head.

"Angela wouldn't even speak to me at the funeral. Maybe I deserve it."

I'm not judging. Dogs don't judge. Dottie may be gone, but your daughter is still alive. Don't give up on her. You're not that guy anymore. It's never too late to be what you might have been.

They sat in silence for a few minutes, a man and his dog.

"I don't know how to fix it." George stood, dropped his cigar butt, and crushed it out with his foot. "Thanks for sitting here and keeping me company."

I'm here for you, man.

"Too bad you can't talk, huh?"

Yeah, too bad.

Chapter Thirty

George received a call on Wednesday that his laptop was fixed and ready to be picked up. Jasmine offered to drive him there, a welcome distraction from Operation Stubble. Gracie agreed to tag along, but only because Savannah was safe at school.

"I'm worried about the new tenant," Jasmine said.

"Well, don't be."

"I Googled him."

"You what?" George exhaled sharply. "And what exactly did you find?"

"I found nothing. The man doesn't exist."

"I'm sure there's a perfectly good explanation."

"You're right. Perhaps he stole the identity of a dead mailman in Florida named Bradley Wolfe."

George wagged an index finger at her. "I'm warning you. I don't want you stirring up trouble in the building or making any calls to the police. You have no proof that Bradley is any different from the other tenants who just need a safe place to live."

Gracie tilted his head. *The police?* According to Mama, the cops weren't to be trusted. He admitted his own personal bias, but wondered why Jasmine hadn't thought of it earlier.

"I don't believe it's a safe place anymore."

"I mean it, Jasmine. This subject is closed."

"Fine! Let's talk about why you won't get your head exam-ined." A smirk crossed her lips. "I mean, your eyes."

"Both are fine, thank you."

"You might see better with the reading glasses I bought you, but you still can't drive. You have a problem, George, and it's not going to get any better."

"So, you're a doctor now?"

I told you he's stubborn.

Gracie waited in the car while they went into the store. They rode home in silence until Jasmine turned off the car.

"Thank you," George said before he opened the door. "I'm going to go work on my story."

When Jasmine opened the back door, Gracie leapt from the seat and ran toward Savannah's corner. His legs had grown more powerful, and they carried him like Secretariat on the last leg of the Triple Crown.

Savannah was nowhere in sight when he reached the corner. He sat and waited, staring down the road. His runaway beating heart eventually synced with the rest of his body, and he settled in for however long it would take. Dogs can sit for hours with-out any effort because they live in the here and now. Humans are more interested in the future.

Soon, his eyelids became heavy, but the noise from his stomach kept him awake. Sometime later, he heard the big yellow box. He sat up, tail wagging, but the box didn't stop. He watched it roll down the street right past where he sat. There must be two of them, he reasoned. He would wait for the other one.

Finally, the other box pulled up and stopped in front of him. Savannah called from inside, which sent his tail spinning out of control.

She jumped down to the ground and ran to him. "Gracie, Gracie, Gracie!"

After all the hugs, he escorted her safely to her door. She offered a snack and a play date, which he reluctantly declined. As self-appointed neighborhood watchdog, he needed to check in on Rita and the others.

Rita and Gracie had settled into a nice little groove. He would sit with her and listen to her stories while he dined on her famous peanut butter cookies or some other tasty snack. She seemed to enjoy their time together as much as he did. With Stubble living in the building now, he made it a point to check on her every day.

They had both dozed off until nearly dinner time, so Gracie said goodbye and headed back home. He slowed as he passed apartment 2E. No sounds came from behind the closed door, but he hugged the opposite side of the hall as he passed.

He pushed his way through the doggy door and found his apartment empty. He barked, but no reply. The newly repaired laptop sat open on the kitchen table, like George had left in a hurry. It wasn't like George to forget dinner, so he sniffed around to make sure Stubble hadn't been there and taken him hostage, or worse.

Convinced there had been no foul play, he set off to check the usual spots. George wasn't out front, or on the patio, or in the garden. He even checked the basement, but no George. Gracie's stomach had been fine-tuned to the dining schedule that he and George had established, and it reacted adversely to any deviation. So, he abandoned his search for George in favor of a search for food.

He started with the low-hanging fruit, or in this case, vegetables. George had warned that the produce stand in the lobby was for tenants only, but desperate times required desperate measures. He stood on his hind legs and knocked a cucumber off the edge of the stand. He curled up around it on the floor and bit off one end.

As he chewed on the last piece and considered a second course, the elevator door opened. Stubble stepped out and walked toward the front door. Gracie tried to play it cool, but he remembered what Luna had said about dog serial killers and panicked. Jasmine had denied their existence, but Gracie wasn't about to take any unnecessary chances. He skedaddled in the opposite direction, missing a perfect opportunity to follow the suspect and gather some intel.

Realizing his mistake, Gracie skidded to a stop at the end of the hall and turned around, but Stubble had gone. He raced out the back door and ran to the parking lot. Stubble slipped into one of the cars and drove off.

Back inside the apartment, George sat at the table, staring at his computer screen. He hadn't noticed Gracie come in.

You gave me quite a scare. Where have you been?

George poked the keyboard a few times.

This would be a lot easier if you were fluent in dog. He barked, and George looked up.

"Gracie. I didn't see you come in." He paused. "Where have you been?"

I asked you first.

"I'm sorry. I guess I got carried away here and lost track of time." He patted his thigh and Gracie approached. "I started writing a story for that contest. Been at it most of the afternoon, except for the half hour I spent with Sam ironing out a few details. He's off on today."

Mystery solved.

He scratched behind Gracie's ears. "I can't believe I'm writing again, and I have you to thank. It feels good."

Gracie closed his eyes. *It sure does. Don't stop scratching. A little more to the right.* He turned his head. *Yeah, that's it.*

George continued scratching. "What do you say we get some dinner?"

Dinner? What's that? he said from his trancelike state.

George stopped scratching and stood.

Gracie opened his eyes and shook his head to clear it. *So, what's for dinner?*

Apparently, it was a kibble night. He watched George fill his bowl and refresh his water. George opened a bag of potato chips and a can of beer. He set them on the table and returned to his seat in front of the computer.

Is this how it's going to be? You'd better hurry up and finish that story.

Chapter Thirty-One

Gracie, Savannah, and Chloe played in the grass after school the following day. Chloe introduced him to a new game called Frisbee—another variation of fetch, but with a colorful plastic disk that floated on the air. If you timed your jump just right, you could snatch it out of the air before it landed.

They played until the girls' arms were too tired to throw. Time for a snack and something called a juice box. He bit into it and showered himself with a deliciously sweet liquid. After he cleaned himself with his tongue, Gracie set out for the parking lot with the girls in tow.

"Where are we going?"

I need to check something. He walked down the row of cars until he found the one he'd seen Stubble drive away in the day before. He followed his nose around the vehicle and found Stubble's scent all over it.

"What's he doing?" Chloe asked her sister.

This is Stubble's car.

Savannah turned to Chloe. "It's the bad man's car."

Gracie stopped at the license plate. He sniffed again, then walked over to another car and sniffed its plate. After he sniffed Stubble's plate again, he tilted his head and stared.

"What is it?"

The other plates smell like metal and paint. This one has another scent that I'm not sure about.

Chloe bent down for a closer look. She scratched it with her fingernail and a strip of plastic peeled off in her hand. "There's tape on it that's covering up part of the E to make it look like an F." She scratched some more. "And the P is really an R."

Why would he do that?

"Maybe he stole the car or the plate, but either way, it's illegal."

You'd better put the tape back the way you found it.

"You were right, Gracie," Savannah whispered. "He's a criminal."

Chloe's eyes widened. "We need to call the police."

No. George told Jasmine no police. He sounded pretty mad when he said it. We don't want to get her in trouble. Let's talk to her first. She'll know what to do.

Savannah relayed the message to Chloe, who replaced the tape before the three ran back to the relative safety of the yard.

"Let's go see if Jasmine is home."

Unfortunately, she was not. Gracie sat outside Jasmine's door and waited after the girls were called home for dinner. Stubble lived down the hall, so he kept a close eye on his door, as well.

We need to talk, Gracie said when Jasmine stepped off the elevator.

"Shouldn't you be home having dinner?"

Ever since George started writing that story, he's forgotten about everything else.

"At least he's writing. It'll be over soon."

Not soon enough. What are you having for dinner?

She unlocked the door, and they walked into a quiet apartment. Luna sat on her perch, staring out the window.

Where's the welcoming committee? A dog would have jumped up and down, thrilled that their master had returned.

"Luna, I'm home."

That's nice.

Gracie looked up at Jasmine. *You really need to get a dog. Just sayin'...*

She nodded like maybe she might consider it.

Wait. I forgot why I came here. Oh, yeah. He told her about Stubble's car and what he and the girls had found. *Chloe suggested we call the police, but after what George said, I advised against it.*

"You let me worry about George. But you shouldn't be taking risks like that, especially with the girls around."

I didn't involve them on purpose, but we were playing together and—

"And you just had to go snoop around his car."

Well... uh... something like that. Gracie hung his head. *In my defense, I didn't tell them to follow me.*

"I don't suppose you told them not to." She raised an eyebrow. "How did you know which car was his?"

He stood a little taller. *I saw him driving it yesterday.*

"That's good work, but you need to be more careful."

Roger that.

"I did a little detective work of my own yesterday. I heard Bradley leaving his apartment, so I stepped into the hall and 'accidentally' ran into him. We exchanged a few words while I read his energy. Feeling all that negativity was a dreadful experience. I also felt the presence of his mother, who'd passed away several years ago. She's very disappointed in her son's behavior. She tried to tell me his name, but I only got the first letter—A."

That eliminates Bradley.

"He's not working alone. There's someone else, but I don't know where."

You got all that from running into him in the hall?

She nodded. "Let's do a little more digging."

Jasmine sat at her desk with Gracie on her lap. He made it a point to keep his paws off her keyboard this time. They checked for wants and warrants in Washington State. There were over a hundred. She clicked on the first one and the screen filled with information, accompanied by a picture of the perp.

"Look, Gracie, each one has a picture. We may or may not know his real name, but we know what he looks like. All we need to do is check each picture until we find a match."

This might take a while. Got anything to eat?

"Let's check a few more before we take a break."

Jasmine pecked away at the keyboard, causing pictures of angry men and women to appear on her screen. Stubble's was not among them. A half hour later, they broke for a quick dinner. George probably wouldn't even miss him.

After dinner, they returned to the computer screen.

"He's going to be here. I just know it."

Jasmine had been right about a lot of things, so Gracie made himself comfortable and settled in for the long haul. That is, until nature called. They resumed Operation Stubble when he returned.

They were more than halfway through the list when a man resembling Stubble appeared on the screen. They stopped and studied the picture.

He looks the same, but different.

"It's him. I can feel it."

Gracie tilted his head.

"He doesn't have a beard now, and his hair is lighter."

Gracie couldn't control himself once he pictured it. He let out a bark. *That's him! What's it say?*

Luna turned and gave him another stink eye.

"His real name is Andrew Dean. That fits with what his mother told me."

You can't trust a man with two first names.

"It says here that he's robbed three banks in Washington and two more in Oregon."

Stubble is a bank robber? California must be next on his to-do list.

"It also says he's armed and dangerous."

Chapter Thirty-Two

Gracie spent a few hours with Rita until Savannah came home from school. He met her at the corner and escorted her home. When he told her they'd found out the man's real name, he left out the armed and dangerous part.

They tiptoed up the stairs to avoid getting cornered in the elevator. Gracie heard voices when they reached the second-floor landing and stopped to listen.

"What?"

Wait here. He peeked into the hallway. The door to 2E hung open a crack. Ruby had told him the man brought very little stuff with him. Of course, Gracie needed to have a look for himself."

"Where are you going?"

Stay there. I'll be right back.

Gracie crept up to the door and pushed it open a little more with his nose. He sniffed the air, and the hairs along his back prickled.

Stubble stood with his back to the door, looking out the window and talking into a little black board like Chloe's. A chair, a TV, and a large duffel bag were the only other things in the room. The duffel was no doubt full of other people's money.

"I'm in a small town in northern California called, get this, Heaven. I rented an apartment that we can use as a base of operations. It's really laid back here, and I should be able to blend in pretty easily. Besides, no one would ever think to look for me in Heaven." He laughed like a braying mule.

Gracie pushed his nose in a little farther, and the door creaked.

Stubble turned around, and his expression fell. "Hey, dog. What are you doing out there?"

Yikes! Gracie hightailed it back to Savannah in the stairway. *Run!*

A door slammed behind them as they made their way up the stairs. They slipped into her apartment and locked her door. With his heart racing, Gracie wondered how long he would have to play security guard. Why hadn't George listened to Jasmine? She warned him. Now they would have to live in fear for who knows how long.

We need to do something, he said when his heart slowed to a reasonable rate.

They crept back down the stairs and knocked on Jasmine's door. Gracie pushed his way in as soon as she opened it.

"What's going on?"

Close the door.

"The bad man yelled at Gracie," Savannah said.

Jasmine folded her arms across her chest and glared at Gracie. "What did you do this time?"

I might have stuck my head in his apartment.

"What? Just now?"

No, earlier.

"He didn't see you come in here, did he?"

I don't think so. I overheard him talking on the phone. You were right, there's two of them. They're going to use his apartment as a base of operations. I'm not sure what it means, but that's what he said.

"Sounds like they plan to rob some banks in California."

We need to tell George.

"Not yet. I have a better idea."

We can't call the police.

"We can talk to Mike. Technically, that wouldn't be calling the police."

· · · · · ● · ● · · · ·

Gracie, Jasmine, and Savannah paused for a moment outside Mike McGuire's door.

"I'll do the talking." Jasmine rapped her knuckles against the door.

Stubble must have heard the knock and opened his door. He probably didn't realize that he'd moved his illegal operations across the hall from a retired cop, but Gracie couldn't take that chance. Before Stubble's door opened enough for him to see them, Gracie charged. He barked out a warning, and Stubble's door stopped moving. Gracie crept closer to keep the door from opening any farther. He bared his teeth and let out a threatening growl.

"Not you again. Get out of here, you damn dog." Stubble slammed his door.

Mike witnessed everything from his doorway and quickly ushered them inside.

"I hope we're not bothering you," Jasmine said.

"Not at all. I was just working on a crossword puzzle." He tapped his temple with an index finger. "They keep this old detective's mind sharp."

"That's why we're here."

He looked at them through squinted eyes. "Crossword puzzles?"

"No," Savannah said. "The detective part."

Mike checked the hall again before he closed the door. "What happened out there?"

"I think Gracie just saved us."

"I'm sorry. I don't understand."

Jasmine continued. "The man you just heard yelling, moved in across the hall on Monday. I got a bad vibe the first time I saw him, so I Googled him and found that he's a bank robber. His real name is Andrew Dean."

"Do you get vibes from everyone you meet?"

Jasmine appeared to resent his tone. "I do. It's a gift."

"What kind of vibe are you getting from me?"

She blew out a breath. "At the moment, you're skeptical and somewhat condescending. Otherwise, you're a decent guy who gave everything he had to the job at the expense of his health and his family. You're retired, divorced, bored with life, and your cholesterol is too high. Shall I continue?"

He held up his hands. "No, that's enough." He looked from Gracie to Savannah, then back to Jasmine. "So, we're talking about the guy in 2E?"

"Yes. He's wanted for bank robbery in Washington and Oregon."

"And you're sure it's the same guy?"

"They posted his picture online, and Gracie overheard him tell someone on the phone that he plans to use this apartment as a base of operations."

"Wait." He pointed at the dog. "That Gracie? He told you he overheard a phone conversation?"

"It's a long story."

"How did you know about my cholesterol?"

"Do you have a gun?" Savannah asked.

Mike hesitated.

Jasmine rested her hands on Savannah's shoulders. "We hoped you might help us, Mr. McGuire. If not, we'll have to drive down to the police station and talk to someone who can."

He held up his hands again. "I didn't say I wouldn't help. This building is my home, too." He picked up a pad and pen from the table. "You said his name was Andrew Dean?"

"Yes, but that's not the name he used to rent the apartment. He also has a stolen car or license plate, or both. Some of the letters are taped over to make them look like different letters."

Mike stopped writing and looked up. "How do you know that?"

Jasmine gestured with her head toward Gracie, who gave a big tail wag.

"Right." Mike shook his head. "Why don't I just make a couple of calls and get back to you."

Is that a yes? Because it sounds like a no.

"Thank you."

Tell him to hurry.

"Gracie says hurry," Savannah said.

Mike looked up from his pad with a blank expression. A smile broke out on his face, and he nodded. "Now you're just messing with me."

An awkward silence descended upon them.

"Uh... I better go make those calls." He closed the pad and tapped it a couple of times with his pen. "Thanks for the information. I'll let you know as soon as I hear something."

Chapter Thirty-Three

G racie paced in tight circles in George's kitchen.

"Gracie, please! You're going to wear a hole in the floor and end up in the basement."

What's taking Mike so long?

"What's gotten into you today?"

I hate waiting, especially when there are lives at stake. How long does it take to make a couple of calls?

"I'm trying to write, so if you don't mind, please take your spin class outside."

Gracie stopped. *Fine, George. But if I get gunned down by a trigger-happy bank robber, who shall remain nameless, then it's on you.*

"If you give me a couple hours of peace and quiet, I'll put bacon on the cheeseburgers tonight."

Now, there's something worth getting shot at for. Gracie wandered outside. He reached the front sidewalk just as Savannah's box pulled up to the corner. *Yikes! I almost forgot Savannah.*

He ran like the wind to the corner.

"Gracie, Gracie, Gracie."

He misjudged his stopping distance and barreled into her, knocking her to the ground. He landed on top of her and licked her face until she pushed him away, laughing.

"Settle down, Gracie, or you're going to make me pee my pants."

I can't help it. I've literally been going around in circles all day. What's taking Mike so long?

"Let's go have a snack and play while we wait."

Okay. Let's try a new game called running around in circles.

"You're funny."

After a quick change and a snack, Gracie and the girls headed outside. They met Mike in the stairwell, where he told them the FBI was on its way to apprehend Andrew Dean. He suggested they stay in their apartment or leave the premises.

"We're going to the store," Chloe said. "So, we won't be in your way."

We are?

"Okay, you can leave through the back. I'll walk you out."

"Why are we going to the store?" Savannah asked after they were outside.

Yeah. I'm confused.

"If I said we were going to play in the yard, he would have made us go back to the apartment."

But...

Chloe threw a stick and Gracie took off after it.

He brought it back, then noticed Stubble exiting the back door with his duffel bag. What if he'd found out the cops were coming, and he was getting away? Gracie needed to stop him.

Stubble glanced at Gracie playing in the yard. He couldn't have imagined Gracie might be the one to crack the case and lead to his undoing. Just another dumb dog, that's what humans think.

Have Chloe throw the stick at him in the parking lot.

Savannah scrunched up her face. "Why?"

Just have her do it. NOW.

Savannah relayed the message, and as expected, Chloe questioned her request.

Throw it right at him. Gracie barked and took off running for the parking lot. Chloe followed his lead and threw the stick.

"Hey, Mister," Chloe shouted.

Stubble turned. He reached his hand out to block the stick, and Gracie barreled into him, tripping him up and knocking him to the ground. Gracie bared his teeth and growled. Stubble kicked at him, but Gracie ducked out of the way, which gave Stubble a chance to gain his feet.

Now, you're just being rude.

Gracie lunged at his leg, and Stubble swung the duffel. The blow caught Gracie in the side and knocked him to the pavement.

Tires squealed as a black SUV entered the lot from the street. Stubble dropped his bag, jumped over Gracie, and took off toward the woods.

Gracie had been stunned by the hit but recovered quickly. Stubble was heading toward the girls in the back yard.

Run, girls! Get out of his way.

They stood frozen with fear. The situation was spinning out of control. Gracie needed to do something.

He ran like a dog possessed until he positioned himself between Stubble and the girls. He barked as loud as he could so there was no mistake that he meant business. Stubble turned and ran into the woods.

Gracie took off after him with the feds in hot pursuit. A familiar roar nearly stopped him in his tracks. The giant metal snake approached. He slowed his pace momentarily, losing ground as he weighed his options. He'd been up close and personal with that snake once before—not something he ever wanted to do again.

Stubble turned around, and Gracie ducked behind a tree. His heart beat in his throat as he silently thanked Jim Rockford for the advice. Seconds later, Stubble continued his getaway. Without hesitation, Gracie resumed pursuit.

Gracie reasoned that if Stubble escaped, he would move into another apartment and endanger more people, maybe even kill someone. His heart had skipped a beat when he thought Stubble might take the girls hostage during his escape from the yard. Gracie couldn't let that happen to someone else.

Stubble stopped when he reached the steel rails, giving Gracie time to catch up. Gracie launched himself like a rocket and slammed into Stubble from behind, knocking him to the ground. He went down hard on his knee. The roar of the rumbling snake nearly drowned out his cry of pain.

After a quick recovery, they wrestled on the tracks as Stubble tried to fend off the attack. Gracie's opponent was agile and smart enough to avoid his snapping teeth. Suddenly, Stubble scrambled off the other side of the tracks to safety and held Gracie down against the rail.

The snake closed the distance between them and let out a hideous roar. Gracie struggled, but Stubble didn't budge.

He realized that Stubble planned to jump out of the way at the last second, leaving him to die a horrible death. He closed his eyes. The snake roared again. *Mama! Help me. I don't want to die.*

The ground shook like an earthquake and the wall of hot air being pushed along by the ferocious snake made it difficult to breathe. It roared a third time and Gracie braced for impact. The rumbling, roaring snake blocked all sound except Mama's voice. *Dogs are tenacious.*

Gracie summoned every ounce of strength and wrenched his head around enough to sink his teeth into Stubble's hand. He cried out in pain, pulled back, and they both tumbled down the embankment just before the snake would have gobbled Gracie up.

As the snake rumbled by, Stubble shook free and limped away. Gracie caught up with him and grabbed his pant leg to slow him down.

Stubble pulled a gun from his belt and aimed it at Gracie. "I should have done this a long time ago."

The tail end of the snake passed, and the feds ran across the tracks with guns drawn. "Drop it!"

Stubble hesitated. He shook his head at Gracie, then dropped his weapon. Gracie let go with an enormous sigh as the two men forced Stubble to the ground and cuffed him.

Thank you, Mama.

Chapter Thirty-Four

A news crew descended on The Station the following morning, interviewing those who had taken part in the fugitive's capture. They interviewed George for backstory about the building and its inhabitants. Unable to provide his own blow-by-blow account of the incident, Gracie made himself available for scratching and petting.

That evening, George set up a TV in the lounge and invited the entire building down to watch the six o'clock news. He ordered pizza and wings for everyone. Rita baked a giant cake, and the event turned into something of a party to honor the unsung heroes who'd saved the building from peril.

According to Mike, a twenty-five-thousand-dollar reward had been offered for information that led to the capture of Andrew Dean, a.k.a. Bradley Wolfe, a.k.a. Stubble.

Jasmine received the check a week later. She lived comfortably off the money she made from personal readings and appearances at psychic fairs, so she used the reward money to set up a ten-thousand-dollar college fund for each of the girls.

Such a fund would be of no use to Gracie, so she installed a doggy door in her apartment, allowing Gracie to come and go as he pleased. Luna wouldn't speak to her for days.

In the meantime, the writing contest deadline loomed less than a week away. George had been busy poking at his laptop, and

Gracie waited impatiently to hear the finished product. At one point, he overheard George mumbling about throwing it away and starting over.

Yikes! It's too late to start over. Read me what you've got, so I can remind you what a talented writer you are. If only George understood him. He prayed his as yet unconfirmed admiration had not been misplaced.

The printer whirred and clattered before a piece of paper floated to the floor. George picked it up and studied it for a moment before spitting out an expletive that probably shouldn't be repeated here. He crumpled it and tossed it at the wastebasket. It landed on the floor next to a dozen others. Gracie sniffed around the overflowing can, wishing he could read the sea of tiny words printed on all that paper.

Gracie accidentally knocked the can over, spilling its contents on the floor. *Oops!* He lowered his head.

George picked Gracie up and deposited him in his lap. "I'll take care of it. I needed a break, anyway. This isn't going so well. I mean, I finished writing the first draft, but it's no good. Maybe I need to read it once out loud before I give up. How about after dinner, I read it to you? I need an audience, particularly one that won't boo me when it's over."

I can do that, George.

George cleaned up the mess Gracie had made, and they walked it out to the dumpster. He avoided Sam in the hall on the way back, which made Gracie think he might be serious about throwing in the towel.

After dinner, George printed a copy of his story, and Gracie found a comfy spot to listen from. When George had finished reading, Gracie's eyes widened and his tail wagged.

That was by far the greatest story I've ever heard. Of course, it was the only story he'd ever heard, but that didn't make it any less great. *If I could talk, I'd tell you that I think you've got a winner there.* He turned his head sideways. *Look at that tail go. It doesn't do that for just anything.*

George shook his head. "It's no good. Flat. If I'm not feeling the emotion, how will the reader?"

What? No emotion? I felt emotion. I laughed, I cried, I wanted to paint the Sistine Chapel. It's brilliant.

"Well, thanks for sitting through that and not heckling me." He held the papers out in front of him with both hands.

No, George. You don't want to do that.

He tore them in half. "You're the only one who will ever hear it."

You can't give up now.

George stood and dropped the papers in the basket. "Let's see what's on TV."

Are you kidding me right now? Who can watch TV? Gracie paced in a circle. He wanted to throw up.

• • • • • • • • • •

Gracie didn't sleep well, worried that George would miss an opportunity that Jasmine said could change his life. When it came time for the daily trip to the market, Gracie settled into his bed. He closed his eyes and waited for George to leave.

"Guess I'm going alone today," George said.

Gracie opened one eye to an empty room. Satisfied he was alone, he jumped out of bed and ran to the wastebasket by the desk. He stuck his nose inside but couldn't reach the papers at the bottom of the can. The girls were in school, so they were unavailable to help. It would be too big an ask of Jasmine to break into her landlord's apartment. He needed to find a way to do it himself.

He tried again, this time stretching too far. The pain caused him to pull back, knocking the can over and creating a good news/bad news situation. The papers were within reach, but he didn't know how he would stand the can up again.

He removed the papers and attempted to right the can. The third time was the charm as he put his nose inside and flipped it into the air. It landed upright, and he pushed it back into place.

With the papers in his mouth, he ran all the way to Jasmine's and deposited them on the floor in front of her. *We have a problem.*

"What's this?"

It's George's story. He read it to me, then ripped it up. He said he quit. He won't submit it.

"Hmm. That is a problem." Jasmine picked up the papers and walked over to the table.

Gracie hopped up on a chair and watched her put the pieces together. *What are we going to do?*

"You're going to go home and act like nothing happened. I'm going to put this back together and read it. Then we'll decide what to do with it." She scanned a couple of pieces, then glanced at Gracie's wagging tail. "It's good, isn't it?"

I'm just a dog, but I think so.

Gracie stopped in the woods to take care of some business on the way home. He did some of his best thinking out there. Without any meaningful way to communicate with George, he would need to defer to Jasmine to talk some sense into him.

Or... Wait. This is brilliant. We could submit it for him.

He quickly covered up the job site and headed home.

Chapter Thirty-Five

G racie played it cool the rest of the day while monitoring the crime scene. The waste basket hadn't moved from the spot where he'd left it. Likewise, George never mentioned the missing papers. His giants were on TV that night, so they watched the game like nothing had happened.

The next morning after breakfast, George went upstairs to clean Stubble's vacant apartment. Gracie seized the opportunity to check in with Jasmine.

Well?

"With a little editing, it might be good enough to win the contest."

I knew it. He paced in a circle.

"Stop it!"

Don't even try to talk sense into George. I have a better idea...

"So do I."

"We should submit it for him," they said in unison.

Wait. What? That was my idea.

"It's not a competition." She smiled. "It was *our* idea."

Okay. I can live with that.

"After I read it yesterday, I got all jazzed up and retyped the whole thing. My friend Sheila said she can give it a quick edit." She paused. "Sam's been living here for months. How did they finally figure this out?"

I might have had something to do with that. I guess I AM kind of resourceful, aren't I?

"I'd better call Sheila and get this thing polished up. The deadline is only a few days away." She wagged a finger at Gracie. "You can't tell anybody about this."

Anybody?

"This stays between you and me."

They say, 'the best way to keep a secret is to tell someone you love.'

"Nobody says that."

· · · · · ● · ● · · · ·

Gracie had to bite his tongue when he met Savannah after school. He desperately wanted to tell someone their plan, and she happened to be the only other human who understood him. It would be a long night. Hopefully, Jasmine would have more information in the morning.

On the way up to Jasmine's the next day, Gracie smelled smoke when he reached the second floor. The door to 2E hung open, so he walked in and found Jasmine moving around the room, waving a cigar. Her motions were slow and deliberate, as if she painted the space with the lazy gray smoke that swirled in her wake.

What are you doing?

"I'm clearing the space."

Oh, good. I thought you'd lost your mind. He paused for a moment, feeling a subtle shift in energy that made the tip of his tail tingle. *Where's George? I thought he'd be in here cleaning.*

"He took a break for lunch."

Is that one of his cigars?

Jasmine stopped. "Not quite. I'm burning sage. It's an ancient spiritual ritual to dispel negative energy."

I'm not sure what that means, but it smells good.

"I want to make sure our resident bank robber didn't leave behind any... bad vibes. Whoever moves in here will appreciate that."

Oh, the vibes thing again. Did George tell you to do it?

She snorted. "God, no. He cleans his way, and I clean mine." She lowered her voice. "Let's just keep this between you and me."

Keep what?

"Exactly."

Did he find a new tenant?

"WE found one."

What do you mean?

"He asked me to look at all the applications and see what kind of *vibe* I got."

Shut the front door!

"No really. Those were his exact words."

And they say you can't teach an old human new tricks.

"Who says that?"

I'm pretty sure dogs say it all the time.

"I see."

So, who is the new tenant? He's not a bank robber, is he?

"His name is Jonathan Russo. He works for the florist in town, and as far as I know, he hasn't robbed any banks."

That's a relief. When is he moving in?

"I don't know." Jasmine sighed. "Poor Jonathan."

Why do you say that? He's got a job.

"He's a lonely young man."

A lot of humans are lonely.

"When he came out, his family shunned him."

Gracie tilted his head. *Where did he come out of?*

"He just came out."

That doesn't help.

She whispered. "Of the closet."

Why was he in the closet?

"I really need to finish up in here."

She wasn't telling him everything. He gave her the sad-dog eyes.

She put her hands on her hips. "I don't know. Maybe he liked to count his shoes."

You don't have to get snippy. He thought about it for a moment. *George wears the same shoes all the time.*

"That's because he's old."

Is there anything to eat in here?

"I'm sorry, there's no food. I need to keep going. I wouldn't want George to catch me practicing my voodoo."

I think he's coming around if he let you use your 'voodoo' to help pick a tenant.

"It's certainly an improvement."

What's going on with George's story?

"The editor is working on it and will have it back to me tomorrow."

I'm not so good with time. Will that allow us to submit it before the deadline?

"Just barely, but I'll get it in. I promise."

· · · • · • · • · · ·

The next week dragged like a turtle through a tar pit. George never noticed the missing papers, and Jasmine submitted his story before the deadline, as promised.

Jonathan moved in over the weekend, and everyone welcomed him with open arms... and paws. The tenants, who had once been like ships passing in the night, felt like a family now. Gracie checked in on Jonathan, and the two hit it off. He picked up the same lonely vibe that Jasmine had mentioned, so he hung around for a while and helped him unpack. For being so sad, all his stuff was very colorful.

Gracie hung out with Jonathan a couple more times that week, along with his daily visits with Rita. He accompanied George to the store, followed him on his rounds, and helped replenish the vegetable stand in the lobby. Since he'd stopped writing, which had consumed much of his time during the previous two weeks, George had more time to spend with man's best friend.

With the daily chores behind them, Gracie reclined in his bed and watched George open his mail at the kitchen table.

"What's this?"

Gracie's ears perked up.

"There must be a mistake. How can I win a contest that I never entered?"

Gracie crept toward the door. He wanted to do a happy dance, but it appeared George needed a little alone time.

"Stop right there."

Gracie paused for a moment before he jumped through the doggy door and hightailed it toward the stairs. *He won! He won!* Halfway up the stairs, he paused. *We're in trouble now.*

George had won the contest. How he won shouldn't matter. Gracie's jump through Jasmine's doggy door was not as, uh, graceful, and he rolled across her floor.

Luna ran into the next room like her tail was on fire.

Jasmine hurried to Gracie's side. "Are you okay?"

He gained his feet and shook it off. *George won the contest!*

"That's great!"

I'm not so sure George sees it that way.

A knock at the door shattered the momentary silence.

Yikes! He held his nose in the air and sniffed. *That's George.*

Jasmine opened the door. "Hello, George. What brings you up to the second floor?"

He walked in. "I think you know."

She shrugged and closed the door behind him.

He handed her a piece of paper. "What do you know about this?"

Rut-ro.

She studied it. "First of all, congratulations. This is wonderful."

"There's just one problem." He pulled the paper from her hands. "I never entered this contest."

"Are you sure? Because I recall you talking about it."

"Cut the crap, Jasmine. How did you and your little accomplice pull this off?"

"You can't blame the dog."

Good answer.

"Really? Then you must have broken into my apartment and stolen it."

"Okay, maybe a little blame."

Not so good.

George's face tightened and he looked mad enough to toss Gracie out again. Gracie was growing tired of their on-again-off-again relationship. While he'd appreciated Jasmine's hospitality the last time, living with a cat was near the top of his things-I-never-want-to-do list.

"Why don't we sit for a minute?"

"I'll stand, thank you." He paused. "If I sit, I won't be able to hug you."

Wait. What? Gracie shook his head to make sure he wasn't stroking out.

Jasmine's eyes bugged out as George leaned in and gave her a big, awkward hug.

"Thank you," he whispered.

Gracie tilted his head and watched George leave. *So, THAT just happened.*

Jasmine closed the door and leaned back against it. She looked at Gracie and let out a long sigh. "I didn't see it going in that direction, did you?"

I told you everything would be alright.

"That's not how I remember it."

What I remember is you throwing me under the box.

"You mean the bus?"

Is that what it's called?

"Yes, but none of that matters now. We pulled it off, and George is happy."

I guess you're right. Got anything to eat?

Chapter Thirty-Six

George became an instant celebrity after an interview with the local paper and an appearance on Good Morning Sacramento. The show's producers asked to meet Sam and interview them together. George agreed, so they scheduled another appearance.

George had never experienced this kind of attention, but he took it in stride. The manager at the market acknowledged his accomplishment with a couple of free cigars. Everyone he knew showered him with praise. Everyone but Angela.

Except for the situation with his daughter, his life seemed to be moving in the right direction. He had a faithful companion in Gracie, he'd forged new relationships with many of his tenants, and his books were selling again. He hadn't seen any of it coming, least of all finding Sam and feeling like something positive had come from the time he spent in that hellhole halfway around the world.

He didn't understand it, or want to admit it, but that stray dog he'd been shamed into bringing home by a five-year-old girl had somehow been responsible for all the recent positive changes in his life.

• • • • • • • • • •

Jasmine drove George to the bookstore to pick up his prize money. Gracie stayed with Luna. He pitied her sheltered life.

So, you've never rolled in the grass?

You mean that green stuff outside? No.

It's wonderful. You don't know what you're missing.

You ever climb a cat castle or scratch a hole in a sofa?

No. He had to admit the sofa thing sounded like fun. *How about we go for a walk outside sometime, and I'll show you around?*

Luna shrugged her little cat shoulders. *I'll think about it.*

Gracie was pretty sure that meant no. Her loss.

The adults returned, and Gracie followed George up to Sam's apartment.

"Hey, Sam." George handed him an envelope. "I want you to have this."

Gracie sniffed around, curious about today's special.

Sam opened it and squinted a little more than usual. "What this for?"

"It's part of the prize money. I want you to have it."

"Why? You write story."

"That's true, but there wouldn't be a story without you."

He shook his head and pushed the envelope away. "Too much money. I can't accept."

Gracie stopped sniffing. *Too much money? I didn't know there was such a thing.*

"Come on, Sam. Everybody can use a little extra cash."

"Since interview, restaurant been very busy. My boss give big raise and bonus. I'm happy. No need to pay me."

"Okay, then..." He took the envelope. "You don't need to pay ME either."

"I no understand."

George shook his head. "Don't bother dropping off a rent check next month. I won't accept it."

Sam hesitated. "You tricky, George. I suppose you win. I not pay rent next month. Thank you."

A broad smile crossed George's face.

Instead of returning to the apartment, George looked at Gracie. "Come on, girl. We're going to the market. They have some beef jerky down there with your name on it."

What? Personalized meat? Why is this the first I'm hearing of it?

On the way home, they stopped to sit on the front steps. George pulled a piece of jerky out of his bag and fed it to Gracie.

"You know... I had my doubts about you."

The feeling was mutual.

George fed him another piece and watched him gobble it up. "I guess you proved me wrong."

Right back at ya.

The two sat for a while—no words, just scratching and petting. Gracie wagged his tail and licked George's hand from time to time to let him know he approved. He didn't know what had gotten into George, but he enjoyed the attention.

Inside the building, George stopped in front of their apartment and stared at a piece of paper taped to the door. He slipped on his glasses and remained silent for, well, Gracie couldn't tell how long, but it felt like a long time.

George removed the paper and looked down at Gracie, his eyes full. "It's from Angela."

Your Angela? She was here?

George wobbled like he would topple over in a stiff breeze.

Let's get you inside and find you a seat.

George fumbled with his keys before finding the right one and letting them in. He set his bag on the table. "I don't believe it. She came to see me."

That's a good thing, right?

"She says she wants to talk."

Talking is good.

George flopped down into his chair in the living room. He turned the paper toward Gracie and tapped it a couple of times with his finger. "Look at that. She left her phone number."

Gracie stared like he could read the digits. *What are you waiting for? Call her.*

"Did you hear that, Dot? Angela was here. She wants to talk to me."

You're leaking again, George. Pull yourself together and make the call.

George sat there for a moment before he wiped his eyes and picked up the phone. When he hung up, he turned to Gracie. "I don't believe it. We're meeting next door for coffee on Saturday."

Did you say next door? Watch out for the angry dude with the apron.

"I'm a little nervous. Want to tag along?"

Gracie walked over to his bed, lay down, and placed his paws over his eyes.

"I guess that means I'm going alone."

You don't need me, George. You got this.

· · · ● · ● · · · ·

Gracie and Savannah watched cartoons in her room after school.

"Do you know what tomorrow is?" she asked.

Wednesday?

"It's Halloween."

Judging by the look on her face and the smell of excitement that filled her room, he assumed it was a good thing.

"We get to trick or treat."

The treat sounded good—the trick not so much. *I'm confused.*

"It's a special day, once a year, when kids... and dogs... get to dress up and collect candy from the neighbors."

I hate to burst your little pumpkin spice-flavored bubble, but dogs don't dress up.

"On Halloween they do. And I have the perfect costumes for us." She pointed to the dumbest-looking character on the TV screen. "That's going to be you."

Gracie shook his head. *I don't think so.*

"His name is Shaggy."

That's a terrible name.

"I'll get your costume so you can try it on."

I should be Scooby. You know, because we're both dogs.

"Yes, but Shaggy is always hungry." She raised an eyebrow above a cute little smirk. "Remind you of anybody?"

She had a point. But wasn't Shaggy the goofy sidekick? *Wait a minute. You think I'm the sidekick in this relationship? I got news for you sister, you're the sidekick.*

"Am not. Besides, Mommy bought ME the Scooby costume."

He had no recourse. *Okay, let's get this over with.*

Savannah opened her bottom dresser drawer and pulled out a green shirt and a handful of brown hair.

What's that furry thing?

It's a wig for you to wear.

Dogs don't wear wigs either.

She sat in front of him and slipped his front legs into the green t-shirt, then pulled it over his head. He squirmed and squiggled.

"Hold still," she said, then placed the ball of fur on top of his head.

It's dark in here.

"Wait a minute." She pushed it up off his face. "There."

He could see again.

Gracie looked at himself in the mirror. *You've got to be kidding.* He turned one way then the other to get the full picture. He looked ridiculous. *Maybe we can trade costumes. After all—*

"No, silly. You won't fit. Besides, you look awesome."

They obviously had two different definitions for that word.

The excitement in the room spiked as Savannah donned her dog costume. He checked himself again in the mirror and shook his head.

The things we do for humans.

Savannah pulled the hood up over her head. "What do you think?"

She bore a remarkable resemblance to the bumbling, crime-solving dog he'd seen on TV. *You look awesome.* Her definition, not his.

Mrs. Miller opened the bedroom door and stuck her head inside. "Time for your little sidekick to go home."

Wait. I'm not the sidekick.

Savannah tilted her head and gave him an I-told-you-so grin.

At dusk the following night, Chloe accompanied the two cartoon crime fighters around the building as they partook in the annual, sugar-coated ritual. They knocked on doors, called out trick-or-treat, and collected their reward. Well, only one of them spoke, the other hid his face to avoid recognition.

Can we go someplace where no one knows me? I'll never live this down.

"Mommy said we need to stay in the building."

Chloe frowned. "I know, dork. That's why I'm here."

"I was talking to Gracie."

Chloe rolled her eyes and hung back while Scooby and Shaggy knocked on another door.

Why does Chloe look like Chloe, and I look ridiculous?

"She made a deal with Mommy to babysit us."

What does she get for her trouble?

"Half our candy."

Did you say OUR candy? I object. I wasn't privy to this negoti-ation.

"You can't object. You're not a lawyer. You're a sidekick."

Everyone keeps telling me that.

Chapter Thirty-Seven

George sat at a table in the Heavenly Café, waiting to meet the daughter he hadn't seen or spoken to in seven years. He closed his eyes and tried to picture her, hoping to avoid the embarrassment of not recognizing her when she walked in—*if* she walked in. He looked at his watch again. Ten minutes late. Maybe this was a bad idea.

He played with the sugar packets, straightening and rearranging them in the little glass container. The table had a slight wobble, an imperfection that seemed to mirror the unease settling in his chest. Each time the bell above the door jingled, it cut through the hum of clinking cups and murmured conversation and signaled his heart to stop.

Could this be a twisted attempt at payback for all the times he'd let her down? He prayed she would walk through that door and let him prove he'd changed.

An inconspicuous glance at his watch told him Angela was going on twenty minutes late. Carl, the owner, stopped by twice to offer a cup of coffee while he waited. Despite the tantalizingly rich aroma that hung in the air, he politely declined each time. How much longer? Ten minutes? Fifteen? He would wait all day if he knew she would show.

The next jingle of the bell signaled the answer to his prayer. Angela stood in the doorway, scanning the room. Even with his bad eyes, he recognized her and waved her over. He stood as she approached.

"I'm so sorry I'm late. I got stuck in traffic for a half hour."

"No worries. You're here now."

The waitress came over and they ordered two coffees.

"It's been a long time," George said.

"I had no intention of ever seeing you again."

He winced.

Their coffee arrived. Angela added a splash of cream and stirred, tapping the spoon on the edge of the cup when she finished.

"What changed?"

"I saw the interview on *GMS*." She took a sip. "Then I looked you up and read the story you submitted."

"What did you think?"

"I learned some things about you that I didn't know."

"It's true. All of it."

"Let's face it, George, you were a horrible father."

That hurt, but she wasn't wrong. He shifted in his chair.

"I didn't know why and probably wouldn't have understood at the time, but it felt like my fault."

"None of it was your fault. I was sick." He paused. "But I should have handled it better."

"The anger and the drinking... I thought you were just a jerk. Then you would disappear for weeks at a time."

"I spent those times in the VA hospital and did a couple of stints in rehab. I was pretty messed up, but I kept trying to get better. You can't imagine how difficult that was."

"For both of us. And Mom, too."

"Believe me, if I could do it over, I would do it differently."

She stared at her coffee cup, turning it slowly in her hands. "I didn't know what to expect when I saw you again. After reading your story, I realized that there were reasons why things happened the way they did. I needed to hear you acknowledge your role and maybe show some remorse."

"A day doesn't go by that I don't regret how I screwed up your life." He studied her. "It appears you've done well in spite of me."

"Looks can be deceiving."

"Is everything all right?"

"Things could be better, but that's not why we're here."

"Please, if there's anything I can do to help…"

"What about you? I see you kept the apartments. How's that going?"

"It's lonely here without your mom, but I'm getting by."

For the next half hour, they navigated through awkward moments, offering a controlled glimpse into each other's lives.

"I have a dog now."

Angela nearly choked on her coffee. "Really?" She set her cup down and wiped the edge of her mouth. "I must say, I'm a little surprised."

"Yeah, me too." He finished his coffee. "Her name is Gracie."

"How did that happen?"

"It's a long story."

A small, secret smile crossed her lips. "Maybe you can tell me next time."

"Next time?" George's eyes widened. "Sure. I'd… I'd like that."

She stood. "I'll call to set something up."

"How about I cook you a nice dinner?"

Angela looked at him through squinted eyes. "Since when do you cook?"

"I learned in the army." He sighed. "But I guess you wouldn't know that. I wasn't around enough to show you."

Their eyes met, and she shrugged it off.

"I'm actually pretty good at it."

She straightened and adjusted her purse strap. "I'll think about it."

· · · · ● · ● · ● · · ·

Jasmine stood at her sink washing the breakfast dishes.

He's meeting with Angela as we speak.

"His daughter?" She stopped. "How did that happen?"

She left a note on his door with her phone number. George called, and they're having coffee downstairs in the coffee shop.

"I wouldn't mind being a fly on the wall in that room."

Or a dog under the table. I would have gone if I knew that dreadful man with the apron wouldn't be there.

"I wonder what made her come around after all this time."

I'm sure he'll tell me when he gets home. He's been spilling his guts lately, like he needs to get stuff off his chest. So, I just sit and listen like a therapy dog.

"That's nice."

Yikes! I'd better get back there before he gets home. I'll fill you in later.

Gracie ran downstairs, jumped through the doggy door, and found a spot in the living room where he could monitor the comings and goings through the front door. He watched and waited.

The sound of the key in the lock sent his tail into high gear. When George walked in, Gracie danced around like the floor was on fire.

George laughed. "Hey, girl." He bent over and scratched behind Gracie's ears.

Gracie sensed that George liked the attention almost as much as he did. He wagged his tail some more and licked George's hand.

Well? What happened? What did she say? Are you going to see her again?

"Did you miss me?"

Of course I missed you. I'm a dog. Tell me what happened.

He set his keys on the table by the door, walked into the kitchen, and opened the refrigerator. Ordinarily, this would have erased whatever was on Gracie's mind like a child shaking an Etch A Sketch. But not this time.

"I'm going to have to buy some steaks."

Nice try, George. Tell me what she said.

"Maybe a bottle of wine." He looked at Gracie. "Or do you think that's too romantic?"

I don't know. Did you have coffee with Angela or pick up one of the waitresses? The communication gap was frustrating.

"Maybe I'm overthinking this." He picked up a cigar and headed for the door. "Come on, let's go sit a spell on the patio."

The two assumed their backyard, cigar-smoking, therapy session positions—George in a patio chair and Gracie at his feet. A gentle breeze moved the seventy-degree air around under partly cloudy skies. George lit his cigar and reclined while Gracie savored the smoky George smell.

"So, it went pretty well with Angela today. She read my story." He took a long draw and blew smoke into the air. "I think she might realize how difficult it was for me. She was too young to understand any of it back then. Things appear to be different now."

It's a start. Baby steps.

"I'm praying the love I have for her will overshadow the mistakes I've made in the past." He paused. "I think she was testing me to see if she should let me back into her life."

When do you get the results?

He puffed his cigar, and they sat in silence for a few moments. "I invited her over for dinner."

Here? When?

"She said she'd think about it."

That's better than a no.

The back door opened, and Ruby stepped out.

Rut-ro.

"There you are." She pulled up a chair next to George. "My air conditioner isn't working and it's hotter than a honeymoon hotel in there."

"I'll take a look at it after I finish this cigar."

"I would be much obliged." She sat back in her chair like she might stay awhile. "So, what's new with you?"

Don't do it, George. Don't mention Angela or you'll—

"I had coffee with my daughter today."

... be sorry.

"I didn't know y'all had a daughter."

"She doesn't come around much anymore."

Let's change the subject. Better yet, maybe she'll leave if you blow smoke in her face.

"I'm sorry to hear that. Why?"

Ruby possessed a rabid curiosity that often led her to stick her nose where it didn't belong.

"It's a long story." He held the cigar to his lips and puffed.

"I've always loved the smell of cigars," Ruby said.

Of course you did.

"You have any kids?" George asked.

"A son. He lives in Arizona."

"If I recall correctly, you're from Texas."

"That's right. Rural Texas, with a capital R. We lived so far out in the country that the sun set between our house and town."

"Heaven must seem like a big city to you."

"I like it here. The weather is nicer."

A silence settled in for a few moments.

"Have you seen Tom and Marilyn lately?" she asked. "It's like they're hitched but not churched. He spends most of his time over at her place."

"As long as he pays his rent, I don't care where he stays."

He didn't tell her that Tom had already given his notice. Gracie had overheard Tom talking to George at the kitchen table about his plan to move in with Marilyn. They'd been seeing each other for a while and decided it was foolish to pay rent for two apartments when they spent most of their time together in hers. Tom's rent had been paid until the end of the month, but he planned to move out this weekend.

George took one last puff on his cigar, then crushed it out under his foot. "Well, I guess I'd better go look at that air conditioner."

· · · · ● · ● · · · ·

George's second *GMS* interview, which included Sam, was a ratings success for the local morning show. People loved the feel-good, human-interest story, and many reached out with cards and letters in the week that followed. They wished them both well and thanked them for sharing their story.

A few days after the interview, George worked on a stack of mail at the kitchen table. The phone rang, and the excitement in George's voice caused Gracie to wander over.

"Angela's coming for dinner on Friday," he told Gracie after he'd hung up. He frowned. "She said she's bringing a guest but wouldn't say who."

Maybe it's a boyfriend, or a husband. He paused. *Or her attorney. Okay, maybe not that. This is wonderful news. What's on the menu?*

"This dinner is a big step for us. Everything needs to be perfect."

You can do this, George... just don't wear that shirt.

"How do steaks sound?"

You really have to ask?

"I can grill them out back."

Would it be too much trouble to wrap mine in bacon? Not just one strip around the outside. Wrap that sucker up like a mummy.

"We'll have baked potatoes and sweet corn. I'll do it all on the grill. I can bring out the picnic table and we can eat outside."

Count me in.

"Let's take a walk to the market and buy all the food."

Gracie had never seen George so excited. *Sounds like a plan. Maybe they still have some of those personalized meat sticks.*

Chapter Thirty-Eight

G racie wandered into Jasmine's kitchen, where he found her having a cup of tea and a scone. *Hey, Jazz. Can I hang out for a bit? I need a break.*

"A break? From what?"

George. He's like a whirling dervish down there. Been like that all day.

"Getting ready for the big dinner tonight?" She pushed a chair out and Gracie hopped up. "Maybe you should cut him some slack. I imagine he's pretty nervous."

If he doesn't take a break, he won't have enough energy left to flip the steaks tonight.

She waved a dismissing hand. "He'll be fine." She paused. "How about you? You must be a little nervous. What if Angela doesn't like dogs?"

That's ridiculous. What's not to like? If I was a cat, I'd be worried. He turned on the big, sad eyes. *You got any more of those cookies?*

"They're called scones, and yes, I can get you one if you'd like."

Gracie jumped down off the chair as Jasmine set a scone on the floor.

"You'd better eat quick. Luna loves scones."

Where IS the queen? I didn't see her on my way in.

"She's around here somewhere."

Gracie glanced around the room, then gobbled up his snack. *Hate to eat and run, but I'm going to check in on Rita. Later, Gator.*

After another snack at Rita's, Gracie sat at her feet and listened to her drone on about this and that. It wasn't so much about the quality of conversation as it was about spending time together. He still sensed sadness in her voice and knew she needed him. After an hour, they both nodded off.

Gracie's eyes opened, and he looked around, confused. When the fog cleared, he jumped to his feet. *Yikes! Did I miss dinner?* He gave Rita a quick goodbye bark. *Gotta bounce.*

He dove headfirst through the doggy door and somersaulted into the apartment. *Sorry. I lost track of time. Are they here yet?*

"There you are. You'd better calm down. They'll be here soon."

George had cleaned up, and the apartment smelled like flowers. He appeared nervous, but he'd stopped running here and there like he had been when Gracie left. A bouquet of flowers sat in the middle of the kitchen table.

"I figured we can sit and have a drink in here before we go outside."

Make mine a Salty Dog. Hold the grapefruit juice.

George paced in front of the door. "I really wish you were here, Dot. You always knew how to calm me down." He wrung his hands. "Don't let me screw this up."

The nervous energy in the room was contagious, and Gracie paced in tighter and tighter circles. It looked like a scene from a sitcom.

The bell finally rang a few minutes later, and George jumped like a dog on the Fourth of July.

This is it, George. You can do it.

He took a deep breath and composed himself before opening the door. Gracie hung back and watched from a few feet away. A forty-something, dark-skinned woman with shiny black hair offered a wide but tentative smile from the doorway. A tiny hand, with a young girl about Savannah's age attached, held her finger tight. Her curly hair had been gathered on each side of her head like mouse ears. The older one blinked her large, ebony eyes and waited.

Say something, George.

When he didn't, the woman said, "May we come in?"

"Of course," George replied after he recovered from his mini-stroke. He stepped aside, and they entered.

"This is my daughter, Maya."

Neither of them saw that coming. George's eyes widened, and his mouth hung open. Not a good look for him.

And you must be Angela. Where's your manners, George?

The girl's eyes were as big as her mother's, and they studied him with uncertainty.

Gracie felt the need to take over before the whole thing went sideways. *Hello, Maya.*

She turned her head.

My name is Gracie, and that's your grandpa over there.

Maya looked up at George with a mix of wonder and confusion. "Grandpa?"

George glanced at the woman. She nodded.

"Yes, little one. I'm Grandpa George." He sat and patted the seat next to him.

She waited for her mother's approval before climbing up. George reached for his glasses, which he'd begun wearing around his neck. "You're a real cute one, just like your mommy."

Maya nodded and hopped off onto the floor. "I like your dog."

Smart kid.

"That's Gracie." He paused a moment to clear his throat. "Gracie, this is Angela and my... my granddaughter, Maya."

Gracie sensed George liked how that sounded. Dogs had a way of knowing what humans feel, and he wagged as he felt the years of pain and regret begin to melt away. George sprung a leak when he turned to Angela. "Thank you for bringing her. I had no idea."

Angela tucked her hair behind one ear and nodded. Her vibrant smile faded momentarily, and Gracie saw a glimpse of the wound that had never really healed. A quick glance at Maya revealed Angela's unselfish motivation.

"I didn't even know you were married." George said. "When did that happen?"

"About a year after the funeral."

"You should have brought him."

"He's not in the picture anymore."

"I'm sorry."

"Yeah, me too. Let's talk about something else."

Let's talk about dinner.

George gestured toward the living room. "Can I get you something to drink?"

"I could use a beer."

"Sure. And Maya?"

"No beer for her."

A brief silence descended before everyone laughed. Gracie wagged his tail. He didn't understand what had happened, but laughing is laughing.

"She'll take juice or soda if you have it."

"Two beers and a soda coming up."

"Can I give Gracie some of my soda?"

I like this kid already.

"I'll put some fresh water in her bowl." He looked over at Gracie, who hung his head. "You can put a little soda in there if you like."

Maya's eyes widened and she clapped her hands.

How would you like to move in with us?

She looked at Gracie. "Mommy said we can only visit."

Ho-lee cow! She had the gift, too. *That's okay, visiting is good. We can still be friends."*

Maya nodded as George returned with the drinks.

Angela took a sip of her beer and studied Gracie for a moment. "Did you say the dog's name is Gracie?"

"Yep. I got her at the pound."

Gracie followed Maya over to his water bowl and watched her pour a little soda in. He lapped at it, enjoying the sweetness on his tongue.

"Was the name your idea?"

He nodded. "Named her after Gracie Allen from one of our favorite TV shows."

"It's a strange name for a male dog, don't you think?"

Gracie turned around. *Rut-ro.*

"What are you talking about? Gracie's female."

Gracie appreciated her honesty but didn't want to see George embarrassed. Besides, he'd gotten used to the name, and so had everyone else.

Angela continued. "Really? When's the last time you checked?"

George's brow furrowed, and he patted his thigh. "Come here, Gracie."

I'm good with the name. You can't change it now.

"I think Gracie is a perfect name." Maya winked at Gracie.

Gracie toddled over to George, who put on his glasses. He picked up Gracie and gave him a quick exam. "Well, I'll be." He spit out a nervous laugh and set the dog down. "Why didn't you say something, Gracie?"

Nice try, George.

"What kind of dog is he?"

George paused. "I never really thought about it. Some kind of mix."

"Looks like he might have some Jack Russell in his bloodline."

Jack? Is that my father's name? Do you know my father? Why had Mama kept it from him?

George studied Gracie and an awkward silence ensued.

"Are you okay, George?" Angela said it like the problem might be more with his head than his eyes.

George sighed. "My eyes aren't what they used to be. Your mother had been after me to see the doctor, but I kept putting it off." He paused. "I made an appointment when I realized I couldn't drive anymore."

"What did the doctor say?"

"I need surgery, but I'm not too keen on letting someone cut my eyeballs, so I haven't done anything yet."

"It's dangerous. If you want to continue to see your granddaughter, you won't put it off any longer."

George took a deep breath and nodded.

Gracie sensed his embarrassment. *Those steaks aren't going to cook themselves. Maybe we should all mosey on outside and talk about something else.* He'd never moseyed before, but it seemed appropriate here.

Chapter Thirty-Nine

Angela pushed her plate away. "I'm impressed. I haven't had a meal that good in a long time."

George shrugged as he rearranged his silverware. "It was a good cut of beef. All I did was cook it."

To perfection. Don't be so modest, Grandpa. I tasted the love.

George turned to Maya. "How was your hotdog?"

"Delish. Thanks, Grandpa."

The back door opened, and Savannah stepped out. Gracie jumped to his feet, tail wagging, and walked toward her.

"There you are. I knocked on your door, but nobody answered," she said as she squatted and stroked Gracie's back.

I made a new friend. Her name is Maya. That's her over there. She's George's granddaughter. He didn't even know about—

"Slow down." Savannah glanced at Maya sitting at the table. "Does she live around here?"

I wish! She's just here for dinner.

"Maybe we can play for a while."

Wait! I forgot to tell you the best part... she can hear me like you.

They walked over to the table, and George introduced everyone.

"Can Maya play with us?" Savannah asked.

Angela hesitated. "Okay, but stay here on the patio."

Gracie positioned himself strategically to hear all conversations. While Savannah and Maya got to know each other, Gracie eavesdropped on George and Angela.

"So, you live in Whitney. What do you do?"

"I'm a social worker for the Sacramento School District."

"You commute to Sacramento?"

"Yes. It's a half-hour drive, but I love my job." She looked away for a moment.

Gracie sensed a tragic futility in her voice. *Rut-ro.*

Apparently, George picked up on it, too. "I get the feeling there's something you're not telling me."

"Everything is fine." She held up her empty can and shook it. "Can I get another one of these?"

Everything wasn't fine, and Gracie knew it.

"You've had two. Maybe that's enough. You're driving."

"NOW you're going to start acting like a father?" She turned to Maya. "Come on, honey, we need to go home."

Yikes! What just happened?

"I don't want to go." Maya stuck out her lower lip and folded her arms across her chest.

"Angela, please."

Angela stood, and George followed suit. "Wait," he said. "We haven't had dessert."

"Dinner was lovely, but we need to get going."

"It's your favorite. Strawberry shortcake."

She studied him but said nothing.

Maya's eyes widened. "I want strawberry shortcake!"

"I'm sorry, honey, but we have to go."

"Why do we have to go?"

Angela glared at her. "Because I said so."

Maya's bottom lip made another appearance.

"Angela, I'm sorry. Please don't go yet."

She put her hands on her hips. "Do you know why my husband isn't around anymore? Of course you don't." She paused. "He died in a car accident three years ago and left us to fend for ourselves. I do the best I can, but..." Her sentence went unfinished.

"I'm sorry, Angela. That must be difficult."

"You don't understand what it's like."

"I think I do."

"I'm not saying it wasn't tough when Mom died, but you didn't have to raise a two-year-old by yourself."

Maya looked at Gracie. "I want to stay with you."

Too bad you can't live here with us.

Maya's lip retracted, and she jumped to her feet. "Mommy? Can we live here?"

The kid's got spunk.

Angela shook her head. "No, honey. Say goodbye to your friends."

"But we have to move, anyway. Why can't we move here?"

"You... you have to move?" George took a step toward her. "Please, Angela. Tell me what's going on."

"It's nothing."

"So, you're moving for no reason?"

"That's not what I meant."

"If there's a problem, I'd like to help."

"I'm afraid you're thirty years too late." She shook her head. "I don't know what I'm even doing here."

George closed his eyes, defeated.

"Mommy, I want strawberry shortcake."

Angela took her hand and led her toward the door. "I'll buy you some on the way home."

Maya turned around and waved to Gracie and Savannah with her free hand. "Bye."

Gracie looked up at George after they left. *Well, THAT just happened. What did you say?*

George pulled up a chair and sat before the evening breeze blew him over. When people are sad, they need their dog. Gracie lay down at his feet and nuzzled his leg.

· · · · · ● · ● · ● · · ·

"Angela, please pick up. We need to talk... I'm sorry about the other night. Let's not let this derail the progress we were making." After a long pause, George added, "Please call me."

He set his phone down and turned to Gracie. "Looks like I blew it. I was just trying to help." He shook his head. "I've been calling all weekend. She won't pick up."

I know, George. Not everybody wants to be helped. Gracie offered his neck for scratching or his head for stroking. Either helped to console humans when they were sad. George chose the latter and let out a loud sigh.

They sat in silence with their own thoughts. Well, Gracie's mind turned to mush as it did when being scratched, stroked, petted or licked. Humans rarely did the last one, but he admitted missing the times Mama had performed that ritual on her pup.

Eventually, George snapped out of it and stood. "I'm going to check the mail."

Good luck with that. It's Sunday.

Unfortunately, George was too old to understand him. The art of canine conversation seemed to be reserved for the very young. And witches.

Wait for me. I'm coming with you.

Gracie followed him to the mailboxes, which were located in the lobby just outside his apartment. George opened the box and bent over to look inside. "Nothing."

I could have told you that.

On their way back to the apartment, Jasmine walked through the front door.

"Hello, George."

He nodded, distracted, probably still wondering why there had been no mail.

Hi, Jazz. George is a little out of sorts today.

"I'm sorry things didn't go so well the other night."

George looked at her through squinted eyes. "Now, why would you think that?"

Uh... I may have said something to her yesterday.

"I'm sorry. Am I mistaken?"

His shoulders slumped, and he shook his head.

"Don't give up on Angela. She needs you."

He's not giving up. I won't let him.

"I tried to help, but she made it clear she doesn't want my help."

"That was just a knee-jerk reaction, but you need to understand that she's embarrassed."

"Embarrassed? Why?"

"She's having a difficult time being on her own, and alcohol numbs her pain." She hesitated. "I'm pretty sure that's something you're familiar with."

George remained silent.

Roger that. But he's been cleaning up his act. I'm proud of him.

Jasmine smiled at Gracie before turning back to George. "She's a good mother, George, but she's treading water. She's living paycheck to paycheck, and now she's losing her home."

"I suppose Dottie told you all this?"

She nodded.

"This thing you do... talking to dead people. It's legit?"

Gracie's tail wagged. *She can talk to dogs, too.*

"Yes, George, that's what I've been trying to tell you."

George considered this for a moment. "Ask her what I should do."

"She said she's working on it. In the meantime, give Angela some space. She'll come around when she's ready."

"How can you be sure?"

"She's drowning, and you're a lifeline. She'll recognize that soon enough."

George inhaled and slowly blew out his breath. "I hope you're right."

Jasmine stooped and placed a hand under Gracie's chin. She lifted it and looked through his eyes into his soul. "When have I ever been wrong?"

Uh... I'm guessing the right answer here is never.

"Good dog." She stood and looked at George. "If you ever need to talk, you know where I live."

Inside the apartment, George picked up his phone, checked for messages, then set it down. A few seconds later, he picked it up again.

Gracie barked, and George turned to face him.

Come on, man. You heard the lady. Give her some space.

George set the phone down and grabbed a beer from the fridge.

Later that night, Gracie heard a whimper from somewhere in the dark apartment and went to check it out. He followed his ears into George's bedroom and found him sobbing in bed.

Gracie felt his pain, and a whimper of his own slipped out.

"Is that you, Gracie?"

What's the matter, George?

"Come on up here."

Me? What about rule number five?

George patted the bed.

You don't have to tell me three times. Gracie hopped up onto the bed and settled in next to George. Sometimes, the best thing you can do to help someone in pain is just to be there.

Chapter Forty

The following day, George scheduled his eye surgery for the week after Thanksgiving. "I guess I have to suck it up and get my eyes fixed if I want to spend time with Maya."

Gracie had never seen George so determined. *I'm proud of you, George. It's long overdue... the eye thing AND the sucking up.*

"And I guess I should apologize for your name."

Step number nine: make amends.

"It took me by surprise when Angela pointed it out. I really like the name and would hate to change it now. It reminds me of Dottie." He reached out and scratched Gracie behind the ears.

Gracie closed his eyes as George continued to scratch. *You can be very persuasive when you want to be.* He turned his head a little to the left. *You missed a spot. Yeah, that's it.*

George held Gracie's head with both hands and looked into his eyes. "Well, what do you think?"

I think you should keep scratching. As far as the name, apology accepted. I've gotten used to it. He barked his approval.

"I'll take that as a yes." George stood. "Now, you'll have to excuse me. I have an idea for a book I want to write."

What? When did this happen? Gracie followed George into the kitchen and watched him sit at the table and open his laptop. *First, you stop reading the obituaries, now you're writing another book? Who are you and what have you done with George?* Gracie barked.

Looking at him over the top of his reading glasses, George said, "I thought you'd never ask. It's about a certain stray dog that opens a grumpy old man's heart and touches the lives of everyone in his building."

Am I that certain stray dog?

"In case you're wondering, that dog is you."

I'm flattered, but I'm just doing what any dog worth his kibble would do.

"They say life imitates art. Why not write a happy ending to our story? See where I'm going with this?"

I think so. If you build it, they will come. Or something like that. It reminded him of a baseball movie they'd watched together.

George pecked away at his computer for the next two days, which didn't leave time for sitting by the phone waiting for Angela's call. Gracie hung around the apartment for moral support until Savannah came home from school. They divided their time between playing outside and talking about how cool it would be if Maya moved into the building. Savannah crossed all her fingers and toes to make it happen. Gracie attempted the same, but, well, you can imagine.

On the third day, George took a break from writing and resumed his daily chores, which he'd overlooked for a couple of days. Sometime after lunch, Gracie's ears twitched. The knock on the door that followed startled George.

He looked at Gracie. "Are you expecting someone?"

If it's the police, tell them I moved and didn't leave a forwarding address.

George opened the door to find Angela and Maya standing in the hall.

"Angela? Shouldn't you be at work?"

"We're playing hooky today."

Maya ran to Gracie and stroked his back. "Hi, Gracie. I couldn't wait to see you again."

Where have you been? I missed you.

She whispered, "After the last time, Mommy said we were never coming back."

Yet, here you are.

George ushered Angela inside. "Before we get started, I want to apologize for the other night. You're a big girl, and I had no right to tell you what to do."

"No need for apologies. You were acting like a father... something I need to get used to." She paused. "I should have controlled myself, but it's just that James left such a mess."

"What happened?"

"I got pregnant a year after Mom died. He asked me to marry him, and I didn't know what else to do. Two years later, he died in a car accident."

"I'm so sorry, Angela." He ran his hand back over the top of his head. "My offer to help still stands."

She looked at him with big, sad eyes, not unlike Gracie's.

They all took a seat in the living room. Maya sat on the floor next to Gracie. George and Angela sat across from each other, making small talk.

You didn't have to be a dog to see they both wanted the same thing. Like a chess match, each cautiously pushed their pawns around the board, afraid to make a real move.

Humans needed to let their guard down once in a while, admit what they were feeling, own it, and move forward. If only Gracie could talk, he might have been able to Doctor Phil them into settling their differences right there and then.

George threw down the gauntlet. "I can help with your financial trouble."

"How do you know I'm having financial trouble?"

George scrunched up his face, undoubtedly embarrassed to admit he'd heard it from a psychic. "Uh... one of my tenants, Jasmine, claims to be a psychic. She told me."

"You went to a psychic?"

He held up his hands. "No, no, not me."

"You just said you talked to a psychic."

"She's a friend. She lives in the building."

"You have a resident psychic?"

He shrugged. "I guess we do."

The look on her face gave Gracie the impression that this was a good thing.

"You need to move. Why not move here?"

"I can't just up and move an hour away. Besides, Maya just started school."

"We have good schools here. She can ride the bus with Savannah, and I can watch her until you came home from work."

Angela hesitated, then shook her head. "We're not moving in with you, George."

"You don't have to. There's a vacant apartment in the building. Just say the word and it's yours."

Well played, George. Check.

"What?"

"You can stay here rent-free until you get back on your feet. I'll even fix up the apartment however you like. I've got this prize money burning a hole in my pocket."

Checkmate.

"That's very generous, but..."

But what? There's no logical way to finish that sentence. Take the deal, Angela.

"Let's think about the future instead of the past," George said.

When Angela didn't respond, he added, "I'll hold the apartment for as long as you need."

"What's going on?" Maya asked.

George is tightening the screws.

"What?"

It's a metaphor.

"A what?"

He's trying to get you guys to live here.

Maya's eyes widened. "Yay!"

Everyone turned to Maya, and she covered her mouth.

Angela's gaze lingered on her daughter. "Okay, I'll think about it, George."

"I wouldn't mind it if you called me Dad."

"Let's not get ahead of ourselves."

Baby steps, George.

He nodded. "I can wait."

After an awkward silence, Angela spoke. "If I'm thinking about taking you up on your offer, I should at least see the place before I decide."

Gracie turned to Maya, tail wagging. *Is this really happening?*

George held up his hands. "Wait right there, I'll get the key." He almost tripped over his own feet.

Careful, George. Don't hurt yourself.

Chapter Forty-One

George unlocked the door to 3B. "I haven't had a chance to clean the place yet."

Angela stepped inside and looked around. "This is bigger than I imagined."

"I plan to paint it and replace the appliances."

She opened the refrigerator and glanced inside. "I don't want you to go through all that trouble."

"No trouble. Probably time to remove these old carpets and put in some of that laminate, as well."

Maya looked up at George. "Where's my room?"

"Right this way, young lady."

Gracie followed them. *You're going to love it here,* he said to Maya. *Savannah lives right across the hall. And yours truly is just an elevator ride away. Don't worry, it's safe.*

"If you don't mind me asking, why did Maya say that you already had to move?"

"Our apartment building has been sold, and the new owner wants to renovate and turn it into condos. We're being forced to purchase or move, and I'm in no position to buy."

"Then this will be perfect. And... you should be able to cut your commute time by at least ten minutes."

"You drive a hard bargain."

"It's a win-win."

Maya wrapped her arms around Angela's leg.

Gracie admired the girl's courage, knowing how much trouble he would be in if he tried something like that.

"Pleeeeze, Mommy. Can we live here?"

Angela met George's gaze and shook her occupied leg. "Was this part of your plan?"

George smiled.

Angela placed her hands on her hips. "I accept on two conditions."

Rut-ro. A counteroffer.

George lifted an eyebrow. "What's that?"

"One. You let me help with the work."

"Can you operate a paint roller?"

"I'm pretty good with a brush, too."

"What's number two?"

"I pay rent."

George rubbed his chin. "Come on, Angela. I'm trying to help you here."

"In case you hadn't noticed, I'm all grown up now. I appreciate the opportunity to live here, I really do, but I can pay my own way."

He ran a hand back over the top of his head.

Yikes! What are you going to do, George?

After a moment of deliberation, George sighed. "It's a deal. Friends and family rate."

Angela pried Maya from her leg and bent down to her level. "I hope it's okay with you if we live here."

Maya glanced at Gracie, who did his happy dance, then gave her mother a vigorous nod.

Angela stood, and her brow furrowed. "I have to be out by the end of the month. Do you think the place will be ready?"

George nodded. "With your help, I'm sure we can have it ready for you to move in Thanksgiving weekend."

Gracie's ears perked up, and he ran out of the bedroom. Ruby peeked her head inside the front door.

"Helloooo."

Gracie skidded to a stop. The others filed out of the bedroom.

"What can I do for you, Ruby?" George asked.

"Nothing, really. I'm just being a Nosy Nellie."

Why am I not surprised?

"I heard all the commotion and figured we must have a new tenant."

"You figured right." He gestured toward Angela. "This is my daughter, Angela, and that's Maya. They're moving in at the end of the month."

"Your daughter…" She nodded her head slowly.

She's probably working on the press release as we speak.

"How nice for you."

"Yes, it is." He paused. "Now, if that's all, I need to go over some things with Angela."

"There's one more thing. It's about Thanksgiving…"

Gracie's ears perked up. *There's that word again.*

"The tenants are all planning a big dinner celebration. Everyone is bringing a dish to pass, and we were wondering if you might provide the turkey."

Gracie didn't understand everything she said, but dinner and turkey in the same sentence had to be a good thing.

George hesitated.

"We'll do all the cooking." The corners of Ruby's mouth twitched into a smile, intent on closing the deal.

"I'll have to think about it." He glanced at Gracie, whose tail spun like a propeller. "On second thought, count me in."

"Thank you, George. I'll tell everyone."

"I'll be bringing my daughter and granddaughter."

Hellooo?

"And of course, Gracie."

"Of course."

After Ruby left, George turned to Angela. "I hope I didn't overstep."

"No, it sounds wonderful. It'll be a great way to get to know my new neighbors." She paused. "Will Sam be there? I'd like to meet him."

"Mommy, is Savannah going?"

"I'm sure she'll be there," George said.

Let's go see if she's home from school yet.

Gracie and Maya headed for the door.

Angela called after them. "Where do you think you're going?"

"To tell Savannah."

"No, you need to stay here with us."

"She lives across the hall," George said. "She'll be safe with Gracie."

Angela hesitated.

"We'll pick them up on the way back to my apartment."

This seemed to satisfy her. She nodded her approval, and off they went.

Savannah's eyes widened when she answered the door.

"Who's there?" Mrs. Miller called from the kitchen.

"It's Gracie and my new friend Maya."

Mrs. Miller appeared, holding a dish towel. "Maya? Where does she live?"

She's moving in across the hall.

"Across the hall."

"That's nice." She smiled. "Welcome to the building."

Her smile disarmed Gracie, and he dismissed the thought that she was sizing Maya up for a pot to cook her in.

"Thank you."

"Come on." Savannah took off toward her bedroom and Gracie and Maya followed. She closed the door and turned to Gracie. "Is she really gonna live here?"

Dogs don't lie.

Savannah wrapped her arms around Maya, and they hopped around the room.

Wait for me!

Gracie performed his happy dance, trying to nuzzle his way in between them. Eventually, the dance party collapsed onto the floor. Gracie filled Savannah in on everything that had transpired that morning.

"When are you moving in?" Savannah asked.

Maya shrugged and looked at Gracie for help.

George said Thanksgiving weekend, whatever that is.

"Thanksgiving is a special holiday where everyone gets together and eats so much turkey and stuffing their stomachs explode."

Sounds messy.

Savannah laughed. "They don't really explode, they just get too full."

Gracie wagged his tail. *Full is good.*

George and Angela showed up a few minutes later to collect Maya and Gracie. They said goodbye to Savannah and returned to George's apartment.

"The Millers seem nice," Angela said. "I'm glad to see that Maya found a friend her age so quickly."

"I have a feeling those three amigos will be—" George stopped abruptly.

"What?"

"I'll be right back." He hurried into the kitchen and returned with a jar full of scratch-off tickets. He presented it to Angela. "This is for you."

"I don't get it."

"For the past couple of years, I've been buying these tickets and saving them for the day I would see you again. You know, the whole positive thinking thing. I didn't know when or if that day might come, but I had to have a reason to believe it would."

Angela examined it. "There must be a hundred tickets in here."

"Let's hope some of them are winners. It could help with moving expenses or, with any luck, Maya's college fund."

Her eyes filled, and her bottom lip trembled. "I don't know what to say except, thank you... Dad."

Both of their eyes were leaking, and Gracie sensed it was a good thing. Humans often communicated with their eyes, but they sent mixed messages. Their eyes leaked when they were happy, and they leaked when they were sad. How the species had survived as long as it had was beyond his comprehension.

Chapter Forty-Two

With Thanksgiving only two weeks away, work began in earnest. Options were discussed and lists drawn up. They all drove to Home Depot for paint, supplies, flooring, and to order new appliances. Angela and Maya picked the paint colors and had input for all the purchases. Appliance delivery and flooring installation were scheduled for the following week.

On Saturday, Angela showed up ready for work. Together, they ripped out the old carpet and threw the pieces in the hall, creating a Ruby magnet.

Gracie and Maya watched as they moved on to painting.

Rut-ro.

George was making a mess. His failing eyesight kept him from doing a neat job, and he nearly stepped into the paint can.

"Helloooo." Ruby knocked on the open door.

"Hello, Ruby." George put down his paintbrush.

"Oh, my." She brought her hand up to her mouth. "That doesn't look good at all."

"What?" George followed her gaze, as did Angela.

"Are you feeling all right, George?"

Angela frowned. "Your eyes are so bad, you can't even paint a straight line."

George hesitated to admit his shortcoming. "Must be the lighting."

"We talked about this," Angela said. "When are you going to get your eyes fixed?"

"I've scheduled surgery for the first week of December."

"Really? That's good, but I'm afraid I'll have to do the rest of the painting."

George shrugged. "I guess I can find other things to do, but it's going to set us back."

"Did I mention I have Thanksgiving week off?"

"I think I would have remembered that."

"School is closed the entire week for the holiday. That'll give us three extra days. If we get done early, maybe I can start moving some of my stuff on Wednesday."

"That's a big IF with only one painter."

"Did I hear someone is looking for a painter?"

"Hey, Mike."

"I thought I'd wander up and see what all the commotion was about."

Ruby took his arm with one hand and pointed at Angela with the other. "This is the new tenant I told you about."

Of course you did.

"Welcome to the building."

Angela smiled and introduced herself and Maya.

"I've had plenty of experience painting. I'd be happy to lend a hand if you need it."

George nodded. "I'm going to take you up on that offer."

That Mike is a stand-up guy... for a cop.

It had been a productive afternoon inside the apartment. Outside had been a different story. Gracie and the girls spent the afternoon talking and playing under the maple tree.

Maya pointed to a second-story window. "Whose cat is that?"

Her name is Luna, and she belongs to a witch.

Savannah snickered. "You need to stay away from her. I heard she likes to eat small children."

Maya's eyes widened, and she covered her mouth.

Yeah. Poor Eddie.

"What happened to Eddie?"

Jasmine, that's the witch, said he was delicious.

"She told you that?"

Savannah burst into laughter. "No silly. We're just kidding."

Maya's face wrinkled. "That's mean."

We're just having fun. You gotta have thick skin around here. My name's Gracie, and last time I checked, I wasn't a girl.

Maya giggled. "Now, that's funny."

No. You're funny, Maya Papaya.

A brisk game of *bet you can't catch me* ensued.

· · · · ●·●· · · ·

By the end of the following week, the floors had been installed, and the appliances were scheduled to be delivered on Monday. Angela and Mike planned to have the bulk of the painting done by the weekend. George fiddled around, cleaning and doing odd jobs.

"I mopped the kitchen floor, so stay off it until it dries." He took a breath. "I think I'll go down to the market and order the turkeys. I want to buy them fresh. They can deliver them on Wednesday." He paused. "I'll get us some lunch. They make a killer roast beef and turkey sub."

Mike nodded. "Sounds perfect. Can you grab me an iced tea?"

"I'll have what he's having," Angela said. "Maya can have some of mine."

"Come on, Gracie. Let's take a walk."

Road trip. What about Maya?

"Mommy, can I go, too?"

Angela looked at George. He nodded.

Gracie and Maya matched George step for step all the way to the market. They studied the rack of individually wrapped meat sticks.

George says they have some here with my name on them.

He didn't have a clear view of the top of the rack, but he didn't see his name anywhere. He wouldn't recognize it even if he did, but he hung his head, nevertheless.

George approached. "Looking for some jerky?" He pulled two packages from the top of the rack and held them up. "But you can't eat them in here."

Gracie's tail shifted into high gear. *What? You found them? I knew they had to be here somewhere. Good job, George.* His happy dance drew the attention of the other patrons.

Before they left, George let Maya pick out some candy for dessert.

When they returned, everyone took a break and ate lunch. Gracie had two meat sticks and Maya's leftovers. It must have been difficult to concentrate on lunch with that candy burning a hole in her pocket.

Work resumed after lunch for Angela and Mike, who painted the living room. George left to replenish the lobby produce stand. After a little horsing around, Gracie and Maya became bored. Sticking around the apartment was as exciting as, well, watching paint dry.

Maya wanted to meet the cat in the window. Gracie tried unsuccessfully to talk her out of it. He didn't understand why anyone would want to meet a cat.

Maya froze at Jasmine's door.

What's the matter? Is it the witch thing?

Maya nodded.

I'm pretty sure she's not a real witch. I've been in her apartment many times and have never seen a broom.

Introductions were made, and Jasmine ushered them inside. Luna sat in her usual spot on the back of the sofa.

"Why is she up there?" Maya asked.

Because she's a psycho cat.

"Luna. Come meet your new friend."

I don't need any more friends, Luna said without turning around.

"Don't be rude. Maya is going to be your neighbor."

She turned her head. *What's HE doing here?*

"Gracie and Maya are friends."

Is that so? If she likes him, she's going to LOVE me. Luna jumped down and moved silently to Maya's feet, where she slithered and slid around them like a snake.

"She's cute." Maya bent down to stroke Luna.

Really? You think that's cute? Gracie restrained himself from putting on his own show to upstage the cat.

"Let them play," Jasmine said. She reached down and held Gracie's head in her hands. "I'm worried about you."

Don't be. I can 'outcute' that cat any day of the week.

She met his gaze, and he detected fear in her eyes. "There's trouble ahead. I'm getting a bad vibe."

Stop it. You're freaking me out.

"I feel like I need to warn you."

You're telling me I finally have a vibe, and it's a bad one?

He shook himself free and took a step back.

"My intuition is never wrong."

Gracie looked at Luna. *It's all her fault. Black cats are bad luck. Come on, Maya, we need to go.*

Luna arched her back. *She can stay here with me.*

No, she can't. I don't want you to jinx her, too.

Gracie and Maya left in a hurry. They returned to the apartment and found their humans packing up.

"There you are. We were just getting ready to leave."

"But I don't want to go yet. I want to play some more." Maya thrust out her lower lip.

You should have thought about that before you dragged me downstairs to see that stupid cat.

"You've been playing all day. It's time to go home and have dinner."

Maya shrugged. "Bye, Gracie. I'll see you tomorrow."

"I'm afraid not, honey. We're taking the day off tomorrow, and Monday the appliances are being installed, but we'll be back on Tuesday."

Tuesday? That's like... a week away.

"When is Tuesday, Mommy?"

"It's only two days. Now let's get going."

Angela and Maya said goodbye. Gracie moped around the apartment. Just when the dynamic duo had become the three amigos, they had to spend two days without their newest member.

Chapter Forty-Three

George let Angela take his truck home on Saturday to move some of her stuff. She pulled into the driveway Tuesday morning, loaded down with boxes and a few small pieces of furniture.

Gracie ran ahead as George went out to meet them.

"We're going to be neighbors," Maya said to Gracie when she climbed out of the truck.

This is really happening. Gracie did a happy dance.

Everyone stopped to watch.

What? This is what I do when I'm happy.

The older humans kept busy all morning cleaning and moving the contents of the truck into the apartment. Meanwhile, the three amigos entertained themselves playing in Savannah's room. After lunch, which Sam graciously provided, they moved their fun and games outside.

Maya produced a fuzzy yellow ball for playing fetch that worked way better than a stick. Sticks don't bounce. The ball traveled farther, and with a well-timed jump, Gracie could snatch it out of the air in mid-bounce. A difficult maneuver, but he had all afternoon to perfect his technique as long as the girls' arms held out.

Keeping an eye on the ball was the key to catching it. Gracie looked away for a second and just missed one. The ball bounced over the fence into the neighbor's yard.

Rut-ro.

The girls joined him at the fence and stared at the ball on the neighbor's lawn.

Savannah called out to the man sitting on his porch. "Hey mister. Can you please get our ball for us?"

He picked it up and threw it in a high arc over the fence.

Suddenly, Gracie was playing center field for the Giants. *I got it!* He ran faster than he'd ever run, his gaze never leaving that ball. It bounced on the sidewalk, and he ran faster. The hot asphalt burned under his paws, but that ball was his. He jumped. *Got it!*

He heard a terrible screeching sound just before the lights went out. When they came back on, Savannah and Maya were screaming.

Oh, no! He needed to help them, but something was wrong. Why was he on the ground? The girls continued to scream. A searing pain prevented him from getting up.

Wait. The girls weren't hurt. HE was. The last thing he remembered was timing his leap to get the ball... THAT BOUNCED INTO THE STREET. *No! No! This didn't just happen, did it?* He tried to move again. *Son of a biscuit! It did.*

He closed his eyes, and his mind flashed back to a picture of Mama lying in the street. The girls had seen him get hit, just like he'd seen Mama. How could he have let that happen?

When he opened his eyes again, he looked down from above his crumpled body lying on the side of the road.

That's gonna leave a mark.

He saw Savannah and Maya crying. Before he had time to react, the lights went out again.

George and Angela ran toward the screams. "What happened?" He bent down to Maya's level. "Are you all right?"

Then he saw it. Gracie laying at the side of the road. He ran to him, and Savannah followed. Angela held Maya on the sidewalk.

Gracie's eyes remained closed, and one of his legs lay bent at an awkward angle. George turned and stopped Savannah before she could get a better look.

"I don't think you should see this."

"Is Gracie dead?"

"I don't think so, but his leg looks broken."

Savannah's shoulders slumped, and she cried.

"Angela, take the girls up to 3D. I don't want them to see Gracie like this."

"Sure. Is he okay?"

"Hard to tell. We need to get him to the vet."

Tom and Marilyn walked out the front door and George called them over as Angela gathered up the girls.

"Tom, stay with Gracie. I'll be right back." He patted Gracie. "Hang in there, boy."

George ran down the driveway as fast as his aging legs would take him.

"Dad! What are you doing?"

He jumped into his truck, flipped the visor down, and the keys fell into his lap. The engine started on the first try, and he gunned it down the driveway.

Mike joined Tom and stopped traffic while George pulled the truck alongside Gracie. He scooped him up and laid him on the front seat.

Angela grabbed George's arm. "You can't drive."

"We don't have time. I need to get Gracie to the vet."

"No. WE need to get Gracie to the vet. I'm driving."

"What about Maya?" He looked at the gathering crowd. "Marilyn, can you take the girls up to 3D?"

She nodded.

Tires squealed as they tore off toward the vet's office.

George's gaze alternated between Angela and Gracie. "Thank you."

"You're not driving until after your surgery."

When they arrived at the vet's, George opened the front door and yelled inside that he had an emergency. Angela held the door while he carried Gracie in. The doctor ushered them into an exam room where George set Gracie on a metal table. He wrung his hands as he watched the doctor examine Gracie. Angela joined him and held his arm for moral support.

The doctor stopped working.

George glanced at Angela, then looked at the doctor. "Is he going to be okay?"

"His left hind leg is broken. I can cast it, but I'm worried that he hasn't regained consciousness yet." He paused, a somber look on his face. "I'll need you to wait outside."

This produced more hand wringing along with a few silent prayers. George had been in similar situations with Dottie over the years. Waiting was always the hardest part.

Chapter Forty-Four

Gracie felt no pain as he watched the scene play out from somewhere above the exam table. His heart ached for George, who paced in the waiting room. George, Savannah, Chloe, Maya, Angela, and Jasmine were his pack now. He belonged with them, and he knew firsthand what it was like to lose a member of the pack.

Gracie was no stranger to feeling alone and helpless. However, the scene below took those feelings to another level.

Then Mama appeared at his side. *Hello again, Son.*

What's happening, Mama?

You're one of the lucky ones.

He didn't see how his present situation could be considered lucky by any stretch of the imagination.

You found your purpose, something I never got to do.

I think you were lucky, too.

How do you figure?

Don't you see? I was your purpose. If you didn't save me from the woman and teach me about life, I never would have found George and Savannah and Maya.

She smiled. *I'm happy you feel that way.* Her expression fell. *Now you have to make a choice.*

What kind of choice?

You can stay here with me, or you can go back.

I don't want to choose. Gracie paused. *Wait. Did you have a choice?*

Everyone has a choice, but sometimes it's complicated.

So, you left me on my own? That's what you chose?

This is where it gets complicated. I knew if I stayed, I'd hold you back from everything you've accomplished. It may be difficult to understand, but my leaving made you better and stronger.

Difficult? Try impossible. The only thing I ever wanted was to be with you.

You never would have found your purpose if I'd stayed.

She had a point. But he couldn't leave his new family the way Mama had left him. You don't have to be born into a family to be part of one. Families care about each other and are always there, in good times and bad.

Gracie had changed The Station since his arrival there. You might say it changed him, as well. It was a match made in, well, heaven. The puzzle pieces were falling into place, but his work there wasn't finished. Savannah and Maya needed him. And who would keep George inspired to finish his new book? A book about, *ahem*, a cute little stray dog.

I appreciate the offer to stay, however, my puzzle isn't finished yet. I understand now what you meant when you told me that someday I'd find my purpose and bring joy to others. George is my person and Savannah, Angela, and Maya are my family now. Gracie paused, and they locked eyes. He never imagined he would say what he was about to say. *I'm going to have to decline your offer, Mama.*

I knew you would, but I had to ask.

Muffled noises grew louder. Gracie tried to bark, but no sound came out. Bright light flooded in as he opened his eyes. Pain shot through his body like a lightning bolt, but all he cared about at that moment was being reunited with his pack.

"Welcome back, boy," the doctor said as he wiped his forehead with the back of his hand. "Looks like you're going to be all right."

The nurse left the room to deliver the good news to George and Angela.

Gracie's return earned him a shot for the pain and a cast on his leg—a reasonable expectation. However, the lampshade that had been attached to his collar, THAT was an unwelcome revelation. Not only did it look ridiculous and crush his self-esteem, it amplified the sound reaching his already sensitive ears.

Because he'd been out so long, he would need to stay overnight for observation and proper medication.

....

George left the building holding his daughter's hand, feeling like a weight had been lifted from his chest. When they arrived home, they went straight up to the Millers' apartment to tell the girls the good news. They were accosted at the door.

"Where's Gracie?"

"Is he okay?"

"When can we see him?"

George held up his hands. "Slow down. Gracie is okay, but the doctor suggested that he stay overnight to make sure he's comfortable."

"He can come home tomorrow," Angela added.

Maya threw her arms around her mother's leg. "I want to stay and wait for Gracie."

"We need to go home and pack up some more things. We'll be back tomorrow when Gracie comes home. I promise."

Maya left reluctantly with her mother.

The other tenants would surely want to know what happened, but no one felt up to knocking on doors, so they stopped at Ruby's on their way downstairs.

On Wednesday, the building buzzed with activity in preparation for the Thanksgiving feast. George and Mike had cleared space in the lounge and were busy setting up tables. Jasmine had volunteered to coordinate the decorations along with Mrs. Miller and the girls.

While the excitement level grew steadily, it was tempered by concern for Gracie, who had not yet returned home.

Savannah approached George. "When is Gracie coming home?"

"The doctor said I can pick him up in one hour."

"Can I go with you?"

"I'm going to need you to stay here with Maya while Angela takes me to get him."

"When is Maya coming?"

"She should be here any minute."

Angela arrived a few minutes later, and George excused himself from the others. He walked Angela to his apartment, where they replaced Gracie's bed with the larger crib mattress Angela had brought. With his leg in a cast and a cone on his head, he needed more room to sleep. They also rearranged some furniture to keep the main pathways clear so there were fewer obstacles for him to run into. It might take some time to get used to the dimensions of his new headpiece and his limited peripheral vision.

"How long does he have to wear the cone?" Angela asked.

"Doc says until the cast comes off in a few weeks. Most dogs will try to chew their cast off if given the chance."

"Oh, no. Poor Gracie."

· · · · ● · ● · · · ·

"You better go get the girls," George told Angela when they returned with Gracie, "or we'll never hear the end of it."

Angela left, and George sat at the table. He patted his leg, and Gracie limped over. George dropped his hand and gently stroked Gracie's back. "You gave me a scare, little fella. I'm glad you're back home."

Stop shouting. I'm right here. Gracie gave his head a vigorous shake.

"I know you're not a happy camper right now, but you'll be back to normal before you know it."

What am I going to do in the meantime? This thing really interferes with my favorite pastime—napping. And playing fetch? No can do. Although fetch is what got me into this mess.

Gracie wandered over to his water bowl and made a mess. The girls arrived and ran to him.

Watch your step. I turn into a water sprinkler every time I take a drink.

Savannah wrapped her arms around his midsection. "I'm so glad you're back."

Why is everyone shouting?

"Be careful of his leg," George said. "He's going to have to take it easy for a while."

"What's that thing on his head?" Maya asked.

I look pretty stupid, don't I?

"It's called a cone."

The cone of shame.

Angela bent down to Maya's level. "He needs to wear it so he doesn't chew his cast off."

"Why would he want to chew it?"

Fun fact: Chewing on hard things is good for a dog's teeth.

"Dogs like to chew things, honey. It's actually good for their teeth."

Told you.

Maya thought about it for a moment. "Okay."

George stood. "Come on, Gracie. I'll show you your new bed."

What? I liked the old one.

Gracie walked into one of the kitchen chairs as he followed George.

I feel like a walking bumper car.

The girls laughed.

It's not funny.

They stopped.

"Poor Gracie."

Gracie circled his makeshift bed. *This is temporary. Right?*

George and Angela walked into the kitchen and left the girls with Gracie.

"Are you excited about tomorrow?" Savannah whispered.

I wish I could go, but I can't be seen in public like this. 'Aww, poor thing,' they'll say, as if I don't already know how stupid I look.

"You look cute."

Cute? I look like I'm auditioning for a role in a Star Trek movie.

"It's really not that bad."

Gracie tried to cover his eyes and hide, but the cone wouldn't allow it. *I'm not going.*

"You have to go!" Maya's voice took on a desperate tone.

I refuse to be that dumb dog at the party with a lampshade on his head.

"There'll be lots of good food."

Bring me a doggy bag.

Savannah hung her head for a moment before it popped up again. "Maybe you can take the cone off for the party."

That won't work. I'll just chew my cast off. That's what dogs do.

"What if you wear something else that doesn't look so...?"

I knew it! I DO look stupid. He hung his head for a moment. *Wait. What kind of something else?*

He looked from one to the other and back with hopeful eyes.

"I don't know," Maya said. "I'm only five."

Savannah straightened. "Me too. Let's ask Chloe."

Is she a doctor?

"No, silly. She's my sister."

Oh, THAT Chloe.

"She can be smart when she wants to."

Let's hope this is one of those times.

Savannah crossed her fingers on both hands, and Maya followed suit.

Gracie couldn't see his paws, but crossing fingers wasn't something a dog could do, anyway.

"Come on."

You go. I'm not leaving the apartment.

Chapter Forty-Five

The girls returned an hour later with Chloe, and they gathered around Gracie. Chloe had cut a pool noodle into three-inch pieces and was attaching them to his collar.

"There. Let's try it on."

She removed the cone and tossed it aside.

Gracie watched it roll around on the floor. *I know just the spot for that thing. In the dumpster.*

Chloe slipped the modified collar around his neck and fastened it.

This doesn't feel half bad. How's it look? Be honest.

"It looks perfect."

Gracie turned his head from side to side. *I can see again.* He attempted to chew his cast, but the noodle collar stopped him from reaching it. *Hey! It works.*

The younger girls clapped while Chloe beamed with pride.

"Great job, Chloe," Savannah said.

I owe you one, sister.

"You can eat with it on, so now you can go to the party."

More clapping.

Gracie strutted around the kitchen with his new collar while *Stayin' Alive* played somewhere in the background.

Angela noticed and nudged George. "Look at Gracie."

George turned. "Where's his cone?"

Chloe smiled. "He doesn't need it anymore."

"So, he can't reach his cast with that thing on?"

"Nope. We tested it."

Savannah took a step back to give Gracie some room. "Show him, Gracie."

Gracie turned and twisted and chomped at the air as he tried to bite his cast.

"Well, I'll be." George said. "Who's the genius that thought of this?"

The little girls spoke in unison. "Chloe."

George turned to Chloe and nodded. "I'm impressed."

She smiled with a measure of humility. "I found it on the Internet."

· · • · ◦ · • · · ·

The big day had finally arrived, and everyone in the building was looking forward to getting together, even Gracie. Guests quickly filled the room, each with a mouthwatering dish to add to the food table. The room smelled like heaven when Jasmine and Marilyn brought in the turkeys.

Gracie hobbled around the room, delirious with delight as he followed the enticing aromas. The only thing that held him back from doing a happy dance was the cast on his leg.

People stopped him to say how glad they were that he'd survived the accident and offer a stroke or scratch, which he graciously accepted. He licked their hands and wagged his tail to show thanks for their concern.

"Come on, I'll show you where we're sitting," Savannah said when she arrived.

He followed her to a small table in the corner.

"This is the kids' table."

I like the sound of that.

A large bowl that resembled a trough rested on the floor between Savannah's and Maya's seats.

"That's your spot."

I'm honored.

He noticed another, smaller bowl near his. *Is that what I think it is?*

"Everyone is welcome at Thanksgiving."

Luna slithered out from under the table.

But I thought cats never give thanks.

Luna flashed a Mona Lisa smile. *I heard they're serving salmon.*

That's the Vietnamese restaurant down the street. Today's special is turkey.

George stood at the head of one of the tables and suggested that everyone say grace.

Really? That's not necessary, George. I don't need any extra attention. I'm just glad to be here.

"It's a prayer," Savannah whispered.

Gracie watched as everyone held their hands together in front of themselves and mumbled a few words, which confused him even more.

Before they ate, each person had a chance to say what they were thankful for—apparently how this particular holiday got its name. Gracie didn't have to think very hard to know what he would say if he could.

Angela introduced herself and Maya and told everyone she was grateful for the opportunity to spend the first holiday in a very long time with her father. And for the twenty-eight hundred dollars she'd won on the scratchers.

George couldn't stop smiling. It's a wonder he was able to keep his food in his mouth long enough to chew it.

Speaking of the food, it didn't disappoint.

After everyone's dinner had some time to digest, Jasmine wheeled in a cart with a huge cake that Rita had baked. The girls ran toward it, eyes wide.

"Look, Gracie."

George held Gracie up to get a better view. Written across the massive cake were the words, "Happy Thanksgiving." Below that, it said, "Welcome Home Gracie."

Aww. Gracie barked his approval.

Someone brought in a big tub of vanilla ice cream. Dogs love cake and ice cream.

Savannah couldn't contain herself. She swiped at the corner of the cake with her finger, then held it up for Gracie to lick.

Butter cream. My favorite.

Jasmine cut the cake and gave Gracie the first piece. He finished it before anyone else had time to pick up their fork. Fortunately, guests of honor were allowed a second piece.

His eyes had always been bigger than his stomach, and he worried the latter might explode at any minute as Savannah had suggested. He dropped to the floor and took a few deep breaths.

Sitting in the center of the room, his stomach full and his heart light, he had a moment of clarity about the transformative power of friendship and a dog's purpose. He'd managed to tear down the walls of this refuge for lonely humans and turn a diverse cast of characters leading separate lives into a family. His family.

They were all different, yet they were all somehow the same. As he gazed around the room at everyone talking, laughing and enjoying each other's company, it occurred to him that love was the ultimate purpose. He'd found his purpose; one he shared with all living things.

That familiar warmth rose in his chest, and his tail swung with wild abandon as he basked in the love of his extended family. This was where he belonged.

A familiar voice said, *Welcome to heaven.*

He turned to see Mama at his side. *This really is heaven, isn't it?*

She nodded. *I'm proud of you, Son.*

· · · ● · ● · ● · · ·

A Note from the Author

Thank you for investing your valuable time in reading my novel. I hope you enjoyed the story. Please visit **www.davidhomick.com** for more information about me and my books and to sign up for my mailing list using the button at the top of the page. You can write to me through the site if you're so inclined. I'd love to hear from you.

Word of mouth is the most powerful promotion any book can receive. If you enjoyed this book, please tell your friends. A shout-out on your favorite social media sites would be cool, too.

I want you, the reader, to know that your review is very important to me and to others that may be considering buying this book. You can leave an honest review on Amazon. It doesn't have to be long, just a sentence or two. Your comments are greatly appreciated.

Thank you, and I wish you all the best.

Books by David Homick

Available on Amazon
Karma Dog: Unleashing Redemption
Changing the Station: How One Stray Dog Found Its Purpose
Don't Curse the Rain (Rain Mystery Trilogy Book 1)
Rain Dance (Rain Mystery Trilogy Book 2)
Fire and Rain (Rain Mystery Trilogy Book 3)
From Time to Time
Broken Angels
Reason to Live